THE RUBY EARRING

Books by Dale Crotts

The Reckoning
Death Watch
The Ruby Earring

THE RUBY EARRING

A MACY MERIT NOVEL BY

DALE CROTTS

Jan-Carol
Publishing, Inc
"every story needs a book"

The Ruby Earring
Dale Crotts

Second Edition Published July 2018
Little Creek Books
Imprint of Jan-Carol Publishing, Inc.
All rights reserved
Copyright © Jan-Carol Publishing

ISBN: 978-0-9850272-6-1
Library of Congress Control Number:2018952307

You may contact the publisher:
Jan-Carol Publishing, Inc.
PO Box 701
Johnson City, TN 37605
publisher@jancarolpublishing.com
jancarolpublishing.com

CHAPTER 1

A slight breeze stirred the warm summer air, causing the front of Josh Stephens' dark wavy hair to lift, separating ever so slightly, as he stepped from his vehicle onto the paved driveway in front of his house. It was four-thirty on a Wednesday afternoon, the same time Josh had been coming home on Wednesdays for the last two years. He kept the same routine, leaving the office for lunch, then heading to the cemetery for a visit with his daughter before making his way home. Today was no different. He walked across the drive to the concrete walkway leading to the back door. Most days, he parked on the left side of the two-car garage, but decided to leave the car out today, for today was a special day. He wondered if his wife, Julie, might like to ride back to see their daughter if he could persuade her to. Last year was just too soon for her to return to the cemetery where they buried their only child one year earlier at the tender age of six. Maybe this year would be different, he thought, as he placed his key in the back door lock. He was somewhat surprised to find the door unlocked since his wife usually kept all the doors locked when she was alone. He slowly turned the knob and stepped inside.

Josh called out to his wife, but heard no answer. He shuddered as a sudden chill swept over his body. He walked through the kitchen to the den where his wife spent many afternoons watching Oprah. There was no sign of her and the television was not on. Josh made his way to the staircase. Maybe she laid down for a nap, he thought, climbing the stairs, walking across the landing to the master bedroom. The bedroom door was slightly ajar. Josh pushed it open and stepped inside. She was lying on her side facing the window. Josh slowly walked over to the bed, calling her name again softly, but she remained silent. As he touched her shoulder, the blood drained from his face as he felt the cold skin of death. He turned her over onto her back, revealing a large circle of blood on the front of her nightgown, a larger matching circle soaking through the sheets and into the mattress. He instinctively pulled her to his breast, sobbing, calling her name over and over, rocking back and forth as if comforting a sick child. After a few minutes, Josh suddenly came to his senses and reached for the phone, dialing 911.

"911 Operator, what's your emergency?" asked the dispatcher.

"My wife is injured," said Josh. "I think she's dead."

"Please stay on the line, sir. I'll dispatch a patrol car to your house."

Josh remained on the line while the dispatcher asked him several questions relating to his wife, like whether she was breathing, what he observed when he came home, and whether anyone else was in the house. After a few minutes a patrol car and ambulance arrived. Josh hung up and walked to the front door to let them in. Each step seemed as if he were walking in sand, his six foot two inch frame slumped from the heavy weight of shock and grief.

The two paramedics pushed past Josh, heading straight for the stairs to the bedroom while the two police officers remained at the front door. One of them could not help but stare at the blood covering Josh's shirt. Then he raised his eyes to meet Josh's and extended his hand.

"Mr. Stephens, I'm Officer Holt," he said, pulling his hand back sharply when he noticed the blood on Josh's fingers. "This is my partner, Officer Baxter," he said, nodding in the direction of the other police officer. Josh nodded at him and motioned for them to enter the house. Josh led them upstairs to the master bedroom where the paramedics were securing their equipment. As they entered the room, one of the paramedics informed Officer Holt that the woman was indeed deceased. He turned to Josh, expressing his sympathy for his loss. They had already covered his wife's body with a sheet. Officer Holt took Josh by the arm to lead him back downstairs to the living room. Josh sat down on the sofa as the paramedics walked through the front door and back to their van. An unmarked police cruiser pulled up in front of the house and two detectives emerged from the vehicle. They made their way steadily to the front door where Officer Holt stood waiting to greet them. He filled them in on the situation and what appeared to be a possible murder. The lead detective was Sergeant Frank Turner. Turner was a twenty year veteran of the force—one of the few black men who had been promoted above the uniform officer ranks. Turner was very proficient when it came to investigations, playing it strictly by the book. His six foot five inch frame hovered over Officer Holt, who stood at five feet seven inches. Turner rubbed his graying temples as he processed the information from Holt, then let out a sigh as he looked in the direction of Josh. Once Holt finished briefing the detectives, he and his partner left while Turner called for the forensic team. Turner and his partner, Mike Brogden, proceeded upstairs to the master bedroom to examine the crime scene.

Sergeant Turner lifted the sheet covering the body, carefully scanning the entire area, hoping to see anything that would explain what had happened. He saw where the blood had covered the front of the woman's gown, along with the bed, but upon closer scrutiny, he noticed there was no weapon either in, or near, her body. He looked around, then dropped to his hands and knees to peer underneath the bed. There was nothing there, which he found unusual considering most people at least had a magazine, a pair of shoes, or something under their bed. It was the cleanest crime scene he had seen in all of his years on the force. Brogden looked over the chest and dresser, but they were equally as clean. Turner and Brogden exchanged glances of understood confusion, having worked enough cases together to know each other's thoughts. No murder weapon and a sterile crime scene usually meant it was an inside job, which put Josh at the top of their suspect list. They would have to wait for the official report from the medical examiner, but Turner felt certain the death was the result of stabbing by some sort of knife, or other sharp object. The autopsy would shed more light on the exact nature of the murder weapon. Having finished their initial examination of the crime scene, it was time to question the husband. Turner and Brogden walked back downstairs to the living room where Josh was still seated on the sofa.

"Mr. Stephens, I'm Sergeant Turner and this is my partner, Mike Brogden," said Turner, gesturing toward Brogden. "We need to ask you a few questions."

"She was murdered, wasn't she?" asked Josh.

"It appears so," said Turner. "There doesn't seem to be any signs of suicide. Do you have any idea who would want to harm your wife?"

"No. She was a wonderful woman," answered Josh. "I can't imagine anyone wanting to do her harm."

"I understand you were the first person to find your wife," said Turner. "Can you tell me exactly what you observed when you got here?"

"Well, I got here around four-thirty, same as every Wednesday. When I came in, I called out for Julie, but she didn't answer. At first, I thought she was taking a nap, but when I touched her to wake her up, she felt cold. I turned her over and saw blood everywhere. I immediately grabbed her and held her for a while, hoping she would start breathing, but I knew she was dead. That's when I called 911."

"You said you usually come home around the same time every Wednesday," said Turner. "Tell me about the rest of today leading up to when you came home."

"I left for work around seven-thirty, got to the office around seven forty-five, worked until lunch. I left the office, grabbed a sandwich at the café, and went to the cemetery. I visit my daughter's grave every Wednesday since she died two years ago," said Josh. "Then I came home. I was hoping Julie would want to go back to the cemetery with me since today is the two year anniversary of our daughter's death, but then you know the rest of my day." Josh pinched the bridge of his nose as if fighting back tears.

"Did anyone see you at the café or cemetery that would remember you?" asked Turner.

"Well, the waitress at the café might, but she probably sees so many people in a day that it would be hard to remember them all," said Josh. "There was no one at the cemetery when I was there."

"And how long were you at the cemetery?" asked Turner. "Let's see, I left the café around one-thirty, so I'd say approximately two and a half to three hours," replied Josh.

"I don't mean to sound unsympathetic, Mr. Stephens, but that seems like a long time to visit one gravesite," said Turner, almost in a half question.

"It's not unusual, though," said Josh. "Time seems to stand still when I'm talking to Rachel. I tell her everything that happened the week before, and before I know it, a couple of hours have passed. Talking to her is the only way I seem to be able to cope with her death."

"Is there anything else you can tell us regarding the death of your wife?" asked Turner.

"I don't know what you want me to say," said Josh. "I've told you all I know."

"Here's my card, Mr. Stephens," said Turner, handing Josh a business card. "If you think of anything that might be important to our investigation, please do not hesitate to call me."

The forensic team, along with the medical examiner, arrived shortly. Turner filled them in on what he knew, barked instructions to the team as to what he wanted printed, bagged, tagged, etc. He turned back to Josh, asking if he had somewhere else he could stay. Now that the house was a crime scene, it would need to remain sealed until they were finished with their investigation. Josh told him he'd stay at a local hotel until they were finished. He asked if he could grab some clothes, but Turner informed him he could not have access to the bedroom until they were finished with their investigation. Josh remembered he kept an extra suit and change of clothes at the office. He'd stop by the office to retrieve the extra clothes, get cleaned up and change. He'd check into the hotel first and wait until he felt certain no one would be at the office before going there.

Turner thanked him for his cooperation and escorted him to the door. He watched as Josh climbed into his car and drove off toward town. He stepped back inside and watched over the forensic team, hoping for a clue he might have missed.

"I noticed you didn't ask him about his daughter's death," said Brogden. "How come?"

"Rachel Stephens was abducted from her school two years ago," said Turner. "Her body turned up in the park three days later. She had been physically assaulted and suffocated. Her murder was never solved."

"You seem to know a lot about the case," said Brogden.

"That's because it was my case," said Turner. "Stephens doesn't remember me, but I remember him. Both he and his wife were devastated when they heard their daughter was dead. It was a difficult time for the entire community."

"I don't know about you, but I'm starting to like the husband for this one," said Brogden.

"Me, too," said Turner. "But let's not get ahead of ourselves. We need to play this one by the book all the way. We don't want to accuse him of killing his wife then find out he didn't do it."

"Did you suspect him at all for his daughter's death?" asked Brogden.

"No way," said Turner. "He had an alibi, besides, there was no way you could fake the amount of grief he was going through. I don't know about his wife's murder, but I'm certain he didn't kill his daughter."

"If he did kill her, what do you think the motive was?"

"Could be a number of things. One or the other could be having an affair. They could have money troubles. Or maybe in some strange way he blamed her for the death of their daughter. That's what we get paid the big bucks to find out," said Turner with a slight chuckle.

As both Turner and Brogden watched, the crime scene investigators carefully poured over the entire crime scene, but found it equally as clean as Turner had surmised. There was no physical evidence that anyone other than the Stephenses had been in the house, much less the bedroom. There was no sign of forced entry at any of the doors or windows. In fact, all of the windows were locked. Whoever killed Julie Stephens was obviously someone she knew and felt comfortable enough to be alone in the house with. The medical examiner told Turner that his preliminary finding was death by stabbing, but could not say what the weapon was until he could do a more thorough examination in the lab. He placed the time of death between one and three o'clock that afternoon. Once the forensic team was finished, they left.

The presence of emergency vehicles and flashing lights had alerted the residents along the street where the Stephenses lived, so by the time Turner was ready to leave, a small throng of people eagerly watched from the street to catch a glimpse of what was going on. One of the local television stations had sent a van to investigate based on a tip. Turner locked the house and sealed the front door with yellow police tape. When he turned around, the reporter began asking what took place earlier that afternoon. He had pictures of the body bag on the stretcher when the forensic team left, so he knew someone was dead. Turner admitted there had been a death, but he did not elaborate any further, as they were just beginning to investigate the incident. He pushed past the reporter with a slight smile and climbed into the cruiser. He and Brogden drove back to the station to begin their initial report and start working on potential suspects.

Meanwhile, Josh arrived at the downtown Radisson Hotel. He opened the trunk to get an old jacket to put on to cover his blood-stained shirt. The jacket was under his cordless drill, so he moved it to the left side of the trunk and grabbed the jacket. He walked into the lobby and proceeded to the front desk where he booked a room for the night. It was now after five o'clock, so he felt confident the office would be empty. He left the hotel and drove the few blocks over to First National Bank, where he took his key and entered the building. There was no alarm on the doors, only the vault, so he was free to enter without having to key in a security code. Josh walked to his office and sat down at his desk. Quickly checking his email, he grabbed the extra suit and clothes from the wardrobe in the corner of his office. Tomorrow he'd advise his assistant that he would be taking a few personal funeral leave days, not that they would not already know his wife was dead by the evening news.

Josh looked around the office, glancing from his desk to the large window which provided a nice view of downtown. His nameplate displayed the title of Vice President, reminding Josh of how far he had come in the past fifteen years. At age forty, Josh was one of the youngest vice presidents in the banking industry, having worked his way up within the bank from the collection department to the loan department, until finally he was given his big break as the vice president for the bank. First National was a small independently-owned bank that was formed by the McAdams family in 1901 in the small town of High Point, North Carolina. It had survived through several wars and the Great Depression to become the leading bank in the community, while the city of High Point grew to become known as the furniture capital of the world, with two major home furnishings markets each year attracting buyers from all over the country, as well as from foreign interests. Josh had steadily become a big fish in a small pond, and was enjoying the fruits of his hard work. Because he and his wife Julie were so well known in the community, Rachel's death felt like a loss to almost everyone in High Point. Josh stifled back a tear as he thought about how successful he had become in business, only to suffer such tremendous personal loss, first with the death of his daughter, and now Julie was dead, too. Josh breathed a labored sigh as if the weight of the world had suddenly settled on top of his chest. He wondered how he would be able to get through this, especially now that he was alone. Then his gaze turned to the picture of his mother on his credenza. She had always been there for him, and was a very important person in his life today. His father died when he was twelve, so his mother had to play both parenting roles throughout Josh's teen years. She was such an important figure in his life that he requested her name be mentioned in the newspaper announcement regarding his promotion when he made Vice President of First National Bank. Now in his hour of need, surely his mother would once again be there for him. This thought provided a small measure of comfort as Josh finished gathering the things he needed.

He left the building and stopped at a local retail store to buy some underwear and socks. Returning to the hotel, he showered and dressed in his jogging suit he wore when he worked out at the gym. He hung his other suit in the closet and stuffed his soiled clothes in his gym bag. It would be best if he disposed of them himself since his wife's blood was on them. Once he was clean and refreshed, he ordered room service and turned on the television to see if Julie's death had made the news. The reporter who questioned Turner at the scene was just beginning his report. Josh recognized his house in the background, and turned up the volume. The reporter confirmed there was a death at the house behind him, but the police had not released any further details. They showed a clip of the body bag being loaded into the medical examiner's vehicle. Josh suddenly felt sick to his stomach and ran to the bathroom to vomit. He wiped his mouth with a wash cloth and walked back to the television, but they had already moved on to another story. He knew there would be more news in the coming days as the police released more information to the press.

A knock on his door announced his food had arrived. He could barely eat under the circumstances, downing half a sandwich and a few potato chips. He set the tray outside his room and locked the door, wished he had a stiff drink, but felt too depressed to even drink. First his daughter two years ago, and now his wife, was gone. He had no one left. He turned off the light and sobbed heavily in the darkness, realizing he was all alone in the world.

CHAPTER 2

The next morning, Turner and Brogden visited First National Bank to speak with Madeline Jones, personal assistant to Josh Stephens. Mrs. Jones verified that Josh left the bank for lunch a little after noon and did not return for the rest of the day. She added a few extraneous comments about what a good boss he was to work for, and how tragic it was that his wife was dead. Turner asked how she knew about Mrs. Stephens and Madeline explained that Josh had already called to let them know he would not be in due to Julie's passing. Turner nodded and continued with a few more minor questions for Mrs. Jones. Next, he asked to speak with Josh's boss, Harvey McAdams. Mr. McAdams was very complimentary about Josh as well. He expressed his sympathy for Josh and all he had been through, what with the death of his daughter and now his wife. McAdams told Turner that he realized they had to explore all avenues, but assured him that Josh was no murderer. Turner simply finished writing his notes without expression, then looked up with a pleasant smile, extending his hand as he thanked McAdams for his time. Turner and Brogden left the bank and headed for the café.

The Villa Café opened at eleven o'clock for lunch and remained open until nine o'clock for the dinner crowd. It was almost ten-thirty when Turner and Brogden arrived. They walked up to the front door and peered in. There were a couple of employees scurrying around preparing the restaurant for opening, so Turner tapped on the window to get their attention. When one of the workers looked toward them, he flashed his badge and shouted for the manager. After a couple of minutes someone turned the lock on the front door and ushered them inside. He was a young man who appeared to be barely of legal age to Turner, but informed them that he was the manager. Turner asked about the waitresses who were on lunch duty yesterday. The manager told him Sharon and Nikki were on duty, yesterday and today as well, apparently helping out in the kitchen until time to open. Turner told the manager he had a few questions for them, and assured him it would not interfere with their job. The manager called out their names in the direction of the kitchen, causing two young ladies to emerge through the double door.

Both were college students at the local university, able to plan their class schedule so they could work part-time for extra money. As they approached, the manager excused himself and disappeared into the kitchen. Turner and Brogden introduced themselves, then all four of them sat down at one of the tables. Turner pulled out a photograph of Josh Stephens and placed it in front of the waitresses. He asked if either of them remembered him being in the café yesterday for lunch. Both ladies looked over the photograph, but neither could be certain they had seen him. He was older than the guys they typically went out with, and tended not to notice men who were not what they considered to be dating material. Brogden could not help but chuckle while Turner remained stoic. He asked them to look again at the photo, but they were unable to say one way or the other about Josh being in the café yesterday. Turner thanked them for their help and nodded at Brogden for them to leave. As they were climbing back into the police cruiser, Brogden chuckled again and asked, "Do you think they would consider me dating material?" Turner just shook his head.

On the way back to the station, the dispatcher came over the radio with a message for Turner—the medical examiner wanted to see him. Hopefully, that meant he had some answers, thought Turner. They carefully weaved their way through the traffic until they reached the lab. As they entered the examination room, Carl Monroe, the medical examiner, glanced over his half-rimmed glasses in their direction. The light from the lamp above the table reflected off Carl's balding head as he peered over the body.

"What's up?" asked Turner.

"I thought you might want to see this," said Carl, motioning for Turner to come closer.

"Do you see the jagged edges around the wound?" Turner nodded his affirmation.

"It appears our murder weapon was some sort of instrument with a rotating motion. Perhaps a power drill, based on the size and shape of the wound."

"A power drill," repeated Turner. "An unusually sadistic weapon, don't you think?"

"That's not all," said Carl. "Take a look at these ligature marks on the victim's wrists and ankles. There is a lot of bruising and tearing which suggests she struggled quite a bit. We also found traces of Rohypnol in her blood stream."

"The date-rape drug," said Turner.

"Yes. Based on the evidence, I would say the victim was drugged, tied up, then the perpetrator waited until she was conscious before taking the drill to her chest, which accounts for the violent struggle as she strained against the ropes."

"This is one sick individual we're looking for," said Turner. Carl nodded in agreement.

"Did you get anything from the nightgown?"

"The blood type was consistent with the victim," answered Carl. "As clean as the crime scene was, it appears our murderer left no traces that would give us a hint of who he is."

"Do you think it could be the husband?" asked Turner.

"It could be anyone. But whoever it is had to be extremely angry and disturbed. In all my years as a medical examiner, I have never witnessed such a heinous crime, and believe me, I've seen a lot in twenty years."

"Thanks Carl," said Turner, as he and Brogden left the lab.

At this point, Josh was the most likely suspect. Turner took what evidence he had and went to the District Attorney's office. Based on the evidence, and the fact Josh could not fully substantiate his alibi, the judge granted a search warrant for the residence, office, and all vehicles owned by Josh and his wife. Turner sent a team to the bank to search Josh's office, while he and Brogden headed to the residence. On the way, Turner phoned Josh at the hotel and asked him to meet him at the house. Josh pulled into the driveway just behind Turner, got out and approached the house as Turner headed toward him.

"We have a warrant to search the premises and your vehicle," said Turner.

Josh took the paper from him and quickly scanned it, then looked up at Turner and asked, "Do I need to call my attorney?"

"That's entirely up to you," answered Turner. "Like I said, we're just here to conduct a search to see if we can find any evidence to assist us in the investigation of your wife's death."

Josh stood by as he watched the detectives go in and out of his home. When they asked for the keys to both his and his wife's car, Josh handed him the set from his pocket, which contained keys for both vehicles. Brogden began combing through Julie's car while Turner started on Josh's. Josh had the vehicles cleaned regularly, so there was very little inside the cars. Turner walked to the back of the car and opened the trunk. He almost jumped when he saw the cordless drill lying there. He carefully lifted it out of the trunk and placed it in a bag. He looked around inside the trunk some more, but was convinced this drill was probably the murder weapon.

After they finished their search, Turner informed Josh he was free to return to the hotel, but warned him not to leave town until they had completed their investigation. Josh asked again if he was a suspect, to which Turner replied they always had to rule out the spouse in these matters. He and Brogden climbed in the cruiser and drove off in the direction of the lab. Turner wanted to get the drill to Carl as soon as he could to determine if it was indeed the murder weapon.

While on route to the lab, Turner radioed in and requested surveillance be placed on Josh Stephens to monitor his activities. A few minutes later, they arrived at the lab. Turner carried the bag containing the drill into the lab, told Carl what he had and handed him the bag. Carl motioned for one of the technicians, handed over the bag to him, and instructed him on how to proceed with the examination. He informed Turner he would let him know as soon as the results were available. Turner thanked him, and he and Brogden returned to the station. They pushed some paper while anxiously waiting to hear from Carl. Turner knew that if the drill was clean, they were at a dead end. They had no suspects other than Josh at this point, and based on what they learned so far, it would be difficult to determine who else might be a viable suspect.

Turner was pouring his third cup of coffee when the phone rang. It was Carl requesting they return to the lab for the results. Meanwhile, Brogden was just completing a phone call. He looked up at Turner with a wry smile and informed him he just found out Josh Stephens had recently taken out a life insurance policy on his wife for one million dollars. This is it, thought Turner. Carl would have told them over the phone if the results were negative. And this new information about the insurance policy on the victim seemed like icing on the cake.

He and Brogden made their way to the parking deck and sped off toward the lab. His hands gripped the steering wheel of the cruiser tightly, as he made his way through traffic. He almost ran from the car to the door, eager to talk to Carl.

Carl, who was crouched over another body, looked over his glasses at Turner as he entered the lab. He walked toward the table along the front wall and retrieved a file, which he handed to Turner.

"We found traces of blood on the bit and handle of the drill," said Carl. "You see this pattern?" he asked, pointing along the handle of the drill. "You can see where blood spattered back, but there is a void where the murderer's hand was.

We analyzed the blood and found it to be a perfect match for Mrs. Stephens. This is your murder weapon," he told Turner, holding up the drill.

"You're positive?" asked Turner, unable to contain a half smile.

"Absolutely," said Carl, as he nodded his approval.

"Were you able to get any fingerprints from the drill?" asked Turner.

"As a matter of fact, we were. The void where the hand held the drill during the murder yielded no prints, which suggests he wore gloves. But when we dusted the rest of the drill, we found a nice set of fingers and thumb along the side and top, possibly where it was later picked up and moved."

"Could you determine whose prints they were?" asked Turner.

"Yes. We matched them to a set we found in a SEC database," said Carl. "It seems the SEC requires anyone who is licensed to sell securities to have their fingerprints on file. At some point, Josh Stephens held a securities license, because these are his prints."

Turner's smile widened as he thanked Carl for the information and bolted out of the lab. He called the District Attorney's office and informed them of the evidence so they could be working on the warrant while he was en route. By the time Turner arrived at the District Attorney's office, they had prepared a warrant for the arrest of Josh Stephens for the murder of Julie Stephens.

Turner and Brogden left immediately hoping to catch Josh still at the hotel. As they rode toward downtown, Turner radioed the patrol unit who was watching Josh. They told him Josh was still there and had not left the hotel since he arrived after the search earlier.

Turner turned the wheel sharply and almost jumped the curb into the parking lot. He and Brogden quickly exited the cruiser and walked to the front entrance. Turner flashed his badge to the desk clerk, who was scanning the pages of the

Sports Illustrated swimsuit edition, and requested the room number of Josh Stephens. The kid glanced up at Turner somewhat annoyed at being interrupted. He tapped a few keys on the computer and informed them Josh was in Room 312. They walked quickly to the elevator and rode to the third floor. Turner knocked on the door and introduced himself loudly. When Josh opened the door, Turner informed him they were placing him under arrest for the murder of his wife, and proceeded to Mirandize him.

Josh stared blankly into space as if he was somewhere else when they placed handcuffs on his wrists and led him to the elevator. Brogden placed a jacket over Josh's cuffed hands for the short walk through the lobby to avoid attention and afford Josh a little dignity. He showed no emotion as they led him through the lobby to the cruiser parked outside. Brogden pushed his head down and helped him slide into the back seat. Josh sat silently during the ride back to the police station, his face still void of expression.

When they arrived at the station, Turner pulled Josh from the car and escorted him inside. They processed him through booking, fingerprinted him, and took mug shots. They led him to an interrogation room, where he sat alone for several minutes before Turner and Brogden joined him. They asked if he wanted something to drink, but Josh said nothing. They began throwing questions at him trying to coerce a confession, but Josh just sat there motionless and expressionless, not even blinking when they shouted directly into his face. The questioning went on for an hour, completely frustrating the detectives by Josh's lack of responsiveness. They tried every trick they could think of to get him to talk, but it was as if Josh was not even there. He continued to stare at the wall in front of him as they pressed on, trying to get him to say something. Finally, there was a knock at the glass of the two-way mirror. Turner and Brogden stepped out of the room for a few minutes.

Callie Devane, the Assistant District Attorney, entered the interrogation room. She walked slowly to the table and sat down across from Josh. She spoke softly as she introduced herself. She explained the severity of the charges against him, and how it would be in his best interest to cooperate.

Josh looked away from the wall for the first time and stared directly into her eyes. He scribbled a name on the pad in front of him, pushed the pad toward Callie, and without emotion or inflection, Josh said, "I'd like to speak with my attorney." He returned his gaze to the wall.

Callie read the name on the paper, paused for a moment as she looked back up at Josh, then she stood up and walked out of the room, carrying the pad with her.

As Callie passed Turner outside the room, she handed the pad to him and said, "Call him."

Turner looked at the name scrawled across the page, shook his head and smiled. He walked to his desk and grabbed the phone, punching in a number he obviously knew from memory. When the receptionist at the other end answered, Turner informed her that one of their clients was being held on a murder charge and had requested his attorney. She told Turner she would have him come to the jail as soon as possible. He hung up and turned to Brogden saying, "This should be interesting."

CHAPTER 3

Spencer Rawlings sat fidgeting in the driver's seat of the rented panel van waiting for his wife, Macy to appear. Suddenly two figures ran out of the darkness toward the van. The back door flew opened and in jumped Macy and Gail. Macy slammed the door closed behind them and yelled to Spence, "Drive!"

They were no more than a hundred yards from the building when they heard a loud explosion. Spence looked into the rearview mirror just in time to see a huge fire ball as glass and metal from the building rained through the air behind them. They continued on their way until they reached the docks, where they left the van and ran onto a waiting boat. Spence released the ropes while Macy raced to the helm. They sped off into the harbor, disappearing under the cover of darkness.

They rode for what seemed hours before Spence saw a light a few hundred yards ahead. Macy eased back on the throttle as they pulled alongside a larger yacht. Spence tossed the ropes to a couple of men on board the yacht, and once the boat was securely beside the yacht, Macy led Gail over the railing and onto the larger vessel. Macy held her arm around Gail as they made their way to the cabin.

As soon as they reached the steps, Macy heard a man's voice from below as he yelled, "Gail!" They had not reached the bottom step before the man ran toward them and threw his arms around Gail, pulling her from Macy's grasp and holding her tightly, kissing her repeatedly while tears streamed down his face. He glanced over at Macy and said, "Thank you," then turned back to his daughter. Macy managed a "You're welcome," as she choked back the emotions of the moment.

She returned topside and made her way back to the smaller boat. Once aboard, she and Spence sped away from the yacht. Their work here was done.

As they sped off into the night, Macy looked over at Spence with a satisfied smile on her face.

"So this is what you do," he said.

"Pretty much," answered Macy with a light chuckle.

"So much for a boring day at the office," said Spence, causing both of them to laugh aloud.

Spence first met Macy Merit last year when her brother George, a good friend of Spence's, sent her to help him. Spence had just been accused of murdering his legal assistant, and was working to clear his name when Macy appeared to help him safely elude capture until they could prove his innocence. They placed their sudden feelings for each other on hold while they worked on the case together. After an elaborate scheme, the charges were dropped.

Spence left his law practice in Kentucky and sailed off to the Bahamas with Macy, where after exploring their relationship a little deeper, they were married. Since Macy was born and raised in Kentucky, they decided to live there after they finished their honeymoon. Macy had tried to explain to Spence the work she did, but the best way for him to fully understand it was to be personally involved. This was his first case with her.

After Macy and George's parents died, they were financially set for life. George went to work for the FBI as a way to help people, but Macy had enough of legal red tape from her days in the Navy. Instead, she decided to help others in more unconventional ways, especially when her clients had exhausted all of the normal avenues the law had to offer. Her special operations and martial arts trainings had prepared her well to deal with any adversity she might encounter during one of her cases. After some successful missions, the FBI, as well as several attorneys, began referring clients to Macy for her unique ability to help them. Spence was one of her cases who eventually became her lover and husband. Instead of continuing to practice law and worry about Macy every time she took on a case, Spence settled on working with her. Even though it was more often her looking out for him, it made him feel better to be with her and know she was okay.

When Macy and Spence returned from their honeymoon, George called Macy about a kidnapping case. The FBI had originally been involved, but when they botched the ransom drop, the kidnapped victim's father refused to allow the FBI to help him. Instead, he was planning to cooperate with the kidnappers fully in order to get his daughter back. George knew from past cases that if the father complied with their wishes, they would simply kill his daughter once they got the money. Macy knew George was right, and immediately contacted Mr. Brady. After a long and sometimes heated conversation, she was able to convince him to let her help secure the release of his daughter.

Gail Brady was a school teacher in Dade County, Florida. Although she worked for nominal wages, her father Malcolm was a wealthy real estate venture capitalist. She was abducted from the school parking lot while walking to her car. However, the witness accounts of what happened offered very little value to the police. The FBI was immediately called in and set up in Mr. Brady's home to await the ransom demand. Everything seemed to be going according to plan until a passing patrol car, unaware of the ransom drop, drove by with lights and siren blaring. The kidnappers never showed, and called Mr. Brady and chastised him for calling in the police. They threatened to kill Gail if he did not make the FBI get off the case. That was when he asked the FBI to leave his house.

The kidnappers told Brady they would wait until they were certain the FBI were not listening in before calling him back with further ransom instructions. Macy knew she had very little time before there might be nothing she could do to save this woman. She immediately began calling in marker from past associates and clients who might possibly be able to offer any information she could use. She was fortunate to uncover the name of one of the suspected kidnappers as a result. She and Spence followed him in case he led them to where they were holding Gail.

They followed him to an abandoned warehouse and watched as he went inside. There was no one outside watching the perimeter, and in view of that, Macy was able to make her way to the side of the building. There she used a rope to climb the wall to an open window several feet off the ground.

When she peeked inside, she saw Gail tied to a chair. She counted four assailants armed only with handguns. She smiled as she said, "Amateurs," under her breath.

Macy climbed down and jogged quietly back to the car where Spence waited. They drove off and headed to Malcolm Brady's. Once there, she outlined her plan, arranging for the boats and equipment she would need. She rented a panel van and loaded it with the necessary items for the mission. Spence stared in awe as he watched her carefully place weapons and explosives in the van. She flashed a wink at him as if to say, "Its okay. I know what I'm doing."

After driving back to the warehouse, Macy went inside while Spence stayed in the van with the engine running, ready to make a quick getaway. Shortly afterward, Macy and Gail appeared. As they drove off, the building exploded, and a father and daughter were reunited.

Macy docked the boat as planned and she and Spence climbed into a waiting car. They drove to the airport and purchased one way tickets to Lexington, Kentucky. Everything had happened so fast that evening Spence felt he had hardly had time to catch his breath. Once the plane took off and reached cruising altitude, Macy looked over at Spence, gave him a knowing wink, and headed for the lavatory. After a few seconds, Spence stood up and walked to the front of the plane to join her. He knocked gently on the door and Macy reached out and pulled him inside holding him tight against her body.

As the adrenaline rush from the evening's events overtook them, they joined the mile high club, finding the cramped accommodations of the airplane lavatory an unnoticed inconvenience to their love making.

Macy left the lavatory first and returned to her seat. Spence joined her shortly afterward as they exchanged knowing smiles and held hands for the remainder of the flight. As soon as the plane landed, they hurried to their parked car and drove home. When Spence turned the key and opened the door, Macy grabbed him and pulled him to her. They entered the house in a passionate display of kissing and groping as they began removing each other's clothes. Spence kicked the door closed behind them before collapsing on top of Macy on the living room floor. They made love again, and fell asleep in each other's arms.

The next day Macy awoke first. She let Spence sleep in since she knew he wasn't used to all of the rigorous work from last evening. When he finally got up, he walked into the study to find Macy busily typing at the computer.

"Hey sweetie," she said as she continued typing. "I think we need a little vacation together, so I emailed an old friend who has a condo at Myrtle Beach and it just so happens to be available for the next couple of weeks. What d'ya think?"

"Sounds perfect," said Spence as he leaned over and kissed her on the back of her neck. Macy spun around and planted a firm kiss fully on his lips, then turned back to the computer.

"If it's okay with you, I'd like to stop in High Point to see an old friend."

"Really? And who is that?"

"Adam Drake," replied Macy. "He's an old friend who went through a rough patch a while back and I thought it would be nice to drop in and say hello."

"You mean an old boyfriend, don't you?" asked Spence with a mocked frown.

"Don't be silly," giggled Macy, tossing a cushion at him as he effectively dodged it. "You know you don't have anything to be jealous about. I met Adam when I was working another case. He was going through a rough time with his marriage and drinking. He wanted to pursue a relationship with me, but there were too many obstacles for me to get involved at the time. We said goodbye and I never looked back. He called me a few times afterward, but that stopped a year ago."

"So why the sudden interest in checking on him?"

"Let's just say unfinished business. I kind of left him hanging and I wanted to make sure he's okay. I guess I'm trying to ease a guilty conscience. I just want to make sure I wasn't the one to drive him over the edge."

"Well you can't blame yourself for what he did or didn't do, Macy. After all, he is an adult."

"I know, but I feel responsible."

"Responsible for what?"

"Okay, I'll level with you. Adam and I had a brief affair. His wife caught us and that's the reason she divorced him. Adam had struggled with alcohol before, but when she left and I bailed, he crawled back into the bottle. I honestly don't know if he got help or not. Can't you see why I need to put this to rest?"

"I understand, Mace," said Spence. "And I trust you. Besides, I intend to be right by your side, just in case you need me."

"That's so sweet," said Macy, as she placed her arms around Spence and kissed him again.

* * *

Adam Drake had just stepped out of the golf cart and was walking toward the tenth green when his cell phone rang.

"Drake," he answered.

"Mr. Drake, I hate to bother you when you're on the course, but Josh Stephens has been arrested for his wife's murder and he requested you to be his attorney," said his secretary.

"Thanks, Betty. I'll be right there."

He ended the call and informed his playing partners something had come up and he needed to leave. He promised to reschedule with them as soon as possible. Of course, this group had been playing golf together every week for the past ten years, so they were used to Drake bailing on them every now and then. He drove the cart back to the clubhouse, quickly showered and changed, and headed to the office.

Drake knew who Josh Stephens was, and about his wife's murder, but was puzzled about why Josh had asked for him. He had never officially handled any legal action for Josh, so why was he referring to Drake as his attorney? Well, there was only one way to find out, and that was to go straight to the source.

Drake swung by his office, grabbed his briefcase, and sped off toward the jail. Once there, he asked to see Josh Stephens and was directed to a vacant room. After a couple of minutes, Josh Stephens entered the room, flanked on either side by a guard. He was in handcuffs and shackles, which was customary for murder suspects. Josh was led to the opposite side of the table, where he sat down across from Drake. Feeling Josh was no threat, he directed the guards to step outside the room. One of them gave Drake a questioning look, but he simply waved his hand, causing the guard to shrug his shoulders and walk out into the hallway. Once they were alone, Drake began his interrogation.

"Mr. Stephens, I'm Adam Drake. I know I've never handled any case for you before, so can you tell me why you asked for me specifically?"

"Because you're the best," said Josh, staring blankly back at him.

"I'm flattered by your opinion of me, but what makes you think that?"

"I read the papers," said Josh. "I've seen you win some major, but very weak cases. This is my life we're talking about, so I want the best."

Drake knew what Josh said was true. He had built quite a reputation over the past several years as the best defense attorney in Guilford County. Many of his cases appeared hopeless, but somehow he managed to pull a rabbit out of the hat and win against all odds. The papers had begun to refer to him affectionately as the "Magic Man." At five feet and eight inches, he would hardly be looked at as a threat upon first glance, but he knew the legal system better than most people knew their own phone number and he used it to his advantage. He took pride in his work and winning was almost more important than getting paid. He never considered himself to be a celebrity, but instead insisted he was simply doing his job—what his clients paid him to do. This case, he decided, would be no different. He retrieved a legal pad from his briefcase and looked directly into Josh's eyes.

"Did you kill your wife?"

"No."

"Look, Mr. Stephens, it doesn't matter to me if you're guilty or innocent," Drake told him. "As long as you pay me, I'll represent you. I just need to know what exactly I'm dealing with in order to properly prepare a defense."

"I did not kill my wife."

"Okay, then let's start by going over the events of that day."

Josh began recalling the same information he had originally told the police. He described how he found Julie, how he grabbed her in his arms covering himself with her blood, and how he called 911 and offered any assistance he could to the police.

"Is this the same story you told the police?" asked Drake. Josh nodded yes.

"If you didn't kill your wife, then who did?"

"I don't know," said Josh, shaking his head.

"Well, we had better come up with an alternative suspect, or we're in trouble," said Drake.

He asked Josh to list all of his wife's known acquaintances, jotting down the names as he called them out. As he wrote down each one, he asked for any details his client could remember that would help them implicate one of them in Julie's murder. Other than a few minor spats that most people have over time, there was nothing serious enough to cause someone to commit murder.

"Now let's look at your acquaintances," suggested Drake.

Josh continued in the same manner as before, spouting out names while Drake questioned him about each one. Most of them were the same people, since he and Julie had many of the same friends. Drake asked about his job and any possible client interactions that seemed negative or hostile, but Josh explained that as Vice President he only dealt with a handful of clients whom he had known for years. They were some of the more prominent citizens in town, and certainly held no grudges against him. All other transactions were handled by junior officers within the bank. He continued to write for several more minutes before suddenly dropping the pen and staring blankly at the paper in front of him. He ran his hands through his blonde hair and around the back of his neck, as if massaging away a headache. He exhaled a huge sigh and looked up at Josh.

"I've got to tell you, Mr. Stephens, this looks pretty bleak. No witnesses, no other suspects, and I haven't even seen the evidence they have against you, but if I were on the jury, I'd convict you. Can't you give me anything to help you?" Drake pressed.

Josh just sat in silence shaking his head. Drake told Josh he would review the evidence the District Attorney had and they would meet again. He shook Josh's hand and left the room, informing the guards he was finished meeting with their prisoner.

Drake drove back to the office, phoning Callie on the way. She told him about the murder weapon with Josh's prints, the life insurance policy on the victim, and the weak alibi the defendant offered. As he processed the information in his mind, he was glad she could not see his face at the moment. He tried to put on a false front as he asked her about a plea. Callie laughed loudly in his ear and told Drake there would be no plea offered. She would be asking for the death penalty.

"See you at the bail hearing," said Drake as he ended the call. He parked in front of his office and hurried inside.

"I've seen that look before," said Betty, her brow furrowed in concern.

"This one's a beauty, Betty," said Drake, striding quickly into his office. "Has the DA's office sent over the pre-trial discovery yet?"

"It arrived ten minutes ago," replied Betty. "But I can tell by the look on your face you already know what's in it."

"Yeah, I spoke to Callie on the way back over here. Did you look at it?"

"You know me, Adam. I can't resist a mystery."

"Well, it doesn't look like there's much of a mystery here," he said. "At least the jury won't think so."

"How do you plan to defend the evidence against him?"

"I'm not sure yet. He insists he didn't do it, but we may have to look at some sort of insanity plea."

"Well, based on what I read in that file, that could be a valid argument. I mean, who takes a power drill to their wife," Betty said, shaking her head. "What a way to go."

Drake poured through the file as if he didn't hear Betty. She shrugged and walked back to her desk. She was all too familiar with his moods, especially when he was concentrating heavily on a difficult case. He frantically scribbled notes as he turned the pages the District Attorney had sent over. Once written on paper, the case looked worse than before. There was physical evidence against Josh, a weak alibi that could not be corroborated, and a rather large motive in the sum of one million dollars, which his client stood to collect if his wife died. Drake decided he had better meet with his client again before the bail hearing. He grabbed his jacket, along with the file, and bolted out the door. He clutched the steering wheel with his left hand as he frantically searched the glove box with his right, weaving a few times over the center line before grasping a half-smoked pack of Camels. He quickly lit a cigarette and took a long draw, waiting a few seconds before exhaling. He had quit smoking for the tenth time three months ago, but just like all the other times, the pressure of an extremely difficult case always led him back to his old friend, Joe Camel. He began smoking Camels when he was in high school as a way to look cool and fit in. His grandfather had always smoked Camels, without the filters, and if it was good enough for Grandpa, it was certainly good enough for him. Besides, he always thought he looked more rugged spitting out the bits of tobacco that entered his mouth, unlike filtered cigarettes, which provided a barrier between the tobacco and his lips.

He puffed away as he drove through traffic. Since it had been three months since his last cigarette, He was buzzing a little from the nicotine by the time he reached the jail. There was no smoking in the building, so the one cigarette would have to hold him until he returned to his car.

Drake made his way through security and was escorted to one of the examination rooms. Josh Stephens was led into the room just as before, shackled and flanked by two officers. Once again, Drake requested he and his client be left alone. He waited until the officer had closed the door behind him before he spoke.

"Mr. Stephens," he began, and was quickly interrupted by Josh.

"Please call me Josh, Mr. Drake," he said. "All of my friends do."

"Okay, Josh, as long as you call me Adam. I received the pre-trial discovery evidence from the District Attorney's office. I have to be honest with you. They appear to have a very strong case against you. Let's start with your alibi. Are you certain there was no one else in the cemetery at the time you were there?"

"I'm positive," replied Josh. "There was one car pulling away as I drove into the cemetery, but with the tinted windows, there was no way they could have recognized me. Besides, I didn't even pay attention to the make, model or color of the car."

"What about the life insurance policy you recently took out on your wife before she died? One million dollars is a pretty strong motive."

"Julie asked me to take out the policy. She wanted to have more children, and wanted to make sure I would have sufficient funds to provide for their care should something happen to her. She said now was the time to purchase the extra insurance while she was young and the premiums were cheaper."

"Then why didn't you take out some on yourself?"

"I did," he answered. "You can check with my agent. He has a copy of both policies."

"And what about the drill the police found in your trunk?"

"What about it?"

"Well, it seems to be the murder weapon and it has your prints on the side of it."

"I remember moving it when I placed my clothes in the trunk before entering the hotel the other evening," said Josh. "Before then, I hadn't seen that drill for months. I couldn't tell you when I last used it."

"Josh, I'm trying to help you, but I've got to be honest with you. These are pretty weak explanations for the evidence against you. Is there anything else you would like to tell me?"

"Like what? Like I killed Julie for the insurance money? I told you, I didn't do it! Don't you believe me?"

"Maybe you blacked out, Josh. It happens sometimes when a person isn't completely in control of their faculties."

"Oh, so now I'm crazy and don't remember killing my wife. Is that what you think, Adam?"

"At this point I don't know what to think. I just wish we had more to work with."

"What about reasonable doubt?" Josh asked.

"Well, the fact that you each took out million dollar life insurance policies certainly raises some reasonable doubt," said Drake, as he rubbed his chin in thought. "It's still going to be hard to sway the jury with just that. I mean, if you did kill your wife and blacked out temporarily, we could opt for a temporary insanity defense."

"No! I was not temporarily insane and I certainly did not kill my wife."

"But, Josh, just hear me out. If they convict you, you'll get the death penalty. If you plead temporary insanity, we can get life in a worst case scenario, and possibly less term in a mental facility, depending on the medical experts we use and how well the jury buys their explanation."

"I told you, Adam, I did not kill Julie, end of story. You'll have to find another way."

"And what if I can't?"

"Then it will be up to the jury. Surely they won't convict an innocent man."

"I hate to tell you this, Josh, but it happens almost every day." Drake paused for a moment and shook his head. "I don't advise it, but I'll respect your wishes. We'll shoot for reasonable doubt and hope we can select an intelligent jury."

"You never answered my question, Adam," said Josh. "What question was that?"

"Do you believe me? Do you believe I did not kill my wife?"

"I believe you, Josh," said Drake. "Let's just hope we can get the jury to believe you, too."

Drake left the jail and headed back to the office for some last minute preparation before the bail hearing at two o'clock. He would argue for release on recognizance based upon no prior criminal activity and his client's good standing in the community. Of course, since this was a murder trial, and a particular heinous murder at that, the judge would definitely insist on some type of bond. It would be his job to obtain the least amount of bail possible for his client. The Assistant District Attorney would argue the worst case scenario in hopes the judge would impose a rather large bond. Either way, it would come down to what the judge decided would be the standard for such a case.

Drake was used to bail hearings and how they were ultimately determined based upon the particular judge and what their mood was for the day. There were several of the judges who he could predict with certainty. The others he had not dealt with enough yet to know which way they would decide. The judge for this case, Judge Robert Abernathy, was one of those Drake was not very familiar with. It would be hard enough to convince a jury that Josh was innocent without the uncertainty of how Judge Abernathy would run his courtroom. He wouldn't concern himself with that for now, and turned all of his attention to defending his client. He'd learn soon enough how the judge would rule once they got in court.

Drake arrived at the courthouse shortly before two o'clock. He took a seat in the gallery along with the other attorneys to wait for his case to be called. He had barely sat down when in walked Callie Devane, dressed in a smart dark gray business suit and heels. She carried her slender five foot five inch frame with the confidence of a poker player holding pocket aces. Even in defeat she never let it show, instead appearing as if she knew the verdict beforehand and was content with it. She walked to the prosecutor's table and opened her briefcase, spreading files out in front of her and removing a pair of dark framed glasses which she used for reading. She brushed back a wisp of her long black hair from her face as she jotted a few final notes while waiting for Judge Abernathy to convene court, then organized her case files in the order of appearance.

A few minutes later the bailiff called the court to order and announced the arrival of Judge Robert Abernathy. Judge Abernathy shuffled into the room wearing his typical black robe. He sat down behind the bench and called the first case, peering over the top of his glasses in the direction of Callie as he asked if the prosecution was ready to proceed. He acknowledged the defendant's attorney and the bidding war for bail began.

Drake logged mental notes on how Judge Abernathy ran his courtroom as he waited patiently for Josh's case to be called. After three cases, Drake was on. Josh was led into the court room in shackles by two guards, and placed behind the defendant's table. Drake stepped up beside Josh and waited for the judge to read the charges.

"State of North Carolina versus Josh Stephens, the charge is murder in the first degree," said Judge Abernathy, and looked at Josh. "Mr. Stephens how do you plead?"

"Not guilty," said Josh as calmly as he could.

"I presume the State is requesting bond, Ms. Devane?"

"Actually, Your Honor, given the nature of this crime, the State requests the defendant be remanded without bail," said Callie. Abernathy peered over the top of his glasses at Callie again, waiting for the inevitable argument from Drake.

"Your honor, Mr. Stephens is a well respected member of this community."

"Who committed a heinous act against his wife," Callie said, looking directly at Drake.

"Please direct the court, Ms. Devane," said Judge Abernathy.

"Your Honor, the defendant took a power drill to his wife's chest while she struggled so hard that the ropes he tied her with dug into her wrists and ankles. In light of the brutality inflicted in this case, we believe the defendant should be remanded."

"You've made your point, Ms. Devane. Mr. Drake, do you have anything to add?"

"Just that this is a first offense and the State still has the burden of proof," insisted Drake. "Until then I believe my client is innocent in the eyes of the court. He has family ties to the community and is not a flight risk, so the defense asks he be released on his own recognizance." Callie gave Drake one of those *you've got to be kidding* looks.

"Nice try, Mr. Drake," said Judge Abernathy. "Bail is set at five hundred thousand dollars." He pounded the gavel and proceeded to the next case. Drake had already obtained the necessary funds per Josh's instructions in case bail was set at one million dollars, and immediately took care of the bond and waited for Josh to be released. He drove him to the hotel, dropped him off, and returned to his office. By the time he got back, Betty was already gone. Drake flipped through the mail Betty had left on his desk, locked the office and headed home. He would get a good night's sleep and start fresh on the case first thing in the morning.

CHAPTER 4

The alarm clock radio suddenly sprang to life as an old disco song interrupted the dream Adam Drake was in the middle of. When he looked at the time and realized what he had to face today, he wished he could return to his dream. In his dream he was in the process of winning a high profile case for a beautiful client whom he knew would want to express her gratitude for providing such great legal prowess. Now, as an illuminated six o'clock displayed in front of him, Drake realized he had the arduous task of beginning to assemble a defense for a case that appeared to be almost hopeless. He sighed as he stood up and walked to the bathroom, his head drooping as if the weight of the world was on his shoulders. He hoped a nice shower would brighten his mood, but even the water appeared to be falling from a black cloud hanging over him.

Drake let out another sigh as he stepped from the shower and dried his body.

Breakfast consisted of a piece of dry toast and coffee. Ever since he and his first wife, Nicole divorced three years ago, Drake lived like the typical bachelor, and ate like one, too. He would occasionally opt for a healthy meal out, but since he was still in fairly good shape, he did not feel the necessity to overdo the health food by subscribing to the newest diet craze. His regular golf games, along with three nights at the gym, kept his figure lean, and helped alleviate the stress that comes with being a criminal defense attorney. He believed he was in good physical condition, and aside from the on and off smoking, had no other bad habits. As he was pouring his second cup of coffee, Sam, his Golden Retriever, squeezed through the doggy door into the kitchen. Drake had installed the door and fenced the back yard so Sam could go out whenever he needed, especially since he often worked late hours. No matter how late he came in, though, he always made sure he spent some quality time with Sam. He reached down and patted Sam on the head before heading out the back door. On his way to the office, he stopped at the Quick Stop for another pack of Camels.

Drake noticed Betty's car already there when he pulled into the parking lot where his office was located. He had leased office space on the third floor of the Williams Realty building situated just one block off Main Street not far from the courthouse. The Realty Company occupied both the first and second floors, while he, an accountant, and an insurance company occupied space on the third floor. It was a former bank building that Williams Realty purchased once the new five story bank building was completed. Although the building was twenty years old, it was still in very good condition.

Drake made his way to the elevator and pressed the third floor button, waiting while it took its time reaching the top floor. He was always amazed when the doors opened, believing he would get stuck on it every time he got on. The elevator was probably as old as the building, and moved like it. Many days he took the stairs, not just for the exercise, but to avoid the elevator. Today, however, he was moving more slowly than usual, and felt he would be unable to climb the stairs carrying all of this extra weight. He feigned a wink at Betty as he walked in, but she could see right through his façade. She jumped up from her desk and took him a cup of fresh coffee as he settled into his chair.

"How are you feeling today?" she asked with a smile, although she already knew better.

"Okay, I guess," he managed to mumble as he took the coffee from her, downing a large swallow. He began to shuffle through the papers on his desk, trying to organize the contents of the file he had started on Josh Stephens.

"How was the bail hearing yesterday?"

"Half a million, which he made with no sweat," he answered, raising his eyebrows at Betty.

"So where do we start?" she asked.

He let out a big sigh. "You tell me. He swears he's innocent, but all of the evidence points to him."

"You've been doing this a long time, Adam, what does your gut tell you?"

"Before I met with him, I would have said he was guilty. But after meeting with him, for some reason I can't explain, I believe him," said Drake.

"Well, your instinct has never been wrong as long as I've known you. We just need to prove it."

"That's the problem," he said with another sigh. "So far he has given me very little to go on."

"So what else is new?" she asked. "You'll come up with something. You always do." Then she smiled, patted him on the shoulder, and turned to walk back to her desk.

"That's easy for you to say," he shouted after her. After a few minutes pouring over the crime scene photographs, Drake suddenly sprang to his feet and announced he was going to examine the crime scene for himself. It was a short drive to the Stephens' residence, but long enough for Drake to smoke one Camel. He took a long drag as he weaved through traffic, holding it longer than usual to get the extra nicotine effect, before exhaling a cloud of smoke in the direction of his window. He was careful not to smoke in the car with the windows completely closed. He also tossed the butts out the window and used air freshener in hopes any passengers would not know he smoked. He was always amazed how his ex-wife knew when he had been smoking, especially since he had always been so careful to cover his tracks. Not realizing how easy it was for a non-smoker to smell the faintest odor of cigarettes, he believed she must have some kind of sixth sense.

He arrived at the house around eleven o'clock. One of the assistants to the District Attorney met him with the key and let him inside. She told him to lock up when he was finished, and left. Drake pulled on a pair of sterile gloves, walking through the entire house checking every door and window for signs of forced entry. What he found was exactly as the police reported. Whoever killed Julie Stephens was someone she either knew or felt comfortable enough with to let inside her home. He scanned the master bedroom to see if there was anything the forensic team missed, but it was as neat as a pin. Except for the blood stain on the mattress, you would never know a crime had been committed.

Inside the closet, he found Mrs. Stephen's purse, which apparently the police had either dismissed or casually examined and left behind. Carefully dumping the contents on the dresser, he studied each item. He noticed an earring in the small zipper compartment, but the mate was missing. It appeared to be a very expensive diamond and ruby earring. He searched through the jewelry chest to see if the matching earring was there, but couldn't find it. For now, he placed it in a plastic bag and took it with him in case it might prove to be useful later in his client's defense. He wondered why she would carry one earring around with her if the other one was missing. Maybe, he thought, she was planning on taking it to a jeweler's to have another one made to match. After looking around some more, Drake was confident there was nothing else of value to his case at the house, so he locked the door and climbed in his car for the ride back to the office. He lit another Camel and took a long drag before cranking the engine and pulling out of the driveway.

When he walked back into the office, he saw Josh Stephens sitting in the waiting area. He remembered he'd asked Josh to join him for lunch today to discuss pre-trial strategy. Actually, he wanted to see if Josh was able to remember anything that could help the case. If not, there was little pretrial strategy to discuss. After he shook Josh's hand, Drake told Betty they were going to lunch and would be back later. Betty just nodded in his direction and continued her work. Drake led Josh down the stairs and out of the building. He did not want to risk taking the elevator and end up stuck inside a small box with a potential murderer. He took them to a steakhouse near the shopping mall on the North end of town. They exchanged idle chit-chat during the ride over, and waited until they were seated and had placed their food order before getting down to business.

"Were you able to remember anything last night that you forgot to tell me, Josh?"

"I racked my brain most of the night, but couldn't think of a thing," he answered.

"So neither of you had any enemies in town?" said Drake.

"Not that I am aware of."

Drake decided to do a little fishing. "I found a diamond and ruby earring in your wife's purse. It appears to be missing the mate. Did your wife have one like it?"

"Yes. She lost one of them and was planning on taking it by the jewelers to have them make a replacement the day she was murdered. I had forgotten about it until you mentioned it, but she must have been killed before she could get there. Wouldn't that mean she was killed while I was at work or something?" he asked hopefully.

"The medical examiner placed the time of death later in the afternoon, the same time you don't have a good alibi. Of course, he did say she was bound and drugged beforehand, so the killer could have actually come to your house earlier that day."

"That has to be what happened."

"If we only had another suspect to investigate, maybe we could place them at your house that morning when you were at work. Who would want to kill your wife?" asked Drake.

Josh sat in silence, staring down at the table. Drake was sure Josh felt bad for not being able to help, but there had to be something he had forgotten. After all, no one kills a person in broad daylight for no reason. Or do they? That's it, thought Drake. They were looking at this all wrong. Maybe it was a random attack, or some kind of gang initiation that had nothing to do with the Stephenses at all. At least that was one place to start. He told Josh he would start questioning the neighbors in case they saw anything. They finished their lunch and Drake took Josh back to the office. They said goodbye in the parking lot and Josh headed back to the hotel while Drake took off in the direction of the residence. He phoned Betty from the car and told her where he was going, and that it might take the rest of the afternoon, depending on who he was able to speak with. He lit another Camel as he made his way back to the Stephens' house.

He parked on the street in the middle of the development, knowing he could walk from house to house without all of the stopping and starting of the car. He began directly across the street since that house had a clear view of the Stephens.

As soon as Drake rang the doorbell, he heard the sound of a dog barking. Obviously, the bell alerted the family guard to his presence. He waited for a few seconds before ringing the bell again. When no one came to the door, he walked to the next house up the street. He was greeted before he reached the front door by a woman in her mid-fifties. She was neatly dressed and fairly attractive. Drake figured she must be the wife of an executive. She introduced herself and held Drake's hand for what seemed longer than normal. Maybe she was one of those lonely housewives, he thought. She invited him inside, but his instincts told him to question her outside the home. She had not seen anything that day because she was at the hairdressers. She brushed a hand through her blonde pageboy like she wanted Drake to notice and compliment her on her hair. He just smiled and continued with a few cursory questions before thanking her and moving on.

No one was home at the next house, so he moved on. He walked on to the next house which was situated on the highest lot in the neighborhood. From here, there was a good view of most of the homes in the neighborhood, including the Stephens' house. Drake rang the doorbell and waited patiently for whoever was stirring inside to answer the door. After several seconds, the door eased open revealing a man in a wheelchair. He looked to be in his thirties, with dark hair and a moustache. When they shook hands, Drake noticed how rough and calloused the man's hand was, most likely from pushing his wheelchair every day. He invited Drake inside, to which Drake complied, closing the door behind him. The man wheeled himself around the great room to a spot where, based upon the carpet wear, must be where he sat most of the time. The spot had a good view of the television, as well as the front door.

Drake sat on the sofa across from the man. As he began his questioning, he noticed a pair of binoculars on the dining room table in the room directly to his right. He remembered a large bay window on the front of the house while he was waiting for the man to answer the door, and surmised the guy must like to watch the neighborhood a lot. It was a logical hobby given the man's physical condition.

"Mr. Evans, my name is Adam Drake. I'm Josh Stephens' attorney, and was hoping you could answer a few questions for me."

"Sure. I always liked the Stephens ever since they moved into the neighborhood," said Evans. "Mrs. Stephens always brought me cookies and fudge at Christmas. It was a terrible tragedy about their daughter, and now with Mrs. Stephens being killed, I don't see how Josh will make it."

"Were you home the morning she was killed?" asked Drake.

"Yeah, I was here until about one o'clock. Then I drove to my sister's in Asheboro to visit for the afternoon. I ended up eating dinner with her and didn't get home until late."

"Did you happen to see anyone at, or near the Stephens' house that day?"

"Well, I saw an air conditioner repairman pull into their driveway around ten. I can see their driveway and the front of their house, but the back of the house is blocked from view. He was there probably an hour before he left."

"I noticed you have a pair of binoculars. Were you able to get a good look at the repairman?"

"Just his uniform and car," he said. "He was wearing a cap and sunglasses, so I didn't see his face. Funny thing, though, the company was called *TruAir*. I've never heard of them before."

"Was there anything else unusual about him?" asked Drake.

"Well, he was driving a Pontiac, which is very unusual for an air conditioning repairman. They usually drive around in company vans, especially for service calls."

"Do you think you would be able to identify this man if you saw him again?"

"Like I said, I didn't see his face," the man said.

Drake thanked him for his time and left a business card with him in case he remembered anything else. He worked his way around the rest of the neighborhood, making sure he asked about anyone seeing an air conditioner repairman. None of the other neighbors were able to provide any helpful information, but Drake felt the repairman lead was a good start. Now all he had to do was find a number for the TruAir Company and see if they received a service call from the Stephenses. It was four-thirty by the time Drake finished canvassing the neighborhood, and he headed straight home. Once there, he tossed a frozen pizza in the oven, opened a soda, and turned on the television to catch the evening news. He was halfway through his meal when the phone rang.

"Hi, I hope I'm not intruding," said a female voice.

"Nah, I was just watching the news. What's up?"

"Well, I thought I would invite you over for a home-cooked meal, that is, if you don't already have plans."

"That sounds great, but I've already eaten. Rain check?" he asked.

"Certainly," she replied. "I'll call you later in the week."

Drake smiled as he hung up the phone. Debbie Ryan had been trying to break through his defenses for a couple of months now. She was a very attractive woman who worked at the county records department. They ran into each other when he was searching for information related to a case. Once she found out he was a bachelor, Debbie immediately began a steady dialogue with Drake. They had been on a couple of dates, but nothing serious. Drake never considered himself to be the marrying kind, at least not for several more years. At thirty-five, he was not ready for married life. Besides, Debbie was divorced and had a three year old daughter. Even if he decided he was ready for marriage, Drake felt he certainly was not ready to be a parent. But with date prospects not plentiful, he continued to maintain a dialogue with Debbie, deciding it was okay to simply date without commitments. After a few hours of television, and a couple more sodas, Drake called it a night. He'd begin fresh in the morning tracking down the TruAir Company.

Chapter 5

Betty was already at her desk when Drake entered the office, which was nothing new considering she always arrived before Drake ever since she began working for him. Drake could tell by the way she beamed at him when he entered that she took pride in her early arrival, as if it were a great accomplishment, so on days when Drake was running unusually early, he made sure to linger at the café or convenience store long enough to ensure Betty would be there waiting when he walked in. He valued her as an employee, and did not want to do anything to dampen her pride and spirit.

"Back on the Camels, I see," said Betty, looking up at Drake with a frown. He had already smoked three before walking in, and his jacket gave him away. He looked sheepishly at her and said, "Now you know how hard it is for a smoker to quit, especially in such a stressful job."

Betty just shook her head in disapproval. "You might be able to get someone who doesn't know better to believe that, Adam, but I used to be a smoker myself, remember? You've just got to want to quit bad enough."

"Well then, I guess I don't," he said with a grin. Betty raised her eyebrows and turned back to her computer.

"Where's the case at?" she asked, not looking up.

"I need you to look something up for me," he said. He gave her the information the neighbor gave him and asked her to find a phone number or address for a company called TruAir. He disappeared into his office to go over the information he had so far and see where he should begin today. He had barely sat down when Betty buzzed him to let him know Callie was on the other line.

"Hello," he said.

"Adam, this is Callie. I just wanted to let you know the Stephens house has been released as a crime scene, so Mr. Stephens can return to his home while he awaits trial. I thought you might want to deliver the good news."

"Thanks, Callie," said Drake, and hung up the phone. He informed Betty he was headed to the hotel to meet with Josh, and could be reached on his cell phone if necessary. She casually tossed up her hand as he walked by, not looking up from her computer as she was searching for TruAir.

Drake arrived shortly at the hotel and knocked on his client's room door. Josh opened the door slightly and peered out the opening. When he realized who it was, he swung the door wider and let him in. Drake told him the police had released his house so he could return whenever he was ready. He asked Josh if he wanted a professional cleaning crew to go through the house first so he wouldn't have to deal with the reminders of his wife's death, such as the mattress, etc., but Josh assured him he would be okay. He would need to shop for a new mattress first, though, before returning home.

"Any new leads on the case?" he asked Drake.

"As a matter of fact, there is. I spoke with one of your neighbors yesterday and he remembered seeing someone at your house that morning. The man had a uniform on that said TruAir, so he assumed it was an air conditioner repairman."

"That's funny," said Josh. "Our air conditioner has been working fine and I've never heard of a company called TruAir. We bought the unit from Quality Air when we built the house. If I needed it worked on, I would call them."

"I'm hoping we can track down this TruAir and see if we can determine who was at your house," said Drake. "Even if we can't locate them, your neighbor's testimony will help to establish some reasonable doubt."

"Is there anything I need to be doing to help?"

"No. Just take care of things at your house and sit tight. I'll be in touch."

Drake left the hotel and headed back to the office. Josh finished cleaning up, checked out of the hotel, and drove to a local furniture store. There he purchased a new mattress and foundation and requested it be delivered later that day. He went home to straighten up before the new bed arrived. Everything seemed surreal as he stepped into the house. He had not been back since his wife's death, and now as he looked around, the eerie silence was almost more than he could take. Josh made his way to the bedroom, stopping in his tracks as his eyes rested upon the blood-soaked mattress. He had made arrangements with the furniture company to dispose of the old one so he wouldn't have to handle it, paying extra for the service. Now, as he stood alone in the place where Julie took her last breath, he couldn't help himself as he walked over beside the bed and ran his hand along the large blood stain that adorned the mattress. Although the blood had long since dried, Josh found himself instinctively rubbing his fingers together as if they were wet. He lifted his hand toward his face and breathed the scent into his nostrils, as a tear rolled down his cheek.

There was very little to be done to ready the bedroom for the delivery. He walked downstairs to wait for the delivery of the new mattress. While he waited, he grabbed a cold soda from the refrigerator and plopped down on the sofa. After a couple of hours, the doorbell rang. Josh opened the front door to see the yellow police tape still attached. He ripped it down and motioned for the men to come inside. He led them upstairs to the master bedroom where they first removed the old mattress and foundation before bringing in the new one. In no time, they had switched out the furniture and were on their way back to the store, leaving Josh once again alone in the house.

Grabbing another soda, he flipped through the television channels, settling on one of the news stations. He watched the headlines until he finished, then stood up and walked out to his car. He needed to visit the cemetery in hopes of finding some form of solace in his time of grief.

Drake walked back into the office, eager to see what Betty had found out about TruAir. His expression was one of a child looking down the stairs on Christmas morning hoping to see that first bicycle. Betty's expression, however, transformed his expectant look into one of frustration, as she shook her head and told him she had been unable to find any company with that name anywhere on the Internet or Secretary of State's database. The words hung in the air like a heavy fog blanketing his already labored mind as he processed the news.

He let out a huge sigh and asked, "Are you sure?" although he already knew the answer. Betty gave him that get-over-yourself look she was famous for, simply nodding in the affirmative. He asked about the blue Pontiac, to which Betty gave him her you've-got-to-be-kidding glare. It would be impossible to track down a certain vehicle without a license plate number and he knew it. It was as if he was drifting along a river about to go over the falls, and was grasping for any twig that would spare him the tumble.

Drake shuffled into his office and collapsed in his chair, rubbing his face between his hands. He ran his fingers through the strands from front to back, interlocking them behind the back of his head. This was quickly becoming one of the toughest cases he had ever been involved with. He looked over his notes again, hoping something would jump out at him, but all he could see were the same notes he'd read many times over. He'd call Mr. Evans to testify about the man he saw, but without a positive I.D., the prosecution will argue it could have been Mr. Stephens. Hopefully, it would create reasonable doubt in the mind of at least one juror, but that was a long shot.

Thoroughly frustrated from the dead end, Drake stood up and walked out of his office. He informed Betty he was going back to the Stephens' neighborhood to scare up any more witnesses. He had another Camel lit before he reached his car.

Drake exhaled a long plume of smoke as he pulled out of the parking lot into the afternoon traffic. He drummed his fingers on the steering wheel to the music from the radio. It was a pleasant sunny day, excellent for field work. The warmth from the afternoon sun invaded the side window of Drake's car, causing his left armpit to sweat. He turned on the air conditioner for some relief. It was a short trip to the Stephens' house and this time he'd start from the other end of the development and work his way backward. There was no need to call on Mr. Evans again, or anyone else he'd already spoken to. He desperately needed to find someone who had seen the repairman close enough to identify him. He told himself there was hope, especially since the police immediately focused on Josh. Surely they didn't question all of the neighbors. Maybe there was one or two who saw something, but didn't want to get involved.

Drake began at the house located behind the Stephenses, which had a perfectly unobstructed view of the entire right side and back of the house. He rang the doorbell and waited patiently for someone to answer. After a few seconds, a young woman in her thirties opened the front door slightly and peered out at Drake.

"Can I help you?" she asked.

"Yes, ma'am. My name's Adam Drake and I'm the attorney representing Mr. Stephens, your neighbor. Did you hear about the incident that happened Monday?"

"The whole neighborhood heard about it. It's simply awful. That poor girl," she said as she bit her lip. "She was so young, it's a shame what happened to her."

"Were you home that day?"

"Yes, I was here all day. I looked out that afternoon and saw a bunch of people standing around, and saw the blue lights from the police cars."

"Did you see anything earlier that day?" asked Drake.

"I try not to pry in other people's business," she replied.

"I understand, ma'am, but did you happen to glance out at any time that morning?"

"Well, I did set a little dish of milk on the back deck for the neighborhood cat. It's just a stray, you know. No one in the community owns it, but we all feed it. I guess you could say we've adopted it," she said with a smile. Drake began to fidget, anxious to find out if she actually saw anything of value, and was not the least bit interested in the neighborhood cat.

"Did you see anyone at the Stephens house when you stepped outside that morning?"

"Now that you mention it, I did see a blue car parked in the driveway, but I never saw anyone."

"Can you describe the car?" asked Drake.

"I said it was blue," she answered shortly, as if she were somewhat offended by the question.

"Did you happen to notice the make or the license number?"

"I'm sorry, but I don't know anything about cars, except that the long pedal which goes up and down makes it go, and the one that goes sideways makes it stop. My ex-boyfriend was a mechanic and knew all about that sort of thing. Are you married, Mr. Drake?"

"Yes, I am," Drake lied, letting out a huge sigh.

"Lucky woman," she said with a wink. "If she don't treat you right, you know where I live." She gave him one of those up and down looks like she was enjoying the view. Drake simply smiled and thanked her for the information. As he walked toward the next house, he began to wonder if there was something in the drinking water causing the unusual behavior he had seen from the neighbors. He thought about his own neighborhood, and could immediately identify a few oddballs there as well. Apparently, it took all kinds to make a community. Even though, she was a little odd, this lady could at least corroborate Mr. Evans' testimony about the blue car.

The house next door was vacant, and had a For Sale sign in the front yard, so Drake headed to the next house. He rang the doorbell twice, and knocked once before the front door opened, revealing a young girl who appeared to be in her early teens. Drake asked if her mother or father was home, but she told him she was alone. She had stayed home from school because she was sick, and was not allowed to let anyone in the house. He asked about the day of the murder, but she said she was in school that day, and was not home to see anything. She added that both of her parents work, so neither was home as well. Drake thanked her and stepped off the front porch as she closed the door. He was afraid many of the residents were at work the day of the murder. That would explain why he was unable to find many at home the last time he went through the development.

Drake spoke to a couple more neighbors, but they did not see anything. At this point, he knew he had more than covered the potential witness pool, except of course, for the murderer and the victim, and unfortunately Mrs. Stephens was not saying a word. Drake climbed into his car, lit another Camel, and headed back to the office. He wanted to go through the file again and organize his notes before beginning to prepare his case in the morning. He had three weeks to get ready before the trial began, and knew from experience it would take all of that, and then some, to prepare his client's defense. As he drove, he played out the different scenarios in his mind of how the case might go, carefully noting the movements and testimony of each and every witness, as well as the prosecutor's actions. As the trial progressed in his thoughts, one thing kept emerging to the forefront of his mind. He was going to lose. He had never felt this way about a case before. Sure, he had doubts about several cases, but none seemed as hopeless as this one. He lit another cigarette as he wrestled with the guilty verdicts from the mock trials swirling in his subconscious. And yet, he believed his client was innocent. This time it was not about winning or losing a case. This time an innocent human being's life was at stake and he felt helpless against the tide of overwhelming evidence that was fast approaching to engulf and drown his client, sealing his fate along with his wife's. As Drake saw the despair in the eyes of Josh Stephens, he gritted his teeth, gripped the steering wheel tightly, and vowed to not go down without a fight. He may very well lose this fight, but not before landing a few punches of his own.

Drake entered the office in a half-run, eager to get started on reviewing the case file. Unfortunately, there was little to look at. He organized what evidence he had into a timeline of events, carefully inserting witness testimony where it would provide the greatest impact. Once he finished organizing his notes, he left the office, deciding to start fresh in the morning, composing a defense strategy based upon the notes he had just gone over. He lit another Camel as he pulled out of the parking lot and headed toward home. As he reached his destination, he suddenly realized he could not remember the ride home. He was so consumed by the case, he could think of little else. It was slowly beginning to migrate from his subconscious to his conscious mind, clouding his senses and mixing thought with reality until it was difficult to discern the difference. He entered his house with a strong craving for alcohol. It had been two years since he took his last drink, but he never lost the urge to crawl back into the bottle. It was a daily struggle with his inner demons that he had won for the past two years, relying heavily on AA meetings and his sponsor, when the pressure to drink became almost overwhelming. It was especially strong when he was involved with a stressful case such as this one. Ever since he dried out, Drake kept a bottle of bourbon in the cabinet, with the seal unbroken, as a reminder of the strength it took to get out from under the suffocating weight of alcoholism. Now, as the pressure began to build from his impending defeat at the hands of Callie Devane, he stood staring at the bottle as he reached for the phone. After a couple of rings, his sponsor answered and began the process of talking Drake down from the ledge.

CHAPTER 6

Drake awoke the next morning to the sound of the radio alarm blaring "Satisfaction" by the Rolling Stones. It had been a long night as he struggled with the urge to drink, and spent several hours talking with his sponsor. Finally he was able to get enough nicotine in his system to help relax his nerves enough to eventually drift off to sleep, but it was a very restless sleep. He dreamed all night, mostly trying cases in court while dressed only in his underwear. Now that he was half-awake, he felt the effects of the night before. As he rubbed his hands through his hair, he thought a hangover would not have felt as bad as this, but then remembered the pain that usually accompanied a night of binge drinking, and was thankful he did not have a headache. Besides, drinking had also left his entire life in shambles, leading to his divorce with Nicole. He stumbled out of bed and headed for the shower, hoping the hot steam would clear the fog from his mind. After he dressed, he swung by the café for breakfast before heading to the office.

Betty was hard at work as usual when he walked in. She jumped quickly from her chair and fetched a cup of coffee, having seen the look on his face that revealed a rough night. She considered herself to be a surrogate mother to Drake, and could always tell when he was not feeling well. She carefully leaned over close to him as she handed him the cup, taking in a big breath through her nostrils. She did not want it to appear obvious she was checking for the scent of alcohol, but after what he went through before, she wanted to know if he was back on the juice. Satisfied that she did not smell any liquor, she flashed a smile and headed back to her work, leaving him alone to silently sip his coffee and collect his thoughts. She could tolerate smoking, but if he returned to the bottle, Betty decided it would be time for her to leave. She was there the first time to help him as he picked up the pieces of what was left of his life, but was determined not to see him destroy himself again.

Drake worked quietly for several hours as he poured over the evidence and began to arrange a defense strategy. His main thrust would center on establishing reasonable doubt in the minds of the jurors. He carefully weaved a plan of witnesses, and potential cross-examination questions for the prosecution's witnesses. Betty could tell he was in one of those creative moods, and offered to get them some lunch and bring it back to the office. He simply grunted his approval, fished in his pocket for some cash and mumbled something about a sandwich without looking up from his desk. She smiled and shook her head, grabbed the money from the top of his desk and walked out the door. There was a small deli just a couple of blocks down the street she used when they needed to have a working lunch. This was definitely one of those situations. She ordered two chicken salad sandwiches, potato chips, and sweetened iced tea. Returning with the food, she sat across from Drake, and removed the paper from around his sandwich, placing it where he could reach it and continue working. She began eating as she watched him work. She always enjoyed seeing him when he was in the middle of preparing a case. She was impressed with his intellect and ability to take a few rough notes and mold them into a winning presentation. This time was somewhat different, though. Drake dropped his pencil, took the sandwich in his right hand and the tea in his left, and sat back in his chair, looking at Betty as he took a bite of chicken salad.

"Wow, you're actually going to stop long enough to eat?" she asked.

"Might as well," he answered between bites. "Going that well, is it?"

"Actually, it's not as bad as I first thought, but it's still going to be a long shot."

"You should be used to that by now," she said with a chuckle.

"Not like this one, though. I've never tried a case with this little to go on."

Sensing his mood beginning to fall, Betty changed the subject, inquiring about Callie Devane and whether he had seen her recently. It was obvious to her the first time she saw the two of them in the same room that Callie was attracted to Drake. They went out a few times casually, but he was in no hurry to make her wife number two, as he still felt some pain from wife number one. Callie, on the other hand, wanted to take their relationship to the next level, and had confided in Betty about her feelings for Adam, hoping she would be able to exert some influence over him. She had tried without success to push him in that direction, but told Callie not to give up on him. Betty thought Callie was a sweet girl, and just what the doctor ordered to get Drake out of his slump. She just hoped he would come to his senses before Callie got tired of waiting and allowed some young junior lawyer to sweep her off her feet. As they continued to eat, the telephone rang. Since it was easier for him to grab it, Drake answered. It was Callie asking if they could have dinner that evening. Betty overheard and began vigorously nodding her head in the affirmative. Since there might be the possibility of discussing a plea for Josh, Drake agreed, offering to pick her up at seven. Betty was all smiles as he placed the receiver back on its cradle.

"What are you smiling at?" he asked, although he already knew the answer.

"Nothing," she replied. "I just enjoy seeing two young people in love."

"It's just dinner," he said with a snort.

"Whatever you say," she said as she hummed a tune on her way back to her desk.

"Besides, maybe she's planning on offering a plea deal on this one," he shouted after her. Betty simply waived her hand in the air as if to say, "If you say so," and went back to work.

Drake shook his head as he wadded up the wrapper and tossed it in the trash can. He took another sip of tea and picked up his pencil to resume preparing his case.

He worked diligently the rest of the afternoon, taking only a couple of breaks to rest his eyes. Suddenly he looked at his watch and realized it was almost six o'clock. Betty had left without him even noticing and if he was going to be on time for his date with Callie, he knew he had to leave now. He finished the sentence he was working on, grabbed his jacket, and headed out the door. He lit a cigarette as he walked toward his car, exhaled a long breath, and climbed in his car and pulled out of the parking lot. He made it home in time to grab a quick shower, change, and still make it to Callie's with five minutes to spare. He checked his hair and teeth in the rearview mirror before getting out of the car and walking to her front door. He barely had time to remove his finger from the doorbell when the door opened and Callie stood there beaming like a high school girl on her way to the prom. He stood silent for a moment, mesmerized by her beauty as the light from inside the house reflected against her dark hair. He was lost in her hypnotizing smile, which revealed two cute dimples at the corners of her mouth. After allowing his eyes to scan the red dress she was wearing, he finally spoke.

"Good evening," he said with a smile.

"It took you that long to come up with that?" she asked, smiling back.

"Hey, don't bust my chops. It's been a long day."

"I'm sorry. I was only teasing," she said, touching his arm. He took her by the hand and led her to the car, where he opened the door for her. Drake was taught at a young age to always show respect for women, which included opening doors, pulling out chairs, and waiting for them to sit before sitting down. Whenever a woman was impressed by his actions, he loved to use the phrase that chivalry was not dead. Drake climbed in beside her, started the engine, and pulled away from the curb. They drove through town for a few minutes, making small talk along the way, until they arrived at The Round Table, a nice upscale restaurant.

After they were seated and the waiter went to prepare their drink order, Callie asked Drake how his day was.

"Long and stressful," he answered with a sigh. "Working on the Stephens defense."

"How's it going?" she asked.

"You know I can't discuss my strategy with you, unless of course you want to talk about a plea deal." Callie lowered her gaze to the table and shook her head. She looked back up at Drake and said, "I'd love to, Adam, but my boss won't budge on this one. He wants to take it all the way. Re-election is coming up in another year, and he doesn't want to appear to be soft on crime in the eyes of the voters."

"So you're content to put an innocent man to death to win an election?"

"I know how you feel, Adam, but all of the evidence points to your client. Frankly, it's going to take another one of your magic tricks to win this one."

"Unfortunately, I must have broken my wand because I'm really struggling with this one," he said, then immediately regretted the words that sprang forth from his lips. Had he just informed the prosecutor that he had no case? Hopefully, she would not key in on what he said, but he knew Callie too well. Although his words appeared to have no effect on her, Drake knew that inside she was jumping with eager anticipation, mentally counting the days until the trial.

"Let's change the subject," he said, just as the waiter returned with their drinks. Callie smiled at him as she lifted the glass of Chardonnay to her soft full lips. He casually sipped his club soda as he tried to appear nonchalant in his admiration of her beauty. Suddenly he found he was staring at her lips, and mentally cursed for being so obvious. She continued to smile at him, basking in the knowledge that he found her attractive. Then his expression changed to one of a more serious tone as he looked directly into her eyes. "This won't work."

"What?" she asked, as if she did not already know.

"Us," he answered. "As long as we sit on opposite sides of the courtroom, how can we ever have more than an adversarial or professional relationship?"

"By starting where we are now," she answered. "Dating is the first step in a relationship. We have lives outside of the courtroom, and should leave the case talk for business hours."

"But it's such an important part of our lives and couples usually talk about their work with each other."

"Well, we'll just have to agree not to," she said. "Look, Adam, any relationship takes hard work, some more than others. Ours will definitely be one of the more difficult ones, but I'm willing to work as hard as I can on it. Are you?"

"If you only knew how much I think of you," he said.

"Then tell me."

"I'm afraid of getting close to you, and then losing you. After all, I did a bang up job with my first marriage."

"Everyone makes mistakes and there are no guarantees," she said, as she took his hand in hers. "But you can't simply give up on love, Adam. Isn't the risk worth the reward?"

"I know you're right, Callie. I guess I'm still a little insecure. Imagine that, a trial lawyer with the reputation of a pit bull is actually insecure about his personal life."

"You're not alone in that respect," she said, squeezing his hand. He gave her a wink as he mouthed the words 'Thank You' under his breath. The food arrived and they finished the rest of their meal in silence, with the exception of a little small talk. As soon as they left the restaurant, Callie invited Drake back to her place for a drink and a chance to finish their earlier conversation. As they drove along, he realized he was rushing to get back to Callie's. Perhaps he wanted to talk about their relationship as much as she did, or more. It had been three years since his divorce, and two years since he had climbed out of the bottle. He was not the man now he was then and it was time to stop beating himself up over the past. He was finally ready to take his relationship with Callie to the next level. He reached across the seat and took her hand, giving it a gentle but firm squeeze. She squeezed back as if to say, "I understand and I love you, too." It seemed like the longest drive he had ever taken before stopping at the curb in front of her house. He came around to her side and opened the door for her as before.

As soon as she closed the door behind them, Callie took Drake by the arm, pulled him closer to her, and reached up for a kiss. He kissed her back, a long wet kiss, as they held their embrace for awhile. Then he released his grip and she walked to the kitchen to get them something to drink while he sat down on the sofa. She returned shortly with a soda for him and a glass of wine for herself. They each took a sip, then placed their glasses on the coffee table, turning to each other for another long kiss. Relationships may be scary, he thought, but they did have their advantages. As their lips parted, he continued to stare into her big brown eyes, seemingly lost in their deep pools of passion. She looked so beautiful to him that he could stare at her for hours.

"Penny for your thoughts," she said.

"I was just thinking how glad I am that you asked me to dinner," he said with a smile.

"I'm serious about what I said earlier," she continued. "I'm ready to take our relationship to the next level. In fact, you're the only man I have been seeing for the past six months."

"Exclusive relationship, huh?" he quipped. She nodded a 'yes.'

"Like I said before, Callie, I'm a little nervous about making a commitment, especially given my past track record. But if you're ready to take the plunge, what with knowing my past, then I'm in it with you. I warn you, though, when I commit, I really commit. I'm in it for the long haul."

"Me too," she replied. "I wouldn't have it any other way." They kissed again, each savoring the flavor of the other as they began the journey of a deeper relationship. Sure they had kissed before, but now everything took on a whole new meaning. Now they were playing for keeps, each one rolling the dice and hoping not to crap out on their partner. Suddenly, Drake pulled away abruptly, a look of concern washing over his face.

"How do we handle the public eye, considering we are on opposing teams?" he asked.

"Easy," she said. "Everything will be on a strictly professional basis when it comes to our jobs. We handle our cases with the utmost integrity, and never give the impression of any impropriety. And I'll make a deal with you. If it ever gets to the point where being professional adversaries threatens our relationship, I'll quit the prosecutor's office."

"Whoa, slow down," he said. "How can you make such a statement so early in our relationship?"

"Because I knew the minute I first laid eyes on you that you were the one for me and I don't intend to let anyone or anything get in the way of my future with you," she said. Then she leaned over and planted another long soft kiss on his lips, lingering for a moment as she let the words sink deeper into his brain, confirming her commitment to him.

He pulled back again and said, "Look, if we get to that point, let's discuss it first before anyone quits anything, okay?"

"Okay," she said. "Now, are we finished over-analyzing our relationship, calming our fears, and settling all of the details in our mind?"

"It would seem so," he replied. "Why?"

"Because I think it's time we began working on the physical aspect of our relationship," she said, as she stood up from the sofa and took him by the hand. She led him to her bedroom, where they immediately embraced, kissing deeply as they hungrily explored each other's intimacies. Callie had waited and worked hard to get Drake to this moment of commitment, and now that they were there, it was better than her expectations. It felt as if they had known each other forever, yet also felt new and fresh, as their lovemaking lasted throughout the night. Eventually they fell asleep in each other's arms, thoroughly exhausted and wonderfully satisfied.

CHAPTER 7

Drake walked into the office feeling the best he had felt in a long time. He was actually whistling as he greeted Betty. "I guess there's no need to ask you how your date went last night," she said. He simply smiled at her and continued whistling all the way into his office. He dove right in on his work, sifting through the file and crafting more strategy and questions. He worked all morning, never looking up the entire time. Betty came in and asked if he wanted her to pick up some lunch for them, but he told her he had other plans. Then in walked Callie with a picnic basket on one arm. She greeted Betty, walked into Drake's office and closed the door. She spread a blanket on the floor and laid out the food from inside the basket.

"This will have to do as a picnic for now, at least until we are not opponents."

"Suits me," he said. "I think the outdoors is overrated anyway." She laughed as she handed him a chicken salad sandwich. He did not have the heart to tell her he ate the same thing yesterday. Besides, she made these, and nothing tastes better than food made with love. She paused for a moment and looked directly into his eyes.

"I think I'll have some dessert first," she said, and leaned forward for a kiss.

Then they descended upon the food, barely speaking between bites. Drake suddenly realized how hungry he was and how long it had been since breakfast. He had become so engrossed in his work that he lost all track of time. They felt like high school sweethearts as they exchanged looks and pecks between bites. It seemed as if they had just started when Callie informed him she had to return to work. His expression was like a puppy whose master was leaving it for the first time. *Where are you going? When will I see you again?* She saw the questions in his deep blue eyes, so she leaned in, kissed him on the lips, and told him she would see him tonight. He felt all warm inside, and would have wagged his tail if he had one.

Betty flashed a pleasant smile at Callie as she left, then walked into Drake's office to grill him for an update, since she definitely sensed a shift in the universe. He simply hit the high spots of their date, and told her they were now officially a couple, so to speak, prompting her to give him a big bear hug. They both returned to their work, struggling to maintain focus in light of the recent events.

At three o'clock, he called Josh and scheduled a meeting for tomorrow to preliminarily go over his testimony, should Drake decide to put him on the stand. He informed Betty he was leaving early and could be reached on his cell phone should an emergency arise. Walking out of the building, he lit a Camel, this time more as a celebratory smoke than one needed to calm the nerves.

He drove through the country, then returned to town, somehow ending up at the cemetery. He stopped and looked around searching for Josh's daughter's grave. As he walked along, he noticed a man standing across the lawn and looking down at a grave. As he drew nearer, Drake saw it was Josh. He walked up behind him and placed his hand on his shoulder, catching him a little by surprise.

Josh described in detail his relationship with his daughter, and how one day someone took all that away from him. Now that Julie was dead, there seemed little purpose to life. Drake tried his best to comfort him, but what do you say in a situation like this, especially if you have never lived through it yourself.

Drake decided to leave Josh alone with his daughter, and patted him on the shoulder again before turning and walking back to his car. This encounter sucked all of the wind from his sails he'd been riding on since last night. He lit another Camel and headed home.

Drake exhaled a huge sigh as he entered his house. There was definitely no mistaking that a bachelor lived here, what with the dirty dishes in the sink, clothes on the floor, and everything in a general state of disarray. Callie was coming over tonight for dinner, so he needed to straighten up quickly. First he picked up all of the clothes lying around and tossed them in the hamper. Next he ran the vacuum over the floor, mainly hitting the high traffic areas. He dusted and straightened up just enough to make things look somewhat neater, and saved the dishes for last, which he loaded into the dishwasher and turned it on. Drake placed his hands on his hips and looked around the room, satisfied he had done a good job cleaning. Now it was time for a quick shower and change before Callie arrived.

At six o'clock the doorbell rang. Drake stepped quickly to the front door in anticipation. He opened the door to see Callie standing there with a big smile on her beautiful face. Her blue jeans hugged every vivacious curve of her body and the blouse she was wearing was cut low enough in the front to reveal her seductive cleavage. As she walked past Drake, he caught a whiff of her perfume, sweet and delicate. He closed the door behind them and scooped her into his arms for a long hello kiss. When their lips separated, Callie took a few seconds to quickly look around the room. Drake was almost beaming with pride at the job he had done cleaning the place.

"Looks like you could use a maid," she said, shaking her head.

"What do you mean?" he asked, a tone of disappointment breaking through.

"Oh, I'm sorry. I didn't mean it was that bad. You can just tell it's a bachelor's place, that's all. Really, all it needs is a woman's touch." Drake knew all too well what that meant. He heard the same thing from his ex-wife before they were married. Of course like most men, he did not really care if they made the place look more feminine, as long as he had food to eat, a bed to sleep in, and the roof did not leak, oh, and also cable television for the sports programs.

He smiled back at her and asked, "Why, do you know any women who might be interested in aiding a poor helpless bachelor in the area of home décor?" Callie gently slapped him across the arm, and laughed that cute high-pitched laugh he found so endearing. He walked into the kitchen and retrieved a glass of wine for her, a soda for himself, handing the wine to her when he returned.

"I thought we would order in Chinese tonight, if that's okay with you?"

"Sounds great," she said.

He placed the call while she sat down on the sofa, suddenly removing a sock from inside the cushions. Drake carried the portable phone over to the couch, where he took the sock from her and tossed it in the closet. She shook her head as he resumed his conversation with the restaurant. Once the order was confirmed, he hung up and joined her on the couch. They embraced and kissed again, caressing each other and holding on tight for several minutes. After making out for awhile, the doorbell rang and Drake sprang to his feet. The food had arrived, so he paid the delivery man and carried the bag to the kitchen. He reappeared from the kitchen with two plates of food, which he carefully placed on the dining room table. He retrieved the bottle of wine and assisted Callie with her chair. With the exception of a few statements of small talk, they remained silent as they ate, neither taking their eyes off the other. Drake thought to himself how new love was so intoxicating, no matter what your age. It was much like an illegal drug, easy to obtain, hard to kick, and can devastate you when going through withdrawal. And yet, human beings cannot seem to get enough, even at the risk of severe heartbreak.

After dinner, Callie helped Drake clear the dishes, then they returned to the living room. He turned on the television to see if there was a good movie they could watch without having to go out to the theater. They settled on a romantic comedy which neither had seen before. He topped off her wine glass again, poured another soda for himself and made some popcorn to eat while they watched the movie. Drake could smell the heavenly aroma of her perfume as she laid her head against his shoulder. Unable to resist any longer, he grabbed her and began kissing her hard. She feigned a weak protest that the movie was not over, but quickly gave in to her physical desires. He scooped her into his arms and carried her to his bedroom, gently laying her on the bed. They immediately began groping at each other like two wild animals, tossing articles of clothing as they went. It was not long before they were deep in the throes of passion, intimately entangled in the sweat and heat of their unbridled love.

Callie spent the night at Drake's, leaving early enough the next morning to swing by her place for a shower and change before heading to work. He lingered in bed, breathing in the sweet aroma from the sheets where she had lain. He smiled as he realized how happy he had been since he and Callie decided to accelerate the relationship. Then, just as suddenly, the smile was replaced by a scowl as he remembered Josh Stephens and how difficult the case was going. Sure, he had spent many hours busily preparing for trial, but there was still a lack of confidence looming over him like a storm cloud about to burst forth a torrent which would wash away any defense he offered. The thought of his client being put to death for a murder he did not commit was a bitter pill for him to swallow, but with no plea offer on the table, he suddenly wished he had a drink to wash it down with. Instead, he took a long shower, hoping it would clear his head and ease his craving for alcohol.

Drake arrived at the office shortly after nine to find Betty hard at work as usual. Josh was coming in around ten, giving him just enough time to finish crafting the practice questions before he arrived. Josh arrived right on time, and they adjourned to the back room in the office, which Drake had converted to a mini courtroom, complete with witness stand and jury seats. He believed in making the setting as close to the actual court as possible, hoping it would alleviate some of the stress by the time the witness actually testified. He spent the next hour firing questions at his client, and reviewing his responses on video tape. He made suggestions to make him sound more appealing and credible, so by the time they finished, he felt confident that Josh was ready. Drake offered to take him to lunch, which he reluctantly accepted. Josh had been trying to keep a low profile in the community ever since he was arrested for Julie's murder. The press had all but convicted him in the newspaper, and public opinion was that he was guilty. He was not sure how people would react to him, but Drake insisted he needed to be seen out so as not to appear in hiding and therefore guilty.

They went to the local café where both Drake and Josh frequented before the murder. Josh felt the cold stares like daggers piercing the back of his skull as people took notice, and exception that he had the nerve to show his face in public. The waitress smiled at Drake as she took his order, then turned to Josh, where her expression went totally blank with a hint of disdain. He quietly placed his order, looking down at the menu in front of him. The waitress flashed another smile and a wink at Drake and walked to the kitchen to place their order. After she was gone, Josh wondered if she would spit in his food before bringing it out.

"Try to relax," said Drake, obviously sensing Josh's nervousness.

"Everyone seems to be looking at me," said Josh, shifting his eyes around the room.

"Just act confident. Remember, you have nothing to be ashamed or embarrassed about. In fact, they should be sympathetic, considering you just lost your wife. Once you're acquitted, they'll feel sorry they ever treated you this way."

"I hope you're right," said Josh.

They finished their meal and headed back to the office. Afterward, Josh left for home and Drake began going over the practiced testimony again just to make sure there was nothing he missed. Satisfied he had done all he could do for now in preparing his client, he turned his attention to his other witnesses. He would go over everything again with Josh just before trial, but for now he needed to get Mr. Evans and the other neighbor who saw the blue car into the office for a witness testimony practice session. He wanted to be as accurate as he could with regard to descriptions of the man and the car, and also prepare them for the prosecutor's cross-examination.

He called Mr. Evans first and scheduled a meeting with him for tomorrow. Then he called Ms. Mason, the other witness, but she was not at home. He left a brief message for her to call his office, deciding it would be best not to leave too much detail on the machine. Drake went back to work organizing his case notes when the phone rang. Betty buzzed him to let him know the call was for him.

"Adam Drake," he said into the phone.

"Hello, sweetie," said the voice on the other end. "This is Sara Mason returning your call. I do hope there is something I can do for you."

"As a matter of fact, Ms. Mason, you can."

"Please, call me Sara," she said. "Now what can I do for you?"

"Ms. Mason, I would like for you to come to my office to review your testimony and prepare for trial. I was hoping we could get together Thursday," said Drake, calling her Ms. Mason for professional reasons.

"Thursday sounds fine," she said.

"Do you know where my office is located?" he asked.

"I have the address on your business card, and am familiar with downtown."

"How does ten o'clock sound?"

"I'll see you then, sweetie," she said.

Drake shook his head as he ended the call, then went back to preparing questions for both witnesses. It was necessary he paint a picture of another suspect, one the police failed to investigate, in order to lay the groundwork for a reasonable doubt argument. He worked feverishly the remainder of the afternoon until it was five-thirty. Heading home to get ready for his date with Callie, he lit a Camel as he walked from the building to his car, and was on his second by the time he reached his house. When he walked in, Sam jumped on him, obviously happy to see him, as well as feeling a little neglected. He walked out back and played with him for several minutes, tossing an old tennis ball for Sam to fetch. When Sam lay down to rest, Drake went back inside and began getting ready for the evening. It was Callie's turn to have him over and she was preparing homemade lasagna from an old recipe her mother handed down to her. He was already salivating at the thought of lasagna, especially homemade, as he remembered the way his grandmother used to make it with lots of cheese.

He suddenly thought, 'what if Callie's cooking was terrible?' Oh well, he would simply make the most of it, get through the meal, and suggest they eat out on future dates. There had to be a subtle way to tell her she could not cook, but hopefully it would not come to that. He wondered why it was that always at some point in the relationship a person imagines the worst of their partner about one thing or the other, when usually their thoughts are way off base. Maybe it was the mind's way of planting roadblocks to hide its own fear of intimacy and commitment. After all, usually everyone carries some kind of baggage into every relationship and no one purposely looks to get exposed or hurt when they initiate contact with the opposite sex. Things just happen sometimes for no certain reason other than the two are not meant for each other, but tell that to the fragile psyche. All of this deep philosophizing about things that may or may not happen was beginning to give Drake a headache. He decided to simply let nature take its course, dealing with whatever came along at that particular moment, and not before. No need to begin inventing problems that were not there, especially when things seemed to be going so well with him and Callie.

Drake arrived at Callie's right on time, and gave her a long lingering kiss when she opened the door. He loved the way she still blushed a little when he caught her off guard like that. As he followed her inside, he smelled the heavenly aroma of fresh baked lasagna. If it tasted half as good as it smelled, he was in for a treat. As he took the first bite, it seemed to melt in his mouth as he soon discovered that not only could Callie cook, but she was very good at it. She was pleased that Drake enjoyed the meal so much, beaming like a new bride after cooking the first meal for her husband. After dinner he helped with the dishes, then they adjourned to the den for a little television and making out, before retiring to the bedroom for the remainder of the evening. Drake spent the night, rising early the next morning to go back to his place for a shower and change before going to work. It was Callie's turn to lie in bed for awhile and bask in the after-aroma of Drake and his Black cologne.

Chapter 8

M r. Evans arrived at ten o'clock the next morning, right on time. Since the building was wheel chair accessible, Drake made certain not to help Mr. Evans unless he was asked first for fear of offending him. Actually Mr. Evans was well adjusted to his physical limitations, and had been driving his specially equipped van for years. It had a lift at the side door for him to enter, and hand controls for the gas and brake. It reminded Drake of the vans kids used for make out dates when he was a teenager, and found himself peeking through the back window when he was at Mr. Evan's house to see if there was a bed in the back. Of course Mr. Evans noticed Drake looking into the van, and laughed, deciding to rib him about it the next time he saw him. That time was today, and as Drake welcomed Mr. Evans into the office, he could not help but ask Drake, "Would you like to see the new mattress I got for the van?" Then he laughed heartily as Drake turned a little red.

"Relax, Mr. Drake," he said. "I remember those days myself, although I didn't own a van back then. Instead I had a Chevy Super Sport, which was just as good for getting girls."

"I just had an old Fairlane," said Drake with a sigh.

"I'm sure a good looking man like you had no trouble with the ladies, no matter what you drove." Drake smiled as he thought about all the girls he had dated in school. Then realizing he was daydreaming, he changed gears and put on his professional face.

"Mr. Evans, I'm not trying to be nosy, but I don't like any surprises during a trial," he began.

"You want to know how I ended up like this," said Mr. Evans, gesturing to his legs. Drake simply nodded in the affirmative, trying not to stare.

"Vietnam," he said. "One of my buddies stepped on a land mine. I was close enough that the blast blew me against a tree. My buddy was not as lucky. He died right there. After a few weeks of intensive care, I was shipped stateside for several months of rehab until I was discharged and told I would have to adjust to life without the use of my legs."

"That must've been tough," said Drake.

"Actually I've managed to get on with my life, having learned I can do almost anything I put my mind to. I'm proud of having served my country and I would do it all over again if the Army needed me."

Drake was impressed by his patriotism and resilience. After a few other incidental questions, he led Mr. Evans to the back room for the trial questions. He asked about the day of the murder, making sure he covered every detail of Mr. Evans's day. Then he asked if he had seen anything that day, to which Mr. Evans told the same story he'd told Drake at his house. He described the man and the car as best he could. Drake was careful to work in why he was watching out the window in the first place, trying to establish a regular routine that the prosecution could not argue might have been missed that particular morning. As Drake hammered away at him, asking any question he could conceive the prosecution might use, Mr. Evans was able to answer each one with polite but plausible answers. He never lost his cool, but maintained his focus throughout the entire process. Drake was very impressed by his manner, and wished all witnesses were this good. After throwing everything he could think of at Mr. Evans, Drake could sense that nothing rattled him. After he finished the question session, Drake invited him to lunch. Mr. Evans accepted on the condition he was the one who would drive since it was easier for him to get into and out of his van. Drake agreed and they headed to the café.

The waitress was much nicer today than yesterday, considering neither of them had been accused of killing their wives. After lunch, Mr. Evans dropped Drake off outside the building and headed home. Drake took the time to smoke a cigarette before he went back inside. He felt a little better about the case after reviewing with Evans, but it would still be an uphill battle. He was almost dreading tomorrow's session with Sara Mason, but that was one of the necessary evils of the job.

He spent the rest of the afternoon working on questions for Ms. Mason. Considering she really did not see anyone, and only saw the car, her testimony would simply corroborate the description in Mr. Evans's testimony. Callie had a late deposition. They took the evening off from their dating.

Tonight, he decided, would be a night to enjoy a frozen pizza while watching the basketball game on the sports channel. He was actually looking forward to an evening where he could relax, although he enjoyed the time he spent with Callie. He always found it interesting how people feel they must be on their best behavior while dating, and it wasn't until after they're married that usually the true colors emerge. Let's face it, we are not all perfect. Sometimes a person just needs to scratch a private area, or pick their nose. But it's not until after the wedding that you see a guy going in for a deep knuckle dig while watching television in the recliner, or a woman scratching her intimate area while sprawled on the couch reading a book. And yet, during the dating phase, we act as if nothing like that ever happens, especially to us.

Drake finished preparing his questions for Ms. Mason, and left the building around six o'clock. He lit a Camel and started the car, easing into the late evening traffic on his way home. Sam was especially glad to see him when he walked in, as if he could sense when Drake would be home tonight. He played with Sam for a little while, tossed the frozen pizza in the oven, grabbed a soda, and flipped on the television. As soon as the pizza was ready, he carried it into the living room where he placed it on the table beside the recliner. Sam joined him in the recliner, licking his lips as he watched him eat. Finally, Drake gave in and gave him a few pieces of the crust, which Sam gulped down as if he had not eaten all day, which was not the case. He simply preferred people food to his regular dog food, but Drake had to be careful not to give him too much. The vet told him that people food was bad for dogs, but a little treat now and then should not hurt, he thought as he handed another piece of crust to Sam. After they finished eating all the pizza, they both settled in to watch the game. Of course, Sam was asleep in minutes, napping while Drake watched the game. Squeezing in beside Drake in the recliner was Sam's favorite place to snooze, and he took advantage of it every opportunity he got.

Drake woke up just in time to see the post game show, having missed most of the second half. He caught up on the local news, then went to bed. Sam had a dog bed in the corner, but sometimes he liked to sleep with Drake. This was one of those nights, so after a few minutes in his dog bed, Sam crept into the bedroom and jumped up on the bed, curling up against Drake's back. The warmth radiating from Sam warmed Drake's back as he drifted off to sleep.

The next morning when he awoke, Drake realized Sam had moved back to his own bed sometime during the night, possibly due to his loud snoring. Sam barely looked up at him as he made his way to the kitchen to start the coffee maker before taking a shower. He let the water run over him as he tried to mentally prepare for the day ahead. He knew the interview with Ms. Mason would be a challenge because apparently she found him desirable. He finished his shower and downed a couple of cups of coffee before leaving for work. Sam was more awake now and had returned from his morning out to say goodbye to Drake before eating his own breakfast kibbles.

Drake lit a Camel as he pulled out of the drive and headed toward the office. A couple of miles from the office, traffic suddenly came to a standstill as cars inched along in front of him. He began drumming his fingers on the steering wheel from nervous agitation at having to wait, opting to light another cigarette in hopes the nicotine would relax him. As he inhaled, he thought about today's meeting with Ms. Mason, and how he planned to make the meeting as short as possible. He had no intention of inviting her to lunch like the other witnesses for fear she might take it the wrong way. He did not want to encourage her with regard to any romantic feelings she might have for him. In fact, he had put on his old wedding band this morning to keep up the ruse that he was still married. Hopefully, she would not ask Betty before he had a chance to coach her on an answer.

As traffic continued to creep along, Drake could tell from the lights ahead there must have been an accident. Traffic continued to crawl until eventually he was near the accident scene. As soon as he saw a vehicle being hooked up to a wrecker, his heart sank as he recognized Betty's car. He suddenly became frantic to find out what happened and make sure Betty was okay. Pulling his car out of traffic, he parked alongside the street, climbing out and making his way toward the police cars. He got the attention of the first policeman he could find and asked about the accident. According to the officer, Betty was on her way to the office when another vehicle ran a red light and struck her car in the passenger side. She was taken to the hospital, but he was unaware of her condition.

Drake noticed another officer was speaking with a man who appeared to be somewhat shaken up. The driver of the other car, he was sure. He estimated the man to be five feet five inches tall, in his mid-forties, bald in the front and top with brown hair around the sides and back of his head. He had beard stubble that looked like he hadn't shaved in a couple of days, and his clothes were rumpled and messy.

Drake watched as they administered a sobriety test on the man, and placed handcuffs on his wrists, easing him into the back of one of the police cruisers. Once the cars were removed and the glass swept to the curb, traffic resumed its normal pace. Drake walked back to his car and climbed in, pulling away from the curb and heading toward the hospital. He wanted to check on Betty before his meeting with Ms. Mason. He thought about canceling at first, but decided he might as well get it over with.

Parking in the outpatient parking area, he raced into the emergency room entrance and walked hurriedly to the front desk. He told them he was Betty's brother, a small white lie, and asked about her condition. They told him she was being examined by a doctor, but appeared to be okay with the exception of a broken leg. He hung around the waiting room until he was told he could go back and see her. Betty was already fussing about the cast they put on her leg, and seemed to be her usual difficult self. He was relieved to see she was doing as well as she was, and aside from a couple of scratches on her face and the cast on her leg, she looked the same as always.

Drake approached her bed and gave her a hug and a kiss on the cheek, causing her to blush and admonish him for making such a fuss over her. She thanked him for coming, but assured him she was okay, and reminded him he had a ten o'clock appointment as she smiled and waved her hand as if pushing him out of the room. He squeezed her hand, winked at her, and walked out of the examination room. He tracked down the doctor who informed him they would observe her for a couple of hours and probably discharge her if everything was okay. Drake left his contact information with them so they would call him to pick her up, left the hospital and drove to the office.

It was fifteen before ten when he arrived at his office, which gave him just enough time to get settled before his appointment with Ms. Mason. She arrived five minutes early, wearing a low cut dress and high heels. She had obviously dressed to impress him, especially when she leaned over in her chair, exposing her cleavage. He kept everything on a strictly professional basis, leading her to the back room and directing her to the mock witness stand. He went through the questions he had prepared, sighing every time she tried to sound sexy when she spoke. He reminded her to keep her answers short and business-like, not flirty. After several minutes of questioning, he could tell by the way she answered the questions the prosecution would spend very little time with her. They had been at it for about an hour when the phone rang. It was the hospital informing him Betty had been released and was ready whenever he could come pick her up. He told Ms. Mason he had to leave due to an emergency, but assured her he had finished with the preparation. She expressed concerns about her readiness and asked about the necessity for another practice session, to which he replied there was no need. Based upon years of cross examinations, he was absolutely certain she was ready. She tried to hang around and flirt some more, but Drake excused himself and ushered her out the door. He lit a Camel and exhaled a long sigh of relief as he sped off in the direction of the hospital.

Betty was waiting for him when he arrived, complete with newly-issued crutches. He helped her up and escorted her to his car, which he parked directly outside the emergency entrance so she would not have to walk very far. It was a small struggle to get her situated inside the vehicle, but they were soon on their way. He cleared the rest of his day and stayed with her in case she needed anything. After a short drive, they arrived at her house. Drake all but carried her up the six concrete steps to the back door, with Betty protesting the entire way. She had always been an independent woman, and insisted she needed no help. He just ignored her and continued assisting her until she was comfortably seated in her recliner with her leg propped up. The doctor told her to keep it elevated as much as possible to reduce the swelling, and gave her something for the pain. Once he was satisfied she was comfortable, he stepped outside for a smoke. It was beginning to rain a fine mist, while he stood under the awning at the back door and blew the smoke toward the back of the house, watching the moisture collect on the rose bushes Betty had planted nearby. He was fascinated by the way the water collected on each leaf until it was enough to form a considerable drop which traveled to the tip before falling to the ground. It made him wonder how many people actually took the time to stop and notice such wonders of nature. As he stood there staring at the bushes, he suddenly felt very small in the world, and his own personal concerns seemed so insignificant.

He blinked as if coming out of a trance, took one last draw before tossing the butt into the rain, exhaled a long plume of smoke, and stepped back inside the house, being careful to wipe his feet on the mat, even though he'd remained on the porch the entire time. By the time he walked back into the living room, the pain medication had already taken effect. Betty was sound asleep. Taking a nap on the sofa sounded like an excellent idea. He stayed with her until he was certain she would be okay. After a couple of hours, he awoke to find Betty staring at him and smiling.

"Why don't you go home?" she asked.

"I'm okay," he said with a yawn.

"Really, I'll be fine. Just leave my medication and crutches where I can reach them."

"What if you fall?"

"Then I'll call you," she said, holding up her cell phone. "Besides, I'm sure you have better things to do than babysit me."

"Promise me you'll call if you need me."

"I promise," she said. "Now go!"

"Okay," he said, reluctantly. "I'll call you later to check on you."

Drake stood up and walked to the door, and turned back to look at Betty before leaving. She made a motion with her hand as if to say, "scoot." He turned and walked out the door to his car. It was raining harder now, as the raindrops bounced off the rose bushes and onto the ground. He cranked the engine, turned on the wipers, and lit a Camel. He still felt a little guilty about leaving Betty alone, but he did have a date this evening with Callie. He shrugged his shoulders and pulled out of the driveway, heading toward home.

CHAPTER 9

As Drake pulled into his driveway, his cell phone rang. It was Callie. "Hey, where are you?" she asked.

"I just got back home from Betty's," he said, and went on to explain about the accident and the hospital visit.

"That explains why you didn't answer the phone at your office this afternoon," she said. "And I thought it was just because you were engrossed in your work."

"Why didn't you call me on my cell?"

"I didn't want to disturb you in case you were working on the case. Besides, I knew I would see you tonight."

"So, are we still meeting at Zachary's?" he asked.

"That's why I called," she said. "I was thinking it might be best if we stay out of the public eye, at least until the trial is over."

"What did you have in mind?"

"I thought I would come over and cook for you tonight, if that's okay with you."

"Hey, that sounds great to me. Just give me an hour to shower and change." Drake ended the call and climbed out of his car, jogging to the door to avoid as many raindrops as possible. Sam looked up as he walked in, and came toward him wagging his tail. Drake gave him a pat on the head, and headed to the bedroom, where he stripped and jumped into the shower. He bathed quickly, toweled off, and tossed on a pair of jeans and a polo shirt. He had fifteen minutes to spare before his date was due to arrive, which was just enough time to play a little with Sam. They were rolling around on the kitchen floor when the doorbell rang. Drake jumped up and walked to the front door with Sam following closely behind. When he opened the door, Callie handed him a couple of bags, kissed him quickly on the lips, and stooped to give Sam a few strokes behind the ears. Drake lingered for a moment after she walked by, inhaling the sweet scent of her perfume through his nostrils, before he carried the bags into the kitchen and placed them on the counter. He and Sam retreated to the living room to continue their playtime while Callie prepared dinner. She decided to make meatloaf since it was an easy meal to prepare and required little effort to make. After all, she wanted to squeeze in as much alone time with Drake that she could, without being tied up in the kitchen all evening.

Once dinner was ready, Sam retreated to his bed while Drake and Callie sat down to enjoy their meal. As soon as they finished eating and began clearing the dishes, Sam reappeared to see if they had left anything for him. Since Drake occasionally fed him from the table, it was worth investigating, after all, there was a first time for everything. Of course, it took only a couple of minutes of being ignored to convince Sam that he was not getting any human food, so he gave up the act and walked back to his bed until they finished with the dishes. After the dishes were done, Drake and Callie retreated to the living room—her with a glass of wine and him with a soda. Sam reappeared, gently nudging Callie's leg with his paw to give her the okay to resume the ear rubbing she had started when she first arrived. Callie laughed at Sam, then began talking baby talk to him while she scratched behind his ears. Drake gently touched her on the arm as if to say, "Hey, I'm over here."

Callie looked at Drake, then back at Sam, before shaking her head and exclaiming, "You guys are all the same. All you want is a full belly and a good rubbing." Drake feigned a whimper, rolled onto his back, and placed his arms up like a dog that wants his stomach rubbed. Callie shifted her knees, causing Drake to tumble onto the floor, then laughed at seeing him sprawled out, hands and feet in all directions. He deftly turned on his side, grabbed Callie's hand, and pulled her to the floor on top of him, placing his lips fully on hers. The laughing quickly changed to a soft sigh as her lips melted into his. Sam cocked his head to one side, first confused by what he saw, then returned to his bed when he realized this was one of those human moments.

Drake kept his hands tight against Callie's back, holding her body against his while she ran her fingers through his blonde hair. He released his grip long enough for her to rise up and unbutton her blouse before they resumed kissing. Their bodies rhythmically writhed together as they groped and tugged until they were completely naked and exposed, making love until each was completely exhausted.

Callie collapsed on top of Drake as he smiled and stroked her beautiful black hair. He felt her warm breath against his chest and her muscles relax as she basked in the afterglow. The craving for a cigarette was strongest after sex, but he refrained from giving in, closing his eyes instead as he tried to concentrate on the warm feeling deep within his soul. He squeezed her more tightly in his arms as if he was afraid to let her go. Sensing his possessive feelings, she nestled more snuggly against his body, also closing her eyes as she drifted off to sleep. They slept for a couple of hours before being awakened by the sound of Sam barking as he scurried quickly to the kitchen and out the doggy door to announce his presence to whatever small animal made the mistake of landing in the backyard.

Drake took Callie by the hand and led the way to his bedroom, where they made love again before falling asleep for the night. She awoke early the next morning, kissed the still sleeping Drake on the cheek, and left to grab a shower and change of clothes at her place before going to work.

Drake woke up with the faint scent of Callie still in the air. He was not surprised to find she had already left, especially since she had done it before, and he knew how she wanted to keep their relationship on the Q.T. As he yawned and stretched the length of his body, he noticed Sam was at the foot of the bed.

Sam barely raised his head when Drake climbed out of bed and headed to the shower. He dressed quickly and headed out the door to the café for a quick bite before going to the office, leaving Sam still napping on the bed. Drake was unusually hungry this morning, so he ate a full breakfast of eggs, bacon, grits, and toast, and of course, coffee. He paid the check and had the waitress give him a coffee to go, then walked out to his car and drove off toward the office.

The trial was to begin next week, so it was time to get down to some serious last minute preparations. He worked diligently all morning organizing the various witness testimonies, along with the character witnesses he had lined up. The only thing left was to prepare his opening statement, which he started on right after lunch.

He passed through a fast food drive thru, where he ordered a cheeseburger, fries and a drink. Driving to the city park, he ate under one of the large oaks that shaded the picnic area. It was a beautiful sunny day, and he hated not to take advantage of the weather by dining indoors. Besides, he felt the fresh air would clear his head and enable him to more clearly organize his thoughts as he worked on his opening statement.

There were several mothers with their small children in the park playing on the swings and eating lunch. He smiled as he remembered coming here as a child, eating hotdogs cooked on one of the open grills, and playing on the playground. He thought about the swings and how high he and his three brothers would try to go, each trying to out do the other. Then there were the two slides, one slightly longer than the other, but both equally as fun. Probably the favorite thing in the park, though, was the old fire truck that was situated near the entrance to the playground. The wheels were partially buried in the earth to prevent any accidental movement, but you could still pretend you were driving fast to a fire as you turned the steering wheel and rang the bell. Children would run back and forth, playing on the old engine for hours.

Drake was suddenly awakened from the dreams of childhood by the cries of a small boy who had fallen off the swing and scraped his knee. After a healing kiss, some ointment and a Band-Aid, and a loving hug from his mother, the child was off and running again as if nothing had happened. He marveled at how often children would fall down, but not start crying until they were certain an adult was watching, obviously taking advantage of every opportunity for attention. Oh well, that was just a part of childhood, he thought, smiling in the direction of the little boy and stood up from the picnic table. He tossed the empty paper bag into the trash can, and walked back toward his car, lighting a Camel along the way.

Since it was such a beautiful day, Drake took a drive through the country-side. He liked to ride with the windows open to let the fresh air inside, even though he was smoking at the same time. He rode past his parents' house, remembering how he used to sit outside and watch the farmers work the fields across the highway from where he lived. Today the fields were a golf course, which seemed to be fairly busy for a weekday. A few short miles further and he turned onto another road, which ended where his grandparents used to live. He remembered rocking on the front porch with his grandfather, blowing his homemade whistle while his grandpa dipped snuff. He spent many days with his grandpa while his mother and grandma went to town to shop. It was their male bonding ritual to eat sardines and sunflower seeds, occasionally going to the local store a couple of miles down the road for a Sugar Daddy. Of course, his grandma always brought a small gift for him from town, usually some kind of toy. Perhaps it was spoiling him, but it provided a lot of great memories for Drake. Even today, whenever the wind blew strongly, he remembered looking out the window of his grandparents' home to see the long grass blowing in the fields. His eldest brother had purchased the property from his grandma a few years before she died. She maintained a lifetime right to the property while she was living, but today it was all his. The old house now stood empty just a few yards from where his brother lived in a doublewide he had purchased with his second wife.

Drake waxed nostalgic as he passed by the old house and over the small bridge, looking at the land to the left where there was once a pond he and his dad and brothers fished in when they were young. The old farmhouse had been torn down and the pond filled in long ago, and now a housing develop-ment stood in its place, an ever-increasing sign of what some called progress along the southern landscape.

As he headed back to town, Drake stopped by the cemetery where Josh's daughter was buried. He was not sure why he went there, but for some unex-plained reason his car seemed to automatically steer itself in that direction. Maybe the thought of losing someone so close and so young was difficult for him to understand, or maybe he hoped to run into someone who would mention they saw Josh there the day of Julie's murder, but for whatever reason, he soon found he was outside the car and walking in the direction of

Rachel's grave. As he drew near, he saw Josh standing there the same as the last time he visited the cemetery. This time Drake didn't let Josh know he was there, instead ducking behind a nearby tree to silently observe his client. He could tell by the way Josh moved that he was speaking to his daughter, then he suddenly burst into tears. Drake stifled the impulse to offer aide and comfort to his client, and remained out of sight and sound as Josh continued his weeping.

Drake looked around the cemetery, but other than the two of them, it was deserted. He noticed there were not many freshly dug graves the first time he visited, and figured that was why there were few visitors who came here. After Josh left, he looked around at some of the other graves to check the dates. Perhaps many of the people who were buried here had no relatives alive to visit them.

Suddenly Drake's peripheral vision identified movement on his left side. He slowly turned his head in time to see an elderly gentleman walk up to a headstone approximately fifty yards away. He watched as the man glanced over in Josh's direction, then returned his gaze to the grave in front of him. When Drake looked back at Josh, he was walking away from Rachel's grave, heading back to his car. He made his way around the side of the tree, careful to remain out of Josh's line of sight. As soon as he drove away, Drake walked up to Rachel's grave and immediately stared down at the engraving which displayed the dates of her birth and death and held the inscription "Beloved Child of God Forever." He was just about ready to turn and head back to his car when he heard a voice behind him.

"That sure was a sad time for this town," he said. Drake turned to see the gentleman from across the way standing directly behind him. He stared at the man intently, searching for something to say. It was probably the first time in his life he had been caught speechless.

"I haven't seen you out here before," the man continued. "Are you a relative?"

"No, sir," Drake managed to choke out. "I'm Mr. Stephens' attorney, Adam Drake." He extended his hand, which the man took, giving a firm shake.

"Roger McNeil," he said. "Most people call me Mac."

"Do you know Mr. Stephens?"

"Only by name and reputation and, of course, the publicity surrounding his daughter's death. I guess most people around these parts are familiar with the Stephens.' And now with the death of his wife, I don't see how he manages to keep going."

"So you've seen him out here before?"

"Many times. In fact, you can pretty much set your watch by him on Wednesdays. He usually comes here around one-thirty and stays for a couple of hours."

"May I ask how you know this?" asked Drake.

"Because I come here every day, rain or shine, to visit with my dear wife, Helen," he said, nodding his head in the direction of the grave he was visiting earlier. "She died six years ago from ovarian cancer, but not a day goes by I don't come and talk to her." Drake was unable to resist the next question, which was whether or not Mac saw Josh here on the day of his wife's murder.

"Yep, I sure did," he said. "He was here like usual and stayed for at least a couple of hours."

"And how long do you usually stay here yourself?" asked Drake.

"Well, that all depends on what I've got to say to Helen. Sometimes it's a quick visit of about thirty minutes or so. Other times I might be here a few hours."

"What about the day Mrs. Stephens was killed?"

"Now that was a special day," replied Mac. "Our son, Bobby, called me that morning to tell me he and his wife, Sarah, are expecting their first child. I just had to tell Helen she was going to be a grandmother. I reckon I spent close to three hours out here, because I was here when Josh came, and still here when he left around three-thirty."

Drake could hardly contain the smile that was fighting to burst forth on his face as he continued his informal conversation with Mac. Before he left, he asked Mac if he would be willing to testify in court about seeing Josh that day, to which Mac told him he would be glad to help anyway he could. He said Josh always seemed like such a nice young man, and anyone who loved their daughter that much was surely not a murderer.

Drake scribbled Mac's name, address, and phone number on a small notepad he kept in his jacket, and thanked Mac for the conversation. Mac headed back in the direction where Helen lay at rest, probably to tell her about the good deed he was about to do for Josh.

Drake climbed back into his car, lit a cigarette, and headed back to the office. He wanted to reorganize his case based upon this new piece of information. It was the first time he actually felt somewhat confident about the case. On the way, he stopped off at Betty's house to check on her.

As he entered the house, she could tell there was something up, especially since Drake looked like a child who was about to burst from trying to keep a secret. He almost exploded as he told her all about his meeting with Mac at the cemetery. Her sudden look of concern stopped him in the middle of his exciting story.

"What's wrong?" he asked.

"Well, just make sure you check out Mr. McNeil before you call him as a witness."

"Why? Do you know this guy?"

"Let's just say he's got a reputation in town as not being all there, if you know what I mean," said Betty. Drake's face sank into an expression of despair. "Oh, don't lose hope," she insisted. "What he told you may very well be what he saw. It's just that he has been an eyewitness in some cases years ago before you got here, and it was proven he did not see things exactly as he originally stated. It seems his mother was very sick with cancer and he was trying to make a little extra money as a witness. He would testify however you wanted for the right price. All I'm saying is just be careful and be prepared to have his character called into question."

"Thanks for the info, Betty."

"Just trying to help. And I'll be back in the office tomorrow morning, cast and all." Betty looked up at Drake and flashed a big smile, hoping her cheery mood would help ease his anxiety over Mac.

Drake left Betty's and drove to the office, where he removed the notepad from his pocket and dialed Mac's number. After a couple of rings, Mac answered. Drake asked if he could come to the office tomorrow to prepare his testimony, to which he replied very enthusiastically he would. Drake hung up and tried to write down a few more questions, but his mind just would not work like he wanted. He exhaled a big sigh and ran his fingers through his blonde hair, realizing it was time to go home for the evening. He walked to the car, lit a cigarette, took a long draw, and exhaled as he pulled out of the parking lot heading toward home. He phoned Callie on the way and begged off from their date tonight. He wanted to be alone for awhile to mull over the day's events and see if he could make some sense out of all of this. Surely he would find a way to present Mac as a credible witness. It was his only hope if he planned to get Josh acquitted. Somehow he knew he had to make it work.

By two in the morning, Drake had yet to fall asleep, turning on the television to break the monotony of insomnia. It was definitely going to be a very long night.

Chapter 10

Drake took an extra long shower trying to shake the cobwebs from the long sleepless night. This would definitely be one of those four cups of coffee mornings he thought, as he dried his body and began to get dressed. He patted Sam on the head as he walked through the kitchen and out the back door to his car. He lit a Camel and headed toward town, deciding to grab a biscuit from one of the fast food restaurants for breakfast. After exiting the drive thru with his ham biscuit, Drake drove to the office, parked in his usual spot, and walked toward the building, dropping his still smoldering cigarette butt in front of him and grinding it out with his left shoe before stepping through the door. When he walked into the office, he immediately noticed Betty with her leg propped up on a stool. She had managed to figure out a way to sit in a sideways position and still reach her computer while keeping her leg elevated at the same time. He paused for a moment and marveled at her ingenuity before smiling and walking into his office. Before he could sit down, she paged him on the intercom.

"I've got something for you," she said.

Before he thought, he asked, "Well, bring it here." Then he remembered her leg and quickly walked out to her desk looking somewhat ashamed.

"That's okay," she said. "I'd like to be able to forget I have this cast on, too."

"What have you got?"

"I took the liberty of doing a little research on Mr. McNeil to prepare you for your meeting with him today," she said, handing him several sheets of paper from the printer. Drake thumbed through the papers as Betty narrated a condensed version of the contents. Apparently Mac had testified in a number of accident cases as an eyewitness, but on three separate occasions it was determined that under the conditions at the time of the incidents, there was no way Mac could have seen what he claimed. According to the reports, it was never proven that Mac was not actually there, but he was discredited as an eyewitness.

He rubbed his chin as he thought about his conversation with Mac yesterday. In this case it was merely the fact that Mac saw Josh at the cemetery on the afternoon of the murder. How could the prosecution find fault with that testimony? After all, it was broad daylight and not a very far distance from Mac's wife's grave to Rachel's. Besides, it was the best shot he had at establishing enough reasonable doubt in the minds of the jurors to acquit Josh. He simply had to use Mac's testimony.

When Mac arrived at the office, Drake immediately took him to the trial practice room. He started right in with the questions, firing one after the other to see if Mac would be easy to rattle. After the first twenty minutes, he had an uneasy feeling about Mac. Not only was he hard to rattle, but he looked like a pro on the witness stand. Mac almost appeared to be too confident and comfortable to be believable. It was an uneasy feeling, but it was all he had.

He continued the practice questions, even playing the part of the prosecutor in a mock cross-examination. Mac answered every question perfectly without hesitation or emotion. He was so compelling he was almost unconvincing. Drake hoped it was merely his own jaded impression from years of questioning unscrupulous witnesses, and the jury would take what Mac said at face value.

After a couple of hours of grueling questioning, Drake suggested they have lunch. Mac declined the invitation, though, and since he appeared to be ready for court, left the office and headed to the cemetery to visit his wife. Drake wondered if he was so excited about testifying he couldn't wait to tell his deceased wife.

Drake went to the café and ordered a couple of burgers to go so he and Betty could have lunch together at the office since it was so hard for her to get around with the cast on her leg. At least the rental car company sent her a small SUV which made it easier for her to get in and out of than a compact. Unfortunately, her car was a total loss, so as soon as the other driver's insurance company settled with her, she needed to buy another vehicle. When Drake returned with their lunch, he found Betty looking at different cars on the internet.

"Find one you like?" he asked, as he placed the food on the side of her desk.

"I was just getting some ideas," she said, still looking at the monitor.

"Well, eat your food before it gets cold," he said with a smile, much like a parent would speak to a child. Betty looked up at him with that 'don't talk to me like that' look. Then she smiled and removed the wrapper from her burger. Drake pulled up a chair and sat beside her while they ate.

"What do you think about Mr. McNeil? Is he going to work as a witness?" she asked.

"He answered the questions okay. I certainly hope he works out, because most of my case is riding on his testimony."

"Is there anything else you need for me to do before Monday?"

"Pray Betty," said Drake.

She smiled at him and gave him a reassuring pat on the arm. They finished their meal, and he returned to his office to reorganize the case file and make sure he had everything ready for Monday. Monday would be jury selection day, and depending on how long it took for them to pick a jury, they would either begin the trial that afternoon or the following day. Getting the right people on the jury was critical to winning a case, especially when it was not a slam dunk. Drake hoped Callie was overconfident enough in her case to let her guard down when it came to selecting the jury. All he needed was a few jurors he could sway with the reasonable doubt argument. At this point in his career, Drake was very good at gauging how an individual would look at a particular case based upon a few simple questions. As long as Callie did not pick up on what he was doing, he should be able to select most of the jury pool to complete his objective. There was always a wild card or two that you could never get a good read on, but he did not need every vote, and after years in a courtroom, Drake was well aware of that fact. Suddenly his thoughts were interrupted by Betty informing him that Callie was on the phone.

"Hello," he said into the receiver.

"Hey yourself," she replied. "How was your evening? Did you get a lot accomplished?"

"A little. How was your evening?"

"A little boring without you, but I was able to catch up on some things I had let go lately."

"Well, I'm completely caught up today," he said, hinting for a date.

"Why don't you come over for dinner this evening, say around six o'clock?"

"Sounds great! See you then." Drake placed the receiver back onto its cradle and leaned back in his chair, unable to contain the smile that spread across his face. He did not want to admit it to Callie, but one of the reasons he had trouble sleeping last night was because he didn't get to spend any time with her.

Suddenly he realized how much he was beginning to think like a married man, and yet he hadn't even discussed that possibility with Callie, much less proposed. He decided to be more patient and allow nature to take its course. After all, there was no need to rush into anything. If he and Callie were meant to be together, they would soon figure that out. Until then, he simply needed to enjoy her company and give their relationship time to mature. Of course, it never hurt to show someone you care about them, so he called a local florist and had a dozen roses sent to her at her office. He made sure they did not put his name on the card, just in case any of her coworkers read it. No one else needed to know about them at this point, and besides, a little mystery always made work more interesting. Later that afternoon his cell phone rang.

"Thank you," said Callie when he answered.

"For what?" he asked.

"You know what. The flowers," she whispered. "Unless I have more than one admirer."

"You're very welcome," he said, unable to contain the smile that erupted on his face.

"It looks like someone wants a special dessert tonight," she said with a naughty giggle.

"I didn't send those just to make a play for something extra tonight," he said, trying to sound offended. "Those came from the heart."

"I know. I was just teasing. Of course, you'll still get dessert tonight," she said in a low sexy voice, then hung up, leaving Drake to his thoughts of what was to come later.

It definitely made it difficult to concentrate on work, as he found his thoughts coming back to Callie. He played out several scenarios in his mind for the evening, seeing Callie's beautiful image in every one. At one point he felt somewhat embarrassed for feeling like a high school boy dreaming about a date, especially when he noticed Betty looking into his office, obviously catching him in the act of daydreaming. She just smiled and shook her head as she turned back to her computer. After torturing himself for another hour, he stood up and announced to Betty he was leaving for the afternoon. He grabbed his jacket and headed out the door, lighting a cigarette on the way to his car. He exhaled a long plume of smoke as he climbed into the driver's seat, and sped off in the direction of home. He would have plenty of time to get ready for his date with Callie, and who knows, he might even show up a little early.

His ever-loyal companion, Sam, was waiting as he walked in the door, standing at attention when Drake spoke his name and reached to give him a pat on the head. Drake quickly headed to the shower for an extra long cleansing, and allowed the hot water to run over his tired muscles. He was always amazed at how tired he felt from a day of office work, when other guys his age spent the day doing hard labor. He had heard about the mental drain of business when he was in school, but never believed it was actually as severe as people described it...at least, not until now. After experiencing it first hand, he was now a confirmed believer in the physically exhausting trials of the mentally challenging vocations. As the warm water cascaded over his body, he could feel his tense muscles begin to relax. He moved his head from side-to-side to loosen his neck as he plunged his head under the shower. As soon as he felt more relaxed, and was certain he was more than sufficiently clean, he stepped out of the shower and dried his body. He got dressed, applied some cologne, and made sure he fed Sam before he bolted out the door.

It was five-thirty, which given the short trip to Callie's, would put him twenty minutes early. He could not help himself, though, as he jumped in his car and drove off. He wanted to see her so much he would risk upsetting her by arriving a little early. Besides, surely she missed him just as much, he thought. He smiled and sang along with the radio, drumming his fingers to the beat, feeling all was right with the world as long as Callie was a part of it. He was even able to forget about the case for a few minutes, which was something that had never happened to him before. Suddenly, he broke out in a cold sweat, wondering if he was losing his edge. He had heard the horror stories of good attorneys who lost their edge, their minds wandering to other thoughts instead of their case, causing them to lose case after case until they realized they were no longer effective at their job. Surely this was not happening to him, he thought, as he gripped the steering wheel so tightly his knuckles turned white. "Get a grip," he told himself as he wiped his brow with the back of his hand. His face was still without color as he rang the doorbell. Callie opened the door before the chime had completely ceased, indicating she had been waiting for him to arrive early. Her smile quickly faded as she saw Drake's face.

"What's wrong?" she asked.

"Nothing," he said, offering a weak smile as he tried to hide his insecurity. He walked past her into the house, kissing her gently on the cheek as he went by. Callie followed him to the living room with a concerned look still on her face. She just stood there and looked at him until he shifted his gaze from the floor to her with an embarrassing look upon his face.

"What's going on?" she demanded, placing her hands on her hips.

"Do you ever forget about a case you are working on?"

"What do you mean?"

"You know, does your mind ever get so focused on something else that the case you're working on is suddenly not occupying your every thought?"

"Oh, you mean am I able to focus on other things like a life outside of work?" she said.

"Not just that," he said. "I'm talking about losing your edge."

"I'm not sure I follow you. What's going on, Adam?"

Drake went on to explain what happened on the way to her house a few minutes ago, and how he had, for a brief moment, forgot all about his current case. Callie listened sympathetically while he went on to explain how he heard of other lawyers who let other things get in the way of their work until they were no longer effective. He described how he felt on the way over and how suddenly his mind had forgotten about the case, and how worried he was that he might be losing his way. Callie touched his arm softly with her hand as she listened compassionately to his outpouring of fear. When he paused, she took the opportunity to speak.

"Adam, you're a great attorney, one of the best. The fact that you allowed something else to occupy your thoughts for a brief second only proves you are a human being with feelings. Believe me, you don't want to become a robotic zombie who thinks of nothing but the law, cranking out case after case with nothing to show for it in the end except a high win rate and no one to share your life with. The horror stories you heard about involving other lawyers is not the same thing you are going through. Those people allowed the wrong influences to take control of their life, like power, success, and money. You're experiencing love, which is a natural and beautiful thing. It will only serve to make you a more compassionate and successful attorney in the end."

"But what if my lack of concentration causes my work to suffer?" he asked. "That would be a huge disservice to my clients."

"Trust me, Adam," said Callie, taking hold of his hand. "When the time comes to perform, your legal instincts will prevail."

"I wish I could be as certain about it as you seem to be."

"Well, the way I see it, you have two choices. You can accept your current situation and use it to become a better lawyer, one with more feeling and compassion. Or you can use this as an excuse to end our relationship. Is that it, Adam? Are you looking to end our relationship?"

Drake sat back suddenly and stared at Callie in disbelief. The thought of life without her had never crossed his mind, and now he was dumbfounded at her straightforward question. He took a moment to compose himself before taking her by the hand.

"Callie, you're the best thing that's ever happened to me," he said. "I love you like I've never loved anyone before. And to even suggest we break up feels like a knife running through my heart. Don't you realize how much I love you?"

"I would like to think I do. But if you're having second thoughts, now is the time to express that before we get in too deep."

"I'm already in too deep, Callie. You left out the third choice available to me."

"What's that?"

"Callie, will you marry me?" asked Drake, dropping to one knee in front of her. Her eyes welled with tears as she struggled to utter the words from her mouth. Finally, she was able to choke back her tears enough to speak.

"Are you sure this is what you want?"

"I've never been so sure about anything in my life," he said with a smile.

"In that case, you'd better believe I will," she said, flinging her arms around his neck and drawing him to her in a tight embrace. Their lips met in a long passionate kiss, then they both erupted in tears of joy. They uncoiled long enough to make their way to the bedroom before becoming entangled again in a lovemaking session as their bodies became one. They forgot all about dinner as they became lost in each other and the turning point of their relationship. They fell asleep in each other's arms, totally exhausted and satisfied in the knowledge they had found their true love.

Chapter 11

Monday morning came quickly enough, as Drake entered the courthouse to begin jury selection for the case against his client. Over the years he had developed quite a process for choosing the right jurors, and attributed his success rate directly to his ability to select a winning jury. Each potential juror was asked the same series of questions, and based on the answers Drake could usually tell which ones would be more inclined to decide in his favor. Although he could challenge a certain number of jurors without cause, he preferred to question every potential juror before deciding to reject one. Today would be no different. He walked into the courtroom and up to the defense table, spreading out his files and papers in front of him. He had the questions on a list inside one of the folders, but since he had used them so many times, he could easily recall them from memory in precise order and detail. He knew from experience that in most cases where a husband was accused of killing his wife, male jurors were more sympathetic than female jurors. The opposite was usually true when a wife was accused of killing her husband. The more male members he could seat today, the better his chances of winning. Of course he realized it would be virtually impossible to have an all male jury, but he only needed enough votes to deadlock the jury. If Josh was not convicted the first time, it would be unlikely the prosecution would go to the trouble and expense of another trial without new evidence. And to Drake, a victory meant his client goes free, however that happens.

Callie looked especially radiant this morning, perhaps as a result of their engagement. She had her game face on, though, as she got right down to business. She also had her questioning technique when it came to selecting a jury, and believed she could pick a juror just as good as any attorney. She laid her files and papers neatly on the table in front of her, smoothed the front of her gray pinstripe business suit, and looked over in the direction of Drake with a stoic expression before giving him a slight wink. He winked back and curled the corners of his mouth in a slight smile. The game was afoot as the judge entered the courtroom and established the ground rules.

The gallery was full of potential jurors waiting to be called and questioned by the attorneys. Most people who are called for jury duty seek ways to avoid serving, which is not difficult if you know how to answer the questions in a way that makes you appear to be more prejudicial toward one side over the other. Typically anyone wanting to avoid serving on a trial like this would state that they believe in the sanctity of marriage and anyone who kills their spouse should hang. That statement, or something similar, will get the defense attorney to dismiss you as a juror. Ones like that are easy for the attorneys. The most difficult people to uncover are the ones who answer every question as the attorney would hope, when all they want is to get on the jury so they can fry the defendant. Drake had been fortunate in his career to be able to spot the tell tale signs of such instigators and dismiss them instead of falling for their false testimony.

As both he and Callie began to question the jury pool, Drake was careful to look for the unspoken clues such as eye movement and body language to determine if the juror is possibly hiding an ulterior motive. After all, there were the few citizens who truly believed and respected their duty to serve as a juror, and would actually look at the facts of the case and weigh all arguments before coming to a conclusion of guilt or innocence. Unfortunately, this type of person was one you also wanted to avoid having on the jury, especially if your case was weak. People serving jury duty as a civic responsibility were less likely to be swayed by the courtroom theatrics of a seasoned lawyer, instead preferring to deal with the facts and actual testimony than opinions or conjecture. This was one of those weak cases for Drake and he desperately needed to find jurors he could sway based on the character and look of his client, and how well of an alternative story he could weave.

They spent all morning questioning various potential jurors, and by lunch time there were only four jurors seated. The judge recessed court for lunch at eleven-thirty, instructing them to reconvene at one o'clock. Drake and Callie made certain not to eat at the same restaurant so as not to give any implication of impropriety. Drake spent the time mulling over the four jurors that had been selected so far, feeling fairly confident that at least two of them would be receptive to the arguments he presented in favor of his defendant. There were still eight more slots plus a couple of alternative positions to fill, so he had to remain on top of his game. It would almost be legal suicide to place all of his confidence in turning two of the initial four jurors. No, he needed to feel confident about the majority of the jurors in hopes that at least one would hold out in favor of Josh.

Drake finished his meal and drove around town, ending up at the cemetery. He stepped out of the car and lit a cigarette, and walked over to Rachel Stephens' grave. After pausing for a brief minute, he walked around looking at the various headstones, making mental notes of the ages of the people buried there. He moved over to where he remembered Mac standing, but was unable to locate his wife's grave. Of course, it was almost like looking for a needle in a haystack, especially when you were not familiar with exactly where someone was buried. He walked around some more until it was time to head back to court. He lit another cigarette for the ride back to downtown. As he pulled into the parking lot behind the courthouse, he took one last long drag from his Camel, flipped the still smoldering butt out the window, and parked his car. He climbed out and walked to the entrance.

Callie was already back at her seat and ready when he walked into the courtroom. He gave a nod of acknowledgement in her direction and sat down to look at some notes while they waited for the judge to enter. It was not long before the bailiff announced the entrance of the judge, requiring everyone in the courtroom to stand until he was seated. He called the court to order and the next potential juror was called to the witness stand for questioning. They continued in this manner until four o'clock, when they finally had all twelve jurors plus two alternates selected. At this time, the judge recessed court until the following morning to begin opening arguments.

Drake wanted the evening alone to mentally prepare for the following morning, although Callie asked for a date. Apparently, she was not as nervous about her opening argument, since she believed her case was air tight. He called her on her cell, while driving home for a short, but intimate, conversation. Then he took a long drag of the cigarette he'd just lit and weaved through evening commuter traffic on his way home. Sam was waiting to greet him when he walked in the back door. Drake gave him a quick pat on the head and walked straight to the pantry, retrieving the necessary ingredients to add to the ground beef he had in the refrigerator to make chili.

When he won his first case several years ago, he had made homemade chili the night before the trial began. Since then, he always made homemade chili for dinner the night before a trial. Much like professional athletes, he wanted to stick to the same routine hoping for the same positive results as in the past. He knew how superstitious, and maybe a little paranoid, it was, but he was not about to question fate or Karma or whatever you wanted to call it, especially when it was crunch time.

He carefully went to work blending just the right amounts of ingredients until he was satisfied the concoction was up to par. Grabbing a soda from the fridge, he headed to the living room to catch the news. When he took the first bite, he closed his eyes and savored the wonderful taste caressing his palate. At least he always had one good meal he enjoyed during a trial, no matter what the outcome. After he finished eating, he turned the television off and retrieved a CD from his stash of music, which was a mix of pop and rock from several different years. This CD was special, though, because it was the only one of its kind in the collection. It was the original soundtrack to the movie *Philadelphia*, which Drake always listened to before, during, and after a big trial. He replayed in his mind the scene where Andrew Beckett cried while listening to opera, sitting in the dark listening to the same music. Because the main character in the movie was a determined attorney fighting against injustice, he felt a spiritual kinship with him. He closed his eyes as he felt the music energizing his entire body, coursing through every fiber of his being, reminding him of why he chose to be an attorney in the first place. He drew an unconscious strength from the sound that flowed from the stereo and through his ears, piercing his soul.

Tonight was not about pouring over details about the case, but rather mental preparation for Drake, much like a warrior prepares before battle. And indeed this would be a hard fought battle that would require every ounce of strength he could muster in order to claim victory in the midst of such a worthy adversary. There was no need to write down any thoughts or words. In all of his years inside the courtroom, Drake never once wrote down an opening argument, preferring instead to allow the spirit from the night before to carry over and take control at the proper moment, providing a more effective soliloquy than he could ever have penned himself. He always spoke from the heart and soul, and not the head. Now, as he listened to the music, recalling flashes of scenes from the movie, he felt the spirit of right and justice welling within him and thought about his client and the death of his beautiful wife. As the singer mourned in the song, Drake mourned in his heart for the victim, scanning the images of the crime scene in his mind. It was a terrible injustice for a life so rich and vibrant to be extinguished at such a young age, but it was even more of an injustice for the love of her life to stand accused of killing his soul mate.

When the CD finished, Drake turned the volume up and allowed it to continue playing through again while he took a long hot bath. He remained in the dark with his eyes closed, listening to the music as his body soaked. Sam had retreated to his bed long ago, being all too familiar with Drake's ritual by now. He was in the zone as he slowly stirred the water with his arms, relaxing his muscles completely, the music sweeping over him. As the CD neared the end again, he climbed out of the tub without grabbing a towel and walked back to the living room. With his body dripping all over the floor, he turned the stereo off and removed the CD, placing it carefully back into its case. He walked back to the bathroom and grabbed a towel, drying his body, the water draining from the tub.

When he was completely dry, he returned to the living room, where he retrieved a DVD from another drawer and loaded it into the player. The completion of his pre-trial ritual culminated with actually watching the movie *Philadelphia* before going to bed. He sat naked in the dark watching the movie and drinking another soda. He had asked Callie not to call him tonight, turning the phones off just in case, at least until he was finished watching the movie.

He'd turn the phones back on before going to bed in case someone needed to get in touch with him during the night.

Once the movie was over, Drake made his way in the dark to his bedroom where he collapsed on the sheets. His body still warm from the bath, he didn't bother climbing beneath the top sheet, instead opting to lay fully exposed on top of the bed. He tried to clear his head of all thoughts in order to more quickly fall asleep, but no matter how hard he tried, the image of Callie kept pressing its way into his mind. He broke out in a sweat as he feared he would no longer be able to concentrate on his career as he should, even though Callie had reassured him that everything would be okay. After an hour of suffering in the dark, he reached for the phone and punched in Callie's number. She answered after two rings.

"Hello?"

"Hey, Callie, it's me," said Drake.

"What's wrong?" she asked somewhat alarmed. "Relax, nothing's wrong. I just needed to talk to you."

"But I thought you wanted the evening all to yourself."

"I did, but I couldn't get you out of my mind."

"Oh, that's so sweet."

"This is serious, Callie. I'm afraid I won't be able to concentrate."

"I know exactly what you need," she said as she hung up the phone.

"Callie? Hello?" he spoke into the phone, but she was obviously not on the other end.

He waited for a few minutes, assuming they were somehow disconnected and she would call back, but the phone did not ring. He called her back but got her answering machine. Now he was really frustrated, and very much awake. As he rose, slipping on a pair of sleep pants, the back doorbell rang. Sam let out an inquisitive bark, but Drake quieted him as he stumbled through the dark toward the kitchen. He peered through the window before opening the door.

"Callie?" he said with a puzzled look on his face. She gave him a quick peck on the cheek, walked past him into the kitchen, and closed the door behind her before grabbing him and pulling him toward her, locking her lips firmly onto his. When she released her grip and stepped back, he noticed she was wearing her long rain coat, which she immediately opened to reveal nothing underneath except a sexy negligee and matching stockings. She slid out of the coat, allowing it to drop to the floor, then took him by the hand as they walked to the bedroom. She shoved him down onto the bed and straddled his body, kissing him deeply. He pulled her closer to him and they made love, unceasing until each was completely spent. Curling up beside him, she placed his head on her chest while she stroked his wavy hair.

"How's your head now?" she asked.

"Amazingly clear," he answered.

"I knew it. All you needed was me. Whenever we're apart, you think of me so much that you can't concentrate on anything else. But when we're together, your mind, body, and soul are so content that you're able to concentrate on other things because you know I'm right here."

"Humph," he grunted, realizing she might have a point. Looking her directly in the eyes, he asked, "So what am I going to do?"

"That's easy," she answered. "We'll simply have to sleep together until we get through this trial, keeping it very hush-hush, of course. Then, once the trial is over, we can get married and everything will be out in the open. I'll probably not be allowed to try cases where you're the defense attorney, but things will work out."

"I certainly hope so," he said, "because I really like having you around."

She smiled and stroked his hair as he fell asleep, completely satisfied and at peace. They slept for a couple of hours, waking up once for another love-making session, before drifting back to sleep.

Callie set his alarm clock for five o'clock so she could leave while it was still dark. It would not do for anyone to see her leaving his house, let alone dressed like this. Drake was still asleep when she turned off the alarm and kissed his forehead. Gathering her clothes, she pulled her coat on, and headed out the door. She had plenty of time to shower and dress before court, and began going over her opening argument in her mind as she drove home. The evidence was very much in her favor. She was not worried about the outcome at all, even with Drake's reputation as a "Magic Man." She smiled as she walked into her place, thinking about how much she enjoyed him being her "Magic Man."

CHAPTER 12

Drake awoke to the realization that Callie was not there.

He rubbed his hands over his face, massaging his eyes with his fingers, climbed out of bed and shuffled to the bathroom. He took a quick shower and dressed in his dark navy suit for the first day of the trial. He put some coffee on to brew while he filled Sam's dish with kibble. He could see the wet paw prints on the kitchen floor indicating Sam had already been outside for his morning routine. As the food rattled in the dish, Sam stood up from his bed and walked slowly to the kitchen to investigate. He gave the bowl a cursory sniff, then turned and headed back to bed. It was too early for him to eat, and besides, he knew it would be there waiting for him when he woke up later.

Drake finished his coffee and toast, called goodbye to Sam, and walked out the back door, lighting a cigarette as he walked to the car. He took one long drag and exhaled before climbing into the driver's seat. Pulling out of the drive, he headed toward Josh's house, deciding it would be best if he took Josh to court and back in order to help him wade through the throng of reporters that would certainly be milling in front of the courthouse like vultures ready to descend upon their prey. It would also give Drake the opportunity to comment or not comment, depending upon how the case was going. He did not want to take a chance on Josh saying anything to the press, preferring to control what information he decided the press should have. He was fully aware that some cases were tried in the newspapers, and wanted to ensure he had complete control over what his side had to divulge, if anything.

He had barely turned into the drive when Josh stepped out of the rear door dressed in a very neat, but conservative dark business suit. Drake had not bothered to give Josh the usual coaching he did for most clients about how to dress for court, considering this was normal everyday attire for his client. Josh threw up his hand in greeting and offered a weak smile, obviously nervous about his first day on trial. As he climbed into the car, Drake offered his hand, which Josh took, grasping it firmly and giving one pump before releasing his grip.

Drake spent the remainder of the drive to the courthouse preparing Josh for the day ahead, giving him a glimpse of what to expect. He hoped the conversation would not only instill more confidence of his ability to defend Josh, but also help alleviate some of the nervousness by requiring him to concentrate on the details.

Drake was just finishing his instructions regarding not speaking to the press when they arrived at the courthouse. He watched as several reporters scrambled into two lines along the steps, much like the red carpet at the Academy Awards, each ready to shout questions while photographers snapped pictures.

Drake climbed out of the vehicle first and walked around to the passenger side, opened the door for Josh and escorted him toward the courthouse. They passed through the gauntlet of reporters without uttering a word until they reached the top step. Drake suddenly turned back toward the crowd and held up his hand, indicating they should be quiet if they wanted to hear an important statement.

"Let me just say one thing," he began. "My client is innocent and is looking forward to his day in court. Thank you."

He turned and entered the building with Josh at his side while the reporters continued to shout questions behind them. Once they were inside, the reporters turned to their respective cameras to give a live update. Drake and Josh made their way past the security checkpoint and onto the elevator. Criminal court was on the third floor. They rode in silence until the doors opened and they stepped off and walked into the courtroom.

Callie was already seated at the prosecutor's table with one of her assistants seated beside her. He appeared to be a recent law school graduate, still wet behind the ears and obviously observing her as part of his training. Drake gave a cursory nod in their direction and escorted Josh to the defendant's table, where they both sat down and waited for the trial to begin. After a few minutes, the bailiff appeared and called the court to order, announcing the presence of the Honorable Robert Abernathy, the presiding judge. Once Judge Abernathy was seated, everyone else was instructed to take their seat. He called the case name and number again and asked if both the prosecution and defense were ready to begin, which both answered in the affirmative, then he instructed Callie to make her opening statement.

She was as eloquent as ever, weaving a tapestry of circumstantial evidence, painting a picture for the jury of a gruesome crime culminating in the death of an innocent victim at the hands of the accused. She assured the jury that she would prove, beyond a reasonable doubt, Josh Stephens killed his wife, Julie, and tried to cover it up by accusing some unknown phantom suspect whom the defense had yet to present. By the time she finished, Drake was questioning the innocence of his client in his mind but snapped to as it was his time to speak to the jury.

He wanted to avoid the more eloquent approach so as not to appear to copy Callie. Instead, he began with the strong character of his client, the tragic death of their daughter, and now the unfortunate murder of his client's wife, which all seemed to be a terrible misfortune of fate that had somehow settled upon this man and his family. He went on to point out some of the evidence the prosecution would use as part of their case, and offered reasonable explanations for each one. Then, at the point of conclusion, Drake looked each juror directly in the eyes and played the 'reasonable doubt' card, seeking to intimidate the jury into reading doubt into every piece of evidence. He made it sound like each and every member of the jury would be accountable for their decision individually, and that somehow he would know if they violated the 'reasonable doubt' imperative.

He was definitely a master at drawing in a jury and influencing their thought process. Yes, the "Magic Man" was on top of his game today, so much so that several of the jurors began taking notes during his opening statement. Walking back to the table, he looked over at Callie, to which she responded by rolling her eyes. Now it was time for the prosecution to present their case.

She began with the testimony of the police officers, providing crime scene photographs for the jury. She wanted to paint the darkest picture she could of the murder to hopefully prevent a juror from feeling any sympathy toward the defendant. Of course, the detective described the scene in great detail, offering his own opinion in the process, to which Drake objected to as facts not in evidence. The judge sustained the objection, but how do you make a juror forget what they heard? It was a tactic used by both prosecutors and defense attorneys—toss out a question you know your adversary will object to, because once it was out there, you couldn't undo it.

She proceeded with the other expert witnesses, including the medical examiner, to provide all of the details necessary for the jury to understand exactly what the prosecution believed happened. The murder weapon was exhibited, along with the testimony regarding Josh Stephens' fingerprints on it. Drake made sure the jury understood exactly where on the drill the prints were found, and there was no evidence to suggest he had actually held the weapon in a manner to inflict the wound upon his wife.

When Callie introduced the life insurance policy as motive for the murder, he made certain the jury knew that both Josh and Julie had purchased policies on each other for the same amount at the same time. In fact, he did a very good job of refuting most of the evidence as circumstantial, except for the lack of a witness at the cemetery, which Callie kept mentioning. She was aware of the witness list, but had no idea why Roger McNeil was on the defense list, unless he was a character witness. Drake was saving him for the defense's turn, where he planned to call Mac and destroy the prosecution's claim of no witness that could place Josh at the cemetery at the time of the murder.

She spent three days calling every witness on her list to substantiate the evidence they had against Josh, and to keep driving home their position that he killed his wife for the money. Then it was Drake's turn. He called Mr. Evans as the first witness, asked about the morning of the murder and whether Mr. Evans had witnessed anyone near the Stephens house. Mr. Evans testified to seeing the air conditioning repairman at the home that morning, described the uniform and vehicle as best he could remember just like they had practiced in Drake's office. Callie asked only one question during cross-examination, and that was for Mr. Evans to describe the man in question. Evans explained he did not get a good enough look at the gentleman to give an accurate description, to which Callie responded by stating the man could have been Josh Stephens. Of course, Drake objected, but she had made her point.

Next Drake called Ms. Mason, making sure he kept the questions brief and to the point, only concerned with her corroboration of Mr. Evans's testimony regarding the car parked at the Stephens home that morning. Again, Callie asked if she had seen the person in question, to which Ms. Mason was compelled to say no. Finally, it was time for Drake to call Roger McNeil to the stand. He began by asking how he knew the defendant, to which Mac replied he had seen him at the cemetery on numerous occasions. Then he asked about the afternoon of the murder, and Mac stated he saw Josh at the cemetery that afternoon from approximately one-thirty until three-thirty. Drake asked if he was positive about the time, to which he replied yes, then went on to elaborate on his visit to his wife's grave. He flashed a subdued smile in the direction of Callie as he said, "Your witness," and walked back to the table to take his seat. He was feeling more confident about the case now, but then Callie began her cross-examination.

"Mr. McNeil, you testified to seeing Mr. Stephens at the cemetery on the afternoon of his wife's death. Is that correct?" she asked.

"Yes."

"And can you tell us again why you were there?"

"Objection, asked and answered," interrupted Drake.

"Sustained," replied Judge Abernathy.

"I'll rephrase the question. You were visiting your wife's grave, correct?"

"Yes."

"Your Honor, I would like to include this diagram of the cemetery as people's exhibit J. This diagram shows where all of the graves are located, complete with names of the deceased," said Callie, holding up a paper and walking toward the witness.

"I know it's different than actually being there, but will you please indicate where your wife is buried on this chart, Mr. McNeil?"

Mac looked at the paper, studying it intently before looking up at Callie with fear in his eyes.

"Is there something wrong, Mr. McNeil?"

"I can't find it," he answered.

"Could that possibly be because it does not exist?"

"Objection," yelled Drake.

"Overruled, answer the question, please," said the Judge.

"Of course, it's there," said Mac, his voice wavering. "Then where is it on this diagram?" Callie persisted. Mac sat silently while Callie turned and walked back to the table. She retrieved another paper and walked back to the witness stand.

"Mr. McNeil, I have here a copy of an obituary for Helen McNeil Barber. Will you please read aloud the highlighted portion?"

Mac peered at the paper she placed in front of him and cleared his throat.

"Mrs. Barber had one son, Roger McNeil, who resides at the same address. Burial will be in Oak Park Cemetery."

"So that is your mother whom you visit at the cemetery," said Callie. Mac simply nodded his head in agreement. "In fact, you've never been married, have you, Mr. McNeil?" Again Mac remained silent and nodded, until Callie instructed him to speak up.

"Yes," he said. Drake could feel the wheels beginning to come off as he struggled to think of some way to object, but instead was forced to listen as Callie continued her assault.

"Mr. McNeil, considering you lied about a deceased wife, why should we believe anything you say?"

"Because I was there," he pleaded.

"Then why were you not honest about whose grave you were visiting?"

"I was afraid what people would think, you know, there aren't many grown men who have never been married and yet still visit their mother's grave almost every day."

"You two seem to have had a special relationship," said Callie.

"Very special," he replied.

Callie suddenly changed direction and asked, "Have you ever testified in court before?"

"Yes."

"And were these also criminal trials?"

"Objection! Relevance, Your Honor," yelled Drake. "Your Honor, if you will allow me a little latitude I believe I can demonstrate the relevance of this line of questioning," said Callie.

"Proceed, Ms. Devane, but connect the dots quickly or I'll cut you off."

"Thank you, Your Honor," she said, and continued, "Mr. McNeil, how many criminal trials did you testify as a witness in?"

"I don't remember. Maybe a dozen or so."

"And you were compensated for your testimony, which later was determined to be false in at least three of these cases, isn't that true?" Mac hesitated for a moment.

"I remind you, Mr. McNeil, that you're still under oath."

"Yes, I testified for money. But I needed the money to pay all of the medical bills that accumulated when my mother was sick." Drake felt weak as he remembered what Betty had told him about Mac earlier.

"So you lied under oath for money," said Callie.

"Yes."

"And were you paid for your testimony in this case?"

"Yes," he answered, avoiding eye contact with Drake.

"Mr. McNeil, who paid you to testify on Josh Stephens' behalf," she asked.

"I don't know. I assumed it was Mr. Drake, but someone called me and told me that Mr. Drake would be coming to the cemetery that day we met, and that I should tell him I saw Mr. Stephens the afternoon of his wife's death. Shortly after I met Mr. Drake in the cemetery, I received a package delivered to my front door, but I didn't see who dropped it off. I just figured since the attorneys paid me in the past, it must be Mr. Drake."

"How much money was in the package?"

"Fifty thousand dollars," he said, causing a collective groan to sweep across the courtroom, followed by many whispering voices. Judge Abernathy rapped the gavel to call the court back to order.

"Mr. McNeil, did you or did you not see the defendant Josh Stephens in the cemetery on the day his wife was murdered?"

"No, I wasn't there that day," he said, looking down at his lap.

Another groan followed by more whispering swept across the courtroom as the judge hammered his gavel to regain order. Callie informed the judge she had no more questions for this witness. Drake asked the court to recess until the following morning, which the judge granted. This would give him time to discuss the option of putting Josh on the stand with him. In most cases, the defendant is instructed not to testify for fear of opening up too many avenues for the prosecution to explore with regard to character, motive, and opportunity. It was usually better if the defendant did not testify, instead relying on the other witnesses. Today's events had destroyed what little foundation of reasonable doubt Drake had been able to create with the jury, though, and now he was almost forced to call Josh to testify.

Drake escorted Josh through the throng of reporters as they shouted questions regarding the day's testimony. This time Drake offered no comment as they hurried to his car. He drove directly to the office without uttering a single word. Then he and Josh entered the building, walked directly past Betty without speaking, and closed the door to his office behind them. Once securely inside, Drake broke the silence.

"Okay, Josh, care to tell me what the hell went on in there today," he said, his red face almost boiling with anger.

"What do you mean?"

"You know what I mean. Did you pay McNeil to lie for you?"

"I'm sorry about all of that, Adam. I just felt I needed a little insurance in order to win, that's all. I never thought he would collapse like that once he got on the witness stand. Besides, I didn't know his history. He contacted me and offered his services for a price."

"Well, that's just dandy! You not only failed to get your so called insurance, but you totally maligned my case. His testimony basically wiped out everything I had accomplished up to that point. Nice job!"

"So what do we do now?" asked Josh.

"We don't do anything. I have no choice but to put you on the stand and try to repair some of the damage. Do you think you can answer some simple questions without messing that up?"

"I'll do my best."

"You'd better. And no more funny business or I'll ask the judge to release me as your counsel."

"Adam, if I can't convince the jury I'm innocent, they'll put me to death."

Drake let out a huge sigh as he stared at the floor. He knew what Josh said was correct. As the case was crumbling before him, he felt as if he were stranded on a railroad track watching a train as it barreled toward him, and try as he may, he could not get out of its way.

"Go home and get some rest," he said.

"Shouldn't we practice my testimony?" asked Josh.

"You can play through it in your head, but it all boils down to simply telling the truth. I'll give you a lot of leeway to talk, but it's up to you to tell your story. I can't prep you on that because I wasn't there." He shook Josh's hand and escorted him to the door. Drake waited until Josh was out of sight before turning to Betty and announcing that he was going home for the evening. He lit a Camel as he made his way through the afternoon traffic toward home.

After dinner, which consisted of a couple of corn dogs, Drake sat in the dark listening to the soundtrack again as he sipped his soda. Around midnight a soft knock sounded on the back door, and he made his way through the dark house to let Callie inside.

Chapter 13

Callie was gone when Drake climbed out of bed and headed to the shower. Yesterday had been such a dismal day in court, he wished he didn't have to go back in there and face the jury today. But his client was counting on him and if he was going down, he was determined to go down swinging. He let the warm water cascade over his body as he kept replaying the testimony from Mac, wondering if there were any questions he missed, or something else he could have done to provide damage control. After beating himself up for several minutes, he realized he had done all he could. Sometimes these things happen and there is really no way to prepare for them. Now the task at hand was to focus for today's round, and try to somehow make the jury believe Josh.

Drake ate breakfast again at home, his usual routine during a trial, unless of course he wanted press attention. If that were the case, he would go to the café or a local restaurant. Not this time, though, as this case was much too difficult to positively spin the local reporters, especially after yesterday. It would be best to maintain a low profile for the remainder of the trial, especially since losing was now a very strong possibility. As he ate, Drake cursed under his breath for letting himself get into this position. He hated the thought of losing, especially when he believed his client was innocent. But he took every loss as a personal defeat, often stewing over a case for weeks after the trial was over. For as much of a "Magic Man" as he was, he was also a master at self-criticism, dissecting every word of a lost case to determine what he missed, or what he could have done differently to alter the eventual outcome.

Having witnessed many times the self-loathing he inflicted upon himself after a loss, Betty gave up trying to help him out of a funk. Instead, she opted to sit quietly on the sidelines while he gave himself a good thrashing until he was completely a shell of the "Magic Man." She would then intervene to assist him in picking up the pieces of his shattered self-esteem, and build him up for the next battle. She was glad his success rate was so high because the entire process was completely exhausting, both physically and mentally. Now that Callie was a part of his life, Betty hoped she would take over the role of reassembling Drake after such a meltdown.

Drake pulled out of the drive and headed to Josh's house to once again accompany him to the courthouse and through the throng of reporters that waited each morning like a pack of hungry wolves for Drake to toss them a morsel they could print for their byline. He flicked the still smoldering cigarette butt through the driver's side window as he turned onto the street where his client lived. He walked past Josh's car to the back door and knocked firmly. He waited patiently for a minute, but upon hearing no movement from inside the house, he knocked again and called out to Josh. As he stood there debating whether to kick in the door, his cell phone rang.

"Hello?" he answered.

"Adam, it's Josh."

"Where are you?"

"Never mind that, Adam," said Josh. "I'm sorry to put you in such an awkward position, but the way I see it, I simply have no choice."

"Don't do anything stupid, Josh."

"Relax, Adam. I know the trial is not going my way, and frankly I don't believe my testimony will save me. I just can't go to prison, Adam. I'd never survive."

"Josh, tell me where you are and I'll come get you. Then we can talk this thing out and determine the best course of action."

"I'm afraid I can't do that," he replied. "If there is any way you can stall the judge to buy me a little time to get a head start, I'd appreciate it. If you can't, though, I understand."

"Don't do this, Josh, please. You're making a big mistake."

"It's my life on the line. I have to do this."

"Will you at least call me later?"

"Don't worry, Adam. I'll stay in touch as best I can. I want you to continue working on the case to see if you can find the man Mr. Evans saw that day. If you can get enough evidence to exonerate me, I'll come in. Until then, I need to stay out of sight."

"Josh, listen to me. Every cop and bounty hunter in the country is going to be looking for you."

"I realize that, but I can't face going to prison. I'll call you later." And with that, Josh ended the call.

Drake stood for a moment trying to let the words sink into his brain. He quickly lit a cigarette and took a long drag, hoping the nicotine would afford him a little relaxation. He walked back to the car and climbed in, driving off toward the courthouse. As he drove, he tried to formulate exactly what he would say to the judge when it became apparent his client was not there.

Drake waded through the rows of reporters, offering no comment as he entered the courthouse. Callie was already inside and seated when he walked in and took his seat at the defense table. She could tell by his pale complexion that something was wrong, but she didn't speak to him. Instead, she tried to concentrate on some of the papers lying in front of her, carefully glimpsing over at him from the corner of her eye every few seconds. She wanted to offer comfort for whatever was bothering him, but under the circumstances that was impossible.

Suddenly, she realized the defendant had not entered with him as he had every other day of the trial, which sent her internal alarms blaring at full alert. Just as her curiosity was about to get the best of her, the bailiff called the court to attention as the judge entered, took his seat, and proceeded to call the court to order. He asked Drake to call his next witness, to which he replied by asking for a continuance. He went on to explain his client was supposed to be his next witness, but he was at home sick with food poisoning, and was not feeling well enough to testify today. He could tell by the expression on the judge's face he was not pleased with the motion, but when Callie had no objection, he granted a two day recess, warning Drake that if his client was not able to appear by then, he would need a doctor to testify to his continued illness. Drake thanked the judge just before court was dismissed, and left as quickly as he could to avoid Callie and the multitude of questions he was sure were swimming in her head. He wanted to make sure he was in his office before Josh called again so he would have more privacy. Once he was past the reporters, Drake lit a Camel, taking a deep drag, hoping the intake of smoke would calm his fraying nerves as he continued to his car. He climbed in and drove off toward the office, releasing a huge plume of smoke from his lips as he rubbed his forehead trying to ease the mounting tension that had been building since he spoke to Josh earlier that morning.

Drake hit the office door on a half-run, not even noticing the couple speaking with Betty as he continued into his office and closed the door. He had barely sat down when there came a gentle knock on the door, followed by it opening slightly to reveal Betty's questioning eyes.

"Aren't you supposed to be in court?" Drake motioned for Betty to enter and close the door behind her, continuing to beckon with his fingers until she was leaning over the desk directly in front of him.

"Our bird flew the coop," he said in a half whisper.

"What do you mean 'flew the coop'?"

"Exactly what it means," replied Drake. "Josh is on the run. I stopped by his house this morning to drive him to the courthouse, but he wasn't home. He called me on my cell phone and explained he didn't believe his testimony would be enough to acquit him, especially after yesterday's events. He wants me to continue to work on proving he is innocent, but unless we get lucky, he doesn't plan on coming back." Drake let out a huge sigh.

"But I thought we were pretty much at a dead end regarding the air conditioner repairman Mr. Evans saw that morning," said Betty.

"We are. That's what makes this so frustrating. I don't know where else to look. Oh, by the way, Betty, who're your friends outside?"

"Oh my, I forgot all about them," she said, and raised her hand to her mouth and exclaimed, "That's it!" Before he could ask her what, she rushed out of the office, grabbed the lady by the hand, and practically dragged her back into his office, moving with one crutch and herding the lady with the other, with the gentleman not far behind.

"Adam, meet Macy Merit," she exclaimed, almost thrusting Macy's hand into Drake's. He took Macy's hand and stood staring into her eyes before speaking.

"It's been a long time, Macy. You're looking well," said Drake. "What brings you to High Point?"

"You look well, too, Adam. We were on our way to Myrtle Beach for a vacation and thought we would stop in and say hello," said Macy. She gestured toward Spence. "Adam Drake, I'd like you to meet my husband, Spencer Rawlings."

"Its just Spence," said Spence, shaking Drake's hand.

"How have you been?" asked Macy.

"Well, I don't have to tell you it was pretty rough going for awhile. But I managed to pull it together, thanks to Betty here." He smiled and winked at Betty. She handed him a business card with the words 'The Avenger' printed in bold face type along with a single phone number and said, "It just happens Ms. Merit helps people who have suffered an injustice. She told me the story about how she met her husband Spence. He had been wrongfully accused of murder and Macy helped prove his innocence. I was thinking maybe she could do the same for Josh."

"Didn't you say your last name was Rawlings?" asked Drake.

"It is. Macy decided to keep her maiden name for professional reasons." Drake nodded his understanding as he looked at the business card again, then paused for a minute as if reflecting on something deep. Betty decided to snap him out of his trance.

"Well, what do you think, Adam?" she asked. "Should we ask Macy to look into this for us?"

"I'm well aware of what Macy does, Betty. And I'm sure she could help, but you heard her say they're on vacation. I don't think we should drag them into this."

"That's okay," Macy interrupted. "Please tell me about it and I'll be glad to give my professional opinion as to whether or not I can possibly help." Drake let out a sigh, rotating his shoulders, and motioned for them to have a seat while he began to recount the entire story about Julie Stephens' murder all the way up to this morning when his client decided to take flight. When he finished, Macy looked over at Spence, gave him a wink and a smile, and asked, "Does any of this sound familiar?" Spence merely nodded and smiled back.

"Well, what do you think?" asked Drake.

"It sounds like your client is innocent and could use our help. Is there any way for us to meet with him in person?"

"Unfortunately, I don't know where he is. He's supposed to call me again, so I can try to set up something then, but for now I'd have to say no."

"Do you have any taped testimony of your client that we can review?" asked Spence.

"Yes, I have the tapes where we practiced for court."

Drake led them to the practice trial room, which garnered an exclamation from Spence as he was unable to hide the fact he was impressed by the setup. Drake put the first tape into the VCR and began playing Josh's testimony on the wide screen television. The room was as quiet as a classroom on the Fourth of July as they all watched the screen. Spence and Macy were especially engrossed, as they seemed to be making countless mental notes. They watched every minute of Josh's testimony, carefully studying the last one as intensely as the first. When the tape was finished, Drake rewound it and placed it back in its file. Then he escorted them back to his office where he handed Macy the case file with all of the photographs and physical evidence. Spence pulled his chair alongside hers and watched over her shoulder as she flipped through the contents of the file. When she finished, she handed the file back to Drake and smiled.

"I believe we can help your client," she said.

"That is, we may be able to help him," interjected Spence, touching Macy's arm. "We would like some time to review the information and discuss a possible course of action."

Drake gave a quizzical look at Betty, and then returned his gaze to Macy, maintaining an awkward silence that screamed, "What am I missing here?" Then he spoke, "Look, I don't want to put you guys on the spot here. I understand you're on vacation. You really don't need to look into this. I can handle it."

"Maybe you're right," said Spence. "Maybe that would be best."

Macy turned in the direction of Spence as her eyes pierced like daggers into his. Then she turned back to Drake, smiled, and said, "Give us until tomorrow morning to talk about it before anyone makes any hasty decisions." Then they exchanged pleasantries again before Spence and Macy left the office.

"How come I never heard you mention Macy before?" asked Betty.

"That was another time in my life that I don't care to revisit," said Drake.

"Well maybe she can help you now."

"I don't know about this, Betty," said Drake. "They didn't seem very eager to pursue this."

"Nonsense, she just needed to get him alone and convince him to see it her way. Didn't you see the way she looked at him? I believe she wants to help."

"I hope you're right," he said with a sigh. "Because right now I'm out of options and the continuance I got is only good for two days."

"In that case, you'd better be working on how you're going to explain things to Judge Abernathy, because no matter how good she is, I doubt Macy can clear Josh that quickly."

He let out another long sigh and flipped his pen in the air, causing it to land with a thud on the papers in front of him. He picked up Macy's business card and stared at it for several seconds before tossing it into Josh's file. Betty returned to her desk, leaving Drake alone as he wrestled for ideas on how to discuss his client's situation with Judge Abernathy. Finally after thirty minutes of almost pulling his hair out, Drake came to the realization there was only one option at this point, and that was to tell the truth and be prepared to suffer the consequences. Besides, surely he could not be blamed for the disappearance of Josh. Even if the judge felt he was stalling for time for his client to flee, no one would ever be able to prove that is what happened.

He ran his fingers through his hair, dropped his pen on the desk, and stood up to leave. He told Betty to call it a day also and close the office a little early today, which she was more than happy to do. He walked out of the building, lit a Camel, and drove off in the direction of home. With a two day continuance, he knew Callie would be eager to spend some extra time together, which sounded good to him, as long as he could keep her from asking about his client. But considering they agreed not to discuss the case, there should be no mention of Josh or the trial. He tossed the smoldering butt out the window with a confident flick of his wrist, feeling pretty good about his relationship with Callie.

* * *

Spence and Macy rode in silence back to the hotel until they were inside their room. Then Macy spoke, "Okay, now do you want to tell me what that was all about?"

"He's guilty, Macy."

"What makes you think that?"

"Oh, I don't know. Maybe it's twenty years of representing criminal defendants."

"Oh, so you're going to tell me you have some sort of ESP when it comes to determining the guilt or innocent of a client."

"Actually, yes I do. I know it sounds a little bizarre, but for some unknown reason my gut is telling me this guy killed his wife."

"Maybe your gut is simply jealous."

"Jealous? Why would I be jealous?"

"You tell me. I told you there was nothing between me and Adam anymore, but do you believe me?"

"Macy, I believe you and I'm not at all jealous. This Stephens guy is guilty."

"But how many people thought the same thing about you when Sherrie was murdered? I mean, shouldn't we at least give him the benefit of the doubt and look into it, just in case your gut is wrong? After all, we should be able to tell after we delve into it whether or not this man the neighbor saw really does exist and whether or not he killed this woman."

"I suppose you're right," he said with a sigh. "It won't hurt to look into it, except for interrupting our vacation." Macy placed her arms around Spence and gave him a short squeeze. "I'll make it up to you," she said. "I promise."

CHAPTER 14

When Drake pulled into the parking lot at the office the next morning, Macy was waiting for him. He climbed out of his car, flicked the still smoldering cigarette butt to the side, and walked steadily to where her car was parked.

"I didn't expect to see you here this morning, especially so early," he said.

"Well, if we're going to prove your client is innocent, there's no time to waste."

"Where's your husband?"

"Oh, he's already working on the case, canvassing your client's neighborhood for anything the police might have missed. I thought I would come by and have you make a copy of everything for me so we can construct our own file," said Macy.

"So you believe my client is innocent," said Drake.

"Let's just say I'm willing to keep an open mind, for the time being."

"And your husband?"

"Spence agrees with me."

"Fair enough. Come on, I'll get you everything you need." Drake escorted Macy into the building and motioned for her to have a seat in his office while he made copies of Josh Stephens' file. He arranged the papers neatly into a folder and walked over to where she was seated, handing her the file.

"This is all I have," he said as she leafed through the papers. "By the way, we never discussed your fee."

"You know I never charge a fee for my services."

"I didn't know if you had changed your practices, especially since you're no longer working alone," he said. She rolled her eyes as he handed her the file.

"Here's everything I have on the case," he said.

"This should get me started," said Macy as she stood to leave handing him one of her cards. "The next time you hear from your client, have him call me." She turned and walked out of the office, climbed into her car, and sped off in the direction of the hotel.

Drake sat down at his desk and ran his fingers through his hair. He knew he would have to explain to the judge about his client tomorrow after the continuation was up, and felt certain Josh would not return before he would have to face the fire. For a fleeting moment he daydreamed of running away, too, but soon realized that would be impossible, or at least impractical, as he thought of Callie and the thought of never seeing her again. Maybe she would run away with him, he thought, but knew all too well she would never consider that as an option. After several minutes of childish pretending, he returned to the real world and began to formulate in his mind what he would say to the judge. As he began jotting down some notes, his cell phone rang.

"Good morning, Adam," Josh greeted.

"Where are you?"

"Now you don't really want to know that, do you? Especially considering you have to face the judge without me present."

"You can always come back to court with me," said Drake.

"I'm sorry, Adam, but that's just not an option at the moment. I just wanted to touch base and see if you had come up with any new leads."

"Actually, I've enlisted the help of a couple of private detectives, so to speak. The lady wants you to call her so she can discuss your situation directly with you."

Drake gave Josh Macy's name and number and insisted he contact her as soon as they hung up. He promised he would, and after a few additional pleasantries, ended the call. Drake tossed the cell phone on his desk and sat back in his chair, interlocking his fingers behind his head and letting out a long sigh. He shook his head disapprovingly, as if Josh could somehow see him, and went back to work formulating his comments for the judge.

Betty soon arrived at the office right on schedule, eager to find out if Macy and Spence were going to help their client. Having become quite efficient with her crutches, she made her way straight into Drake's office with an expectant look, while he continued writing without looking up at her. After patiently waiting all of five seconds, she cleared her throat loudly, causing Drake to look up at her with disapproving eyes.

"Yes, what is it, Betty?" he asked, trying to sound annoyed.

"Don't play that formal interrupted boss routine with me! You know damn well what it is. Did they take the case or not?" she demanded. Drake leaned back in his chair and rubbed his eyes as he let out a long sigh. He looked up at Betty, unable to contain the smile eagerly trying to burst forth across his face.

"Yes, they did," he finally exclaimed, causing Betty to clench her fist and shout triumphantly, "Aha, I knew they would." She spun on her good heel and confidently hopped back to her desk, smiling smugly.

Drake continued with his writing until mid-morning when Betty informed him that Judge Abernathy's clerk was on the phone. Drake reached hesitantly for the receiver, hoping it was not more bad news.

"Mr. Drake, this is Jill from Judge Abernathy's office," said the lady. "His Honor would like to see you in his chambers at one o'clock this afternoon."

Drake tried unsuccessfully to uncover what the meeting was about before telling her he would be there. As he hung up, he wondered what was going on, then immediately thought the judge must have somehow learned about Josh leaving town. Why else would he ask to see him the day before trial was to resume?

Reaching into his top desk drawer, he retrieved a bottle of antacid pills, popping two in his mouth, hoping to ease the sudden burning in his stomach. He sat back in his chair and closed his eyes, trying to concentrate on what he would say to the judge. He had written some phrases on the legal pad in front of him, but they were based upon tomorrow's court hearing, and were no good for a meeting this afternoon. He suddenly felt weak all over, as he broke out in a cold sweat. He was thoroughly convinced the judge would see right through any attempt to downplay the matter, and would probably believe he knew where Josh was, or at least helped him get out of town. "This is not good," he said aloud as Betty came into the office.

"What's not good?" she asked.

"Judge Abernathy has summoned me to his chambers this afternoon."

"Why?"

"I don't know for sure, but I suspect it has to do with the fact my client skipped town."

"But how would he know that?"

"I don't know. But I can't figure out why else he'd want to see me," said Drake with a sigh. Betty hobbled around behind Drake and began massaging his shoulders, trying to loosen the knots that had immediately twisted through his muscles. She tried to offer some encouragement by pointing out that he did not know for sure what the judge wanted, and it could be something very simple as a point of law, or something to do with the jury. She insisted he try not to believe the worst until it was confirmed, and instead try to prepare for the meeting as best he could. After several minutes of massage and ego therapy, they concluded the best thing to do was confess openly and honestly to the judge that Josh was on the run. Drake could always maintain the illness story, instead using it as the way Josh duped him until he could safely leave town. That way he could not be blamed for knowing of Josh's departure before today. This plan of action alleviated some of

Drake's worries, however, he knew Judge Abernathy would probably hold it against him during future cases.

Since she was still in a cast, Betty called the deli to deliver a couple of sandwiches and drinks. She insisted Drake eat something to keep himself focused on the discussion with the judge and not a rumbling stomach. She also knew from past experience he would have a raging headache later that afternoon if he did not eat lunch. They ate in silence, not knowing what to say. As he swallowed the last bite, he peered up at the clock and noticed it was fifteen minutes before one o'clock. He stood up from the desk, tossed the food wrapper in the wastebasket, and headed out the door. As soon as he cleared the back door threshold, he lit a Camel and took a long drag. He exhaled the smoke as he climbed into his car and drove off in the direction of the courthouse.

He arrived at the courthouse with three minutes to spare, just enough time to walk from his car to Judge Abernathy's office. As he made his way through security and down the hall to the elevators, he barely noticed the other people milling about. His heart was in his throat as he stepped off the elevator and walked to the judge's office, hesitating before knocking on the door. He heard Jill's instruction to enter from within, and carefully turned the knob as if he were afraid of letting out a caged animal.

He peered through the crack in the door until he saw Jill motioning him inside, then his eyes met Callie's and his heart sank further, feeling surely if the prosecution was also here for the meeting, it would probably not go well for him. He flashed a nervous half-smile in her direction and sat down to wait for the judge, barely resting his butt on the seat before the judge emerged from his office and summoned them both inside.

"Mr. Drake," he began, "I apologize for requesting this meeting on such short notice, but something has been brought to my attention regarding the case against Mr. Stephens that I simply had to discuss with you." Oh no, thought Drake. Here it comes. Then Judge Abernathy continued, "The prosecution informed me earlier today that Ms. Devane's father passed away last night and she needs to leave immediately for Georgia to make funeral arrangements, as well as settle his estate. She has requested a continuance for two weeks in order to take care of these personal matters before continuing with the trial. I am aware you intended to call your client as the next witness, however, under the circumstances, I'm sure you and your client won't mind waiting a couple more weeks."

Drake sat silently for a couple of seconds as he let what the judge had just told him sink into his brain. Finally, he looked up and informed the judge that a continuance for an additional two weeks would be satisfactory to him and his client. He went on to offer his personal condolences to Callie for her loss, and asked her to please let him know if there was anything he could do. She wiped a tear from her eye as she thanked Drake for his sympathy. She stood and thanked Judge Abernathy for his understanding before turning and walking out of the office with Drake only a couple of steps behind. As they left the office and headed for the elevators, he grabbed her by the arm, causing her to turn toward him.

"Are you okay?" he asked.

"Yes, I'm fine," she replied with a wink. "This is not the time or place to talk. I'll see you tonight." Callie walked away from Drake and took the stairs to the lobby while he waited for the elevator. He knew she was right—they should not risk being seen together in public for too long. He took his time exiting the building in order to give Callie sufficient time to be gone ahead of him. He climbed into his car and lit another Camel, blowing the smoke out the driver's side window before starting the engine and heading back to the office. He took his time on the way back, allowing what the judge told him to sink in. He was greatly relieved that he was not in trouble, but now his concern had shifted to Callie. He wanted to run to her immediately, take her in his arms, and be there for her in her time of need. And yet, he could not take the chance of anyone seeing them together, especially when they were trying a murder case on opposite sides of the courtroom. He needed to exercise patience until he would see her tonight, when he could hold her close and kiss her tears away.

He climbed out of his car and began walking toward the building, so occupied with his thoughts he almost walked into a parked car. He knew that under the circumstances the rest of the afternoon and evening would drag by at a snail's pace. Passing Betty's desk on his way to the office, he barely mumbled a half-hearted greeting, creating a look of desperate dismay upon her face. She instantly rose on her crutches and followed him into his office, fearing the worst from his meeting with the judge.

"What happened?" she asked.

"We got a continuance for two more weeks."

"That's good, isn't it?"

"Yes, I suppose."

"Then what's wrong?" Betty pressed on.

"Callie's father died. That's why she asked for a continuance, so she can go to Georgia for the funeral and handle the affairs of his estate."

"I see," she said, with a rather puzzled expression on her face. "Her father died two years ago, though. But, hey, we got a continuance, so I wouldn't rock the boat."

"What do you mean her father died two years ago?" asked Drake.

114

"Well, I remember Callie saying something about it last year. It seems like it happened around Easter, but he lived in Tennessee, so there was nothing in the local papers about it."

"If that's true, then why would she lie about it now, especially to a judge?"

"I don't know," replied Betty. "But she must have a very good reason. Why don't you ask her?"

"I intend to do just that," he said, his eyes narrowing into a deep squint as he tried to process this latest bit of information. The rest of the afternoon seemed to last for days while he impatiently waited until time to leave the office. He did not want to leave early in case Josh or Macy called, so he tried to stay busy as best he could. However, with Josh's case being the main thing he had going, there was little else to work on.

Checking the Internet for any news of Callie's father in the Georgia papers, he searched the obituaries, and came across one for a Harry Devane, but since he died yesterday, the article was incomplete, with no next of kin listed. He called out to Betty to see if she remembered the name of Callie's father, to which she replied it was Charles, the same as her own father. That was how she could remember it. He rubbed his chin with his left hand while he worked the mouse with his right. He searched for other listings of Harry Devane's death, but found no additional information. Next he checked if there was anything about Charles Devane in Tennessee from two years ago. After searching for fifteen minutes, he was able to locate an old archived obituary from two days before Easter exactly two years ago. This one contained a full article, complete with next of kin. There in print was Callie's name listed as a daughter of the deceased. He was now more curious than ever as to why she lied about her father. After all, she was winning the case, so why did she want a continuance? It made no sense at all.

After a little more casual surfing, it was finally time to leave the office. He packed up quickly and left the office a few minutes ahead of Betty. He hurried home so he would have plenty of time to feed Sam and play with him some before getting ready for his meeting with Callie. She would come after dark, same as always, and leave before morning light. But this night would be different, he thought. Tonight would be all about Callie and the story she made up for the judge. Drake sat silently in the dark and waited for the familiar knock on the door.

He was suddenly roused from sleep by a familiar kiss. She had used the key he gave her to enter the house, finding him asleep in the chair. Apparently, he was more tired than he realized after the day's events, and had fallen asleep thirty minutes before she arrived. He took her in his arms and pulled her onto his lap, kissing her deeply. As their lips parted, he could see her beautiful brown eyes illuminated from the street light, silhouetted against the backdrop of the wall behind her. For this moment in time all of the questions he had earlier had suddenly left him, as her familiar scent filled his nostrils and heightened his passion. He became totally lost in his desires, scooping her up into his arms and carrying her to the bedroom. There all of their animal instincts were unleashed as they became entangled in the throes of unbridled intimacy. As they collapsed in a heap, fully spent from their love making, Drake succumbed to a deep sleep while Callie drifted off, stroking his hair.

CHAPTER 15

Drake woke to Callie's jostling as she was practically yelling in his ear. "Wake up, you sleepy head. We've got to get going."

"Going where?" he asked in the middle of a yawn. "Georgia, remember, my dear departed Dad?"

"Oh yeah, about that," he said. "I thought he died two years ago."

"He did," said Callie, biting her upper lip. "It was actually my Uncle Harry who passed away, but Judge Abernathy will never bother to investigate the matter, especially since the trial is almost wrapped up."

"I don't understand. The case was clearly going in your favor. Why would you risk the wrath of a federal court judge by lying in order to get a continuance you didn't even need?"

"Because I felt you needed it," she said, smiling at Drake. "After you told the judge your client was sick, and he granted the two day continuance, I had someone go by and check on Mr. Stephens just to make sure everything was okay. When he was not home, but his car was there, I knew he must have bolted on you and you were simply buying some time until you could either talk him into coming back, or at least come up with a good story for the judge. When I received word about Uncle Harry, and your client was still not back the night before last, I decided to take this opportunity to buy you a little more time. Besides, Georgia is not such a bad place to visit for a few days," she said with a smile.

"Aren't you afraid someone at your office will rat you out?"

"No, I asked Norma to cover for me. As far as they know, I'm attending a funeral out of state, but that's all the information they have. This way, they don't know I told Judge Abernathy it was my father. Could you imagine what my boss would say, knowing I took bereavement leave two years ago when my father actually died?"

"I just hope for your sake that Judge Abernathy doesn't run into your boss and express his sympathy for the loss of your father."

"Don't worry," replied Callie. "I have it on good authority that Judge Abernathy is taking a two week sabbatical to his mountain home for a little R & R."

"So why do we need to go to Georgia?"

"Did you forget about Uncle Harry? I mean, it would be nice for me to at least go to his funeral. Besides, we shouldn't be seen in town when I'm supposed to be gone."

"I see your point," Drake said, letting out a huge sigh. "I'll start packing."

"Great! My bags are already in my car, so I'll drive."

Drake tossed some clothes into a small suitcase before he and Callie showered and dressed for their trip. They waited until they were out of town before stopping at a fast food restaurant for breakfast. Then they continued on their way to Georgia. Drake called Betty when he was certain she would be in the office and informed her he was taking a few days off, but could be reached by cell phone if necessary. He also promised to check in with her at least once a day while he was gone. She assured him that since the Stephens case was the only thing he was working on at the moment, there was no need to worry about anything at the office. In fact, she was glad to see him get away for awhile, especially after witnessing firsthand the stress inflicted upon him from his latest client. After he ended the call, he looked over at Callie and smiled, reaching for her hand, and giving it a gentle but firm squeeze. Callie returned the smile, telling him that she loved him, and insisting he now relax and enjoy their time together. With nothing but the open road ahead, Drake eased the seat back and closed his eyes while Callie navigated their way down Interstate 85.

* * *

Macy was staring out of her hotel room window watching the raindrops bounce on the sidewalk below. The rain began sometime after midnight, and had not stopped since. According to the local news channel, the skies would clear sometime late in the afternoon, after this cold front pushed through the area. Macy could not help but think about how bleak and cold everything seemed when it was raining, even though it was actually warm outside. Spence had gone down to the coffee shop on the corner to fetch them a latte, so she waited patiently for him to return as she went over the information Drake gave her regarding the Stephens case in her mind. There was actually very little in the file and Spence had gathered no additional information from his neighborhood canvas the day before. She rubbed her hands over her arms as if warding off a chill when her cell phone rang, causing her to jump. She reached for the phone, speaking rather softly, "Hello?"

"Is this Macy Merit?" asked the gentleman on the other end.

"Yes, I'm Macy Merit. Who am I speaking with?"

"My name's Josh Stephens. Adam Drake gave me your name and number. He said you were helping him with my case, and wanted to speak with me."

"Yes I do," said Macy. "Are you nearby?"

"Yes."

"Good. Come to the Radisson Hotel, take the elevator to the fifth floor, and go to room 523. There will be an envelope taped to the door with a room key inside. I have already reserved the room, so all you need to do is go inside and lock the door. Once you're there, call me back at this number. Oh, you may want to wear sunglasses and a hat, or something to help disguise your true identity to avoid any unwanted attention," she told him before ending the call. She walked over to one of the chairs in the sitting area of the suite just as Spence returned with their lattes.

"They're still nice and hot," he said, handing one to Macy. She thanked him for being such a dear, and flashed her usual winning smile, but he could tell there was something on her mind.

"What's up?" he asked.

"Josh Stephens just called. I gave him the instructions and am waiting for his next call."

"Good," said Spence. "I want to meet him face to face so I can look him directly in the eyes as you question him."

"Now, Spence, I told you this is not an interrogation. We are trying to help this man."

"I still think he killed her," said Spence, as he let out a sigh. "But if you're still convinced he's innocent after you meet him, then I'll help you any way I can."

"Thank you," said Macy, offering a confident nod as she took a sip of her latte.

It did not take long before Macy's cell phone rang. "I'm here," said Josh.

"Good, I'll be right there."

Macy and Spence left their room and headed to the stairwell, making their way up one flight of stairs to the fifth floor. They walked to room 523 and quietly knocked. The door opened slightly as Josh peered through the crack at them. Macy identified herself in a half-whisper, so Josh opened the door wide enough for them to enter before locking it securely behind them. They exchanged pleasantries before sitting down at the small round table that was located across from the bed.

"So, Mr. Stephens, tell me your story," said Macy with an empathetic smile.

"On the day my wife was murdered, I left the bank around lunch time, went by the cemetery, and when I got home around four-thirty, I found Julie lying on the bed, dead. I guess I held her instinctively, hoping she would wake up, but after a few minutes, I called 911."

"So that's how you ended up with her blood on your clothes?" asked Macy.

Josh nodded.

"Were you and your wife having any marital problems?"

"No, we never fought. Of course, Julie had withdrawn somewhat after our daughter died, but I assumed that was typical, and was patient to allow her sufficient time to grieve and heal. She was becoming more like her old self just before she was killed."

"And how are you coping with everything?"

"It's very hard, but I guess men deal with things a little differently than women, so I guess I'd say I'm doing okay, considering."

"I understand," said Macy, patting Josh on the hand.

"Tell me about the unidentified man one of your neighbors saw that day."

"Mr. Evans said he noticed an air conditioning repairman at my house that morning, but we didn't call anyone about our air conditioning. In fact, it was working fine. Adam was unable to find a company by that name, so I guess we're at a dead end on finding out who he was, but I'll bet he was the one who killed Julie."

"Can you think of anyone who would want to do harm to you or your wife?"

"Like I told the police, I don't know anyone who would want to harm us, let alone kill Julie."

"Have you ever had any harsh business dealing with clients who became angry at you?"

"Well, I've had people get mad when we had to repossess their car or foreclose on a mortgage, but people don't usually kill someone over that, do they?"

"You'd be surprised what people will kill for. Do you remember anyone who was particularly animated or threatening?"

"No one comes to mind, but you might want to ask my assistant Madeline. She usually fielded a lot of the irate calls, so she may remember someone I'm not even aware called."

"Where have you been staying?" asked Macy.

"I'd rather not say if it's all the same to you."

"I understand. Listen, I booked this room in Spence's name, so you're welcome to stay here."

"Thank you," said Josh. "It would be much more comfortable than last night's accommodations."

"Just order what you need from room service and have them charge it to the room," said Macy. "Oh and here," she said, handing him a duffle bag. "Here's a disguise should you need to go out for anything. I understand there's a two week continuance on your trial now, something to do with a death in the prosecutor's family, so no one knows you are on the lam yet."

"That's good to know, but I think I'll continue to keep a low profile, just in case," said Josh, gesturing to the bag Macy had just handed him. She thanked him for the information and assured him that he need not worry. She would speak with his assistant and see if they could determine who was at his house that morning. Until then, Josh was to lay low and wait for her to contact him. She gave him a cell phone that was untraceable and instructed him to use that if he needed to call her. Then she and Spence said their good-byes and made their way back to their room. Once inside Spence broke his silence.

"I still believe he is guilty, Macy. Didn't you see how unemotional he was as he discussed his wife's murder? He almost seemed cold to me."

"I remember how you were when you were in a similar situation, and at the time, I didn't think you seemed very emotional either, but I just assumed you were too busy concentrating on proving your innocence. Besides, you men seem to handle stressful situations differently than we women," said Macy, as she smiled and offered a half-hearted laugh in Spence's direction.

"Maybe so, but I still believe he could have been a little more upset. I know how I would feel if something ever happened to you," he said, placing his arms around her and giving her a big squeeze.

"You're so sweet, but he's been through a lot. Trust me. I've seen people in similar situations act much the same way. Stress can manifest itself in many different ways."

"True, but there's just something about this guy that I can't quite put my finger on."

"He needs us Spence."

"I'm with you, Mace," he replied. "Just be careful." Macy smiled back at him and offered a reassuring wink. Then they embraced again, their lips meeting in a long sensual kiss. It seemed to Macy that Spence held on a little longer than usual, but maybe she was just sensing his concern.

"So where do we start?" asked Spence, slowly releasing his arms from around Macy's waist.

"Well, it's obvious from your visit to Josh's neighborhood that we're not going to get any more useful information there, so I suggest we begin with

Madeline, Josh's assistant, and see if she remembers any disgruntled customers who may have been angry enough to take revenge on Josh and his family."

"Okay, why don't you go see his assistant while I take another look at the police file from their daughter's murder? There may just be a connection between the two murders, and if so, the file might hold a clue the police overlooked."

"I like your way of thinking," replied Macy. "But how are you going to get the police to hand over a case file, especially on an unsolved case?"

"You just leave that to me," he answered with a smile. "I have my ways."

"Oh, I'll just bet you do," said Macy with a laugh, as she grabbed him, pulled him on top of her, and planted a long sensual kiss firmly on his lips. Then she pushed him away, stared directly into his eyes, and said, "Just remember that whenever you think about putting any fancy moves on some pretty female detective just to get a peek at a file."

"Don't worry," said Spence with a chuckle. "I only have eyes, and lips, for you." Then he pulled her to him and kissed her deeply, holding her so tightly, a piece of dental floss could not be wedged between them. He released her slowly, stood up, and headed for the door. He offered a wink in her direction as he walked out of the hotel room. Macy tossed him the keys to the car, insisting he take it since it was only a couple of blocks to the bank, and she could walk to her meeting with Madeline. He grabbed the keys in mid-air, blew a soft kiss in her direction, and closed the door behind him.

She remained behind for a few minutes, basking in the warmth and security of knowing she was loved, then grabbed her umbrella and left the room, making her way to the elevator. When she walked across the lobby to the front door, she noticed the rain had stopped. Tucking the umbrella under her arm, she pushed her way through the revolving door and stepped outside onto the still damp sidewalk. She turned right and walked the two blocks north to First National Bank, where she entered and made her way to Josh's office. As she approached, Madeline came to her feet and greeted her. Macy extended her hand and introduced herself and the reason for her visit. Once Madeline learned she was there to talk about Josh, she ushered Macy quickly into Josh's office and closed the door behind them so they could speak privately. Macy explained the reason for her visit and asked Madeline if she remembered any customers who were particularly upset with Josh in the past, or if any had ever threatened to harm him or his family. Madeline told her that she always kept a log of such calls, but some of the information had been placed in storage, so it would take a couple of days to retrieve the information. She asked if there was anything else she could do to help Josh, but Macy assured her that the phone logs would be a big help for now. As she stood to leave, Macy walked over to the credenza and picked up a framed photo of a little girl.

"Is this a picture of Rachel Stephens?" she asked.

"Yes," replied Madeline. "That picture was taken on her sixth birthday two weeks before she was killed. She wanted one of those glamour photos like a lot of the girls at her school had done."

"She almost looks like an adult, especially with the makeup," said Macy.

"She was a beautiful child and Mr. Stephens loved her dearly," said Madeline. Macy stared at the photo for awhile before smiling and placing it back in its place. She thanked Madeline again for her help and gave her the information for the hotel where she could be reached once the phone records were retrieved. Then she excused herself and left the bank and walked back to the hotel. Once inside the room, she grabbed a soda from the mini-bar and turned on the television while she waited for Spence to return.

CHAPTER 16

Spence drummed his fingers impatiently as he waited in the parking lot outside the police station. After several minutes a grey sedan pulled in alongside his car and parked. The elderly gentleman was smiling as he exited the vehicle and approached Spence.

"It's so good to see you," he said, grabbing Spence and giving him a quick hug.

"It's good to see you too, Dad. I'm glad you agreed to help me out."

"What, are you kidding? I was thrilled you even asked me. Now just wait here and leave everything to me," he said as he winked at Spence. He disappeared into the building while Spence climbed back in his car to wait. His mind wandered as he sat there thinking how good his father still looked at seventy-six. Spence hoped when he was that age, he'd still have a full head of hair like his father, even if it was white. He noticed how many women seemed to actually find his white hair attractive, often referring to it as distinguished-looking. And of course, the George Hamilton tan he had developed added to the effect. He smiled as he mused how his father had never seemed more alive than after he was declared dead. Warren Rawlings was an attorney, and later a judge in Michigan where he became entrapped in a conspiracy with the VanWarner crime family. In order to avoid personal harm, and also rid himself of the bonds placed on him by Joey VanWarner, Judge Rawlings had to fake his own death. Macy was the one who helped him, and ultimately helped Spence when he came to administer the estate and became tangled up with the VanWarners. That was when Spence first met Macy and their relationship began. He had been estranged from his father for over fifteen years prior to the judge's faked death, so now he took every advantage he could to make up for lost time. In fact, he and Macy solicited his father's help on certain cases where he still had beneficial contacts in the legal community. This was one of those cases where Spence called upon his father to help him acquire the police file on Rachel Stephens. Now all he could do was wait and hope his father was successful.

After a few minutes that seemed like an eternity, Judge Rawlings walked out of the police station, walked over to Spence's car and climbed into the passenger seat. He removed a file from underneath his overcoat, handed it to Spence, and said, "It sure was good to see you again."

"You, too," replied Spence. "I'll call you and we'll all have dinner together."

"You'd better," said his father, grinning and patting Spence on the shoulder, then climbed out of the car, walked over to the grey sedan, and drove off. Spence tossed the file on the passenger seat beside him and drove out of the parking lot. He would wait until he was safely at the hotel before he opened the file.

As he drove, Spence smiled and shook his head as he thought about how easy it seemed for his father to retrieve the file. Of course, Judge Rawlings told him he had some friends in high places who could assist him in procuring the information. Still, Spence thought it would be more difficult than that, as he chuckled out loud. Yes, his dad still had it, he thought.

He pulled into the parking garage of the hotel and made his way to the room. Macy raised her head and looked at him in expectation, hoping he had the file. She frowned in disappointment as he stood there empty handed. Then he flashed a grin and pulled his left hand from behind his back, revealing the file. Macy shrieked out loud, jumping from the sofa and practically running to him, planting a big wet kiss on his lips.

"Wow!" said Spence. "Considering Dad got the file, I wonder what you would do if I was the one who had retrieved it?"

"I'll show you later. And don't let me forget to give your dad a kiss for this, too. He's been such a good friend and helper ever since we straightened out his predicament."

"Yes, he has. And I have you to thank for reuniting us. I just hope we have enough time left to make up for the missed years."

"Don't worry. I'm sure you will," said Macy as she smiled at him. "So, have you had a chance to look at the file?"

"Now you know I wouldn't dream of getting ahead of you," he replied as he handed her the file. She took the file and carried it over to the dining area table where she opened it and began scanning the contents. Spence walked up behind her and peered over her shoulder as she read the reports. Apparently Rachel Stephens was picked up from school by someone, physically assaulted, then suffocated. Her body was found in the park. She was only six years old. Her father, Josh Stephens, was working with his assistant that evening at the time of the abduction, according to Madeline Jones' statement. The mother arrived at the school to pick up Rachel, only to find she was not there. There were no witnesses who saw her leave. The family received no ransom demand or threats, so there were no suspects. The family posted reward flyers, but no credible suspects turned up. It was almost as if this person did not exist, and yet Rachel Stephens' lifeless and abused body said otherwise. Suddenly Macy's eyes widened as she read the statement of the first detective on the scene. According to him, it was the cleanest crime scene he had ever seen in seventeen years on the force. Afterward, the police assumed because of the lack of physical evidence at the park, the crime must have occurred somewhere else and the body dumped there.

"I believe I've heard that somewhere before," said Macy.

"The cleanest crime scene I've ever seen."

"And what a coincidence it just happens to have been this little girl's mother's murder scene," said Spence. "Are you thinking what I'm thinking?"

"Whoever killed Rachel Stephens killed Julie Stephens. But then your hunch about Josh can't be right since he has an alibi for Rachel's murder."

"I suppose you're right," said Spence, rubbing his chin. "So who's our prime suspect?"

"At this point, we don't have one, but I'm hoping Madeline Jones will be able to provide a few from her phone logs."

"Call me crazy, but I still think something's not quite right with Mr. Stephens."

"Okay, you're crazy," said Macy with a laugh. "Look, Spence, he had an airtight alibi for his daughter's murder. If it was the same killer, there's no way he could have done it. Let's see what Ms. Jones comes up with. Surely there's someone who had a big enough axe to grind with Josh that he wanted to see him suffer."

"When are you supposed to meet with her again?"

"I don't know. She's supposed to call me as soon as she retrieves the phone logs from storage. It may take a couple of days."

"The clock is ticking," said Spence.

"I'm well aware of that, but right now this is all we have."

"So what do we do in the meantime?"

"Wait. And while we're waiting, I believe I promised to show you what I would do if you had been the one to actually retrieve Rachel Stephens' file."

Spence could not help but smile as Macy took him by the hand and led him into the bedroom. As she closed the door behind them, he hoped that whatever it was, it would take the rest of the afternoon.

* * *

Harry Devane was the editor of *The Daily Citizen-News*, and a very prominent citizen of Dalton, Georgia. He was a deacon at The First Baptist Church, and also served on various community boards and committees during his lifetime. Callie had not seen her uncle since the last extended family reunion three years ago, but she kept in touch with her Aunt Jewel. In fact, it was Aunt Jewel who called Callie with the news of Harry's death.

As they drove into town, she couldn't help but think how little the town had changed since she was last there. She always enjoyed coming to Dalton because of the charming older homes with their distinguished southern architecture. Drake almost felt his body relaxing as he felt the laid back atmosphere of small town living. Aunt Jewel had insisted she and her friend stay in their house, but Callie explained she had already reserved a room at the Bed and Breakfast just on the edge of town. After a little cajoling by Aunt Jewel, she finally gave up, telling Callie the invitation was still open if she didn't like the accommodations at The Dalton House Inn. Callie thanked her for her hospitality and promised to see her a lot while in town to make up for the disappointment.

She told Drake about the carpet outlets along Interstate 75, describing the contrast between the charming older downtown compared to the modern world of commerce that had sprung up along the highway. Dalton had become to many, the Carpet Capital of the World.

The warm gentle breeze swept through Callie's hair as she stepped out of the car. She drew in a deep breath as if the air was somehow different, and indeed to her, it was. The house was just as she remembered it from three years ago, complete with hanging baskets of petunias and yellow portulaca along the front porch, and Aunt Jewel's beautiful rose garden in the back. There were some people sitting on the front porch in the white rocking chairs, then she saw Aunt Jewel in the swing to her right. Callie walked straight toward her as if in a trance, not even looking at the others as she passed.

"Aunt Jewel, I am so sorry about Uncle Harry," said Callie, stretching her arms out to embrace the fragile lady whom she remembered as being so strong when she was younger.

"My dear sweet Callie, thank you for coming," she replied, kissing Callie on the cheeks. She held Callie at arms length and said, "Let me take a good look at you. You sure are a sight for sore eyes." She hugged Callie again as a few gentle tears streamed down her face. Callie eased back and introduced Drake. Aunt Jewel swayed back on her heels as if she were sizing him up before she spoke, "So this is the young man you've been tellin' me about. Well I certainly see why you took up with him," she said as she winked at Drake. "He's kinda cute." Callie laughed out loud, which prompted a response from Aunt Jewel. "Listen child, I may be old, but I can still see. And if he treats you half as good as he looks, then you'd better stick with him."

"Don't worry, Aunt Jewel," said Callie as she tucked her arm in Drake's. "I intend to do just that." They all chuckled together and hugged each other. Aunt Jewel sat down and patted the swing on both sides of her, indicating for them to sit on either side. They both complied while Aunt Jewel rocked the swing back and forth ever so slightly.

Drake actually sat back in the swing and let out a relaxed sigh as he felt right at home. He could smell the sweet fragrance of honeysuckle, which took him back to his own childhood. After a few minutes, he closed his eyes and took in the sounds and scents that were Dalton while Callie and Aunt Jewel carried on a conversation he cared little about. He was just glad to be with Callie and hear her sweet soft voice. And for one brief moment, he forgot all about the case, Josh Stephens, and the fact he would have to face the music in front of Judge Abernathy when they returned. For now, he simply relaxed and enjoyed the moment for what it was—sweet southern bliss.

After a few minutes of conversation, Aunt Jewel offered them some lemonade. Callie immediately jumped to her feet and headed off to the kitchen, not wanting her aunt to wait on them. She was back in a flash with three glasses, having to touch Drake so he would open his eyes before handing a glass to him. As he sipped the sweet tangy liquid, Drake thought the only thing missing now was a trip to the fishin' hole with

Andy. Although High Point was not a large city, it was certainly busier and more congested than Dalton, to which he was glad for the relief.

As the afternoon passed, people came and went, each paying their respects to Aunt Jewel. By six o'clock, only Callie and Drake remained. Aunt Jewel suddenly stood up and announced she was going to fix supper, to which Callie mildly protested. After a brief chastising by Aunt Jewel on how she was certainly able to put together a meal even with Harry's passing, Callie agreed with the condition she be allowed to help. Callie and Aunt Jewel retreated to the kitchen leaving Drake alone in the swing. He could not help but smile as he thought how surreal this was...the women heading to the kitchen to prepare the meal while the man sat on the porch and waited to be called to dinner. It was very old fashioned, and yet it felt awfully good to him.

Easing a little bit farther back in the swing, he closed his eyes again, this time trying to identify the different bird sounds he heard. It was not long before his breathing turned into a soft snore when he drifted off to sleep to the peaceful sounds of nature.

Meanwhile in the kitchen, Callie and Aunt Jewel began cooking dinner. It would be a southern meal complete with Aunt Jewel's homemade biscuits and gravy. As they worked they continued their conversation.

"So how are you holding up, Aunt Jewel?" asked Callie. "Well, I won't lie to you. I miss him somethin' awful, but child, when you've been with someone as long as I was with your Uncle Harry, you realize just how lucky you are to have had that many wonderful years with the love of your life. I'm sure it'll be lonely, especially at first, but I have so many good memories to hold onto."

"I can stay a couple of weeks, Aunt Jewel, if that will help."

"Child, that will be wonderful," said Aunt Jewel as she wiped a tear from her eye. "You know, Callie, of all the nieces and nephews you were his favorite. He was so proud of you when you graduated law school, and he always read your local newspaper in case you were mentioned. He followed your career very closely." She walked over to the china cabinet and retrieved a photo album from the drawer.

"Here, he kept this full of clippings and pictures, all about you and your career," she said as she handed the book to Callie. "I'm sure he would want you to have it." Callie took the book from her and began to leaf through the pages. She laughed through tears as she looked at all of the information Uncle Harry had so painstakingly collected over the years. Then she closed the book, held it tightly to her chest, and mouthed a choked, "Thank you," in her aunt's direction, no longer able to control the tears that flowed down her cheeks. Aunt Jewel put her arms around Callie and they wept together as the chicken fried in the cast iron skillet. After a good cry, they wiped away their tears and continued preparing dinner.

Drake was awakened by a sweet soft kiss. "Supper's ready," said Callie as she whispered gently into his ear. He opened his eyes, stretched, then stood, catching hold of Callie's arm. He spun her around quickly, placing his lips fully on hers. Just then he heard the sound of someone clearing their throat and looked up to see Aunt Jewel standing in the doorway with a big smile on her face.

"Okay, you two," she said. "You can finish this after we eat. Supper's gettin' cold." She chuckled under her breath and walked back into the house. Callie took Drake by the hand and led him inside to the kitchen table. After all, this was family, and in the Devane house, family ate at the kitchen table. After they ate, Callie and Drake stayed for awhile longer, but once the light outside began to fade, they left and drove over to the Bed and Breakfast for the night. Aunt Jewel tried her best to get them to stay, but she understood how young people in love wanted their privacy, and actually she preferred to be alone with her dreams of Harry tonight. Callie promised she would come early tomorrow for breakfast. Once they were settled in their room, Drake took Callie in his arms and kissed her deeply. After a long lovemaking session, they fell sound asleep in each other's arms, not stirring until the next morning.

CHAPTER 17

Macy almost jumped out of bed to the sound of her cell phone blaring Beethoven's Fifth Symphony. She changed her ring tone to that one week ago, and still hadn't gotten used to the sound, especially when she was awakened from such a deep slumber. She clumsily reached for the phone and noticed the time was eight-fifteen. "Hello," she said sleepily into the phone.

"Ms. Merit, this is Madeline Jones. I believe I have the information you were looking for the other day."

"That's great. When can we meet?"

"How about eleven o'clock? I should have everything caught up by then."

"That should work for me. I'll see you then." Macy flipped her phone closed and took a long stretch before walking into the bathroom.

"Who was that?" Spence called from beneath the sheets. "Madeline Jones at First National. She said she found the information I asked about and wants me to meet with her at eleven. Are you coming with me?"

"Sure, I've got nothing else to do right now, and besides I'm interested in hearing the information myself."

"Well then, you'd better get up and start getting dressed. I want some breakfast before we head over there. I'm starving."

"Why don't you get your shower first while I get in forty more winks?"

Macy stormed back into the bedroom, ripped the covers off Spence and said, "Get out of that bed right now, mister, or I'm gonna give you forty whacks."

Remembering the time he snuck up on Macy and she almost put him in traction with one of her martial arts moves, he jumped out of bed, flashed a smile in her direction, and hurried into the bathroom. Feeling a little guilty for the threat, Macy joined Spence in the shower to make up for it. After they finished, they headed downstairs to the restaurant for breakfast. By the time they finished their meal, they had just enough time to freshen up before their meeting with Madeline Jones. At ten minutes before eleven, Macy and Spence stepped outside the hotel and headed north, walking the few blocks to First National Bank. There was a gentle breeze stirring, but not enough to disturb Macy's red page boy as it glistened in the bright midmorning sun. Spence smiled as he thought about how much he loved to bury his face in her red locks. It seemed he had a thing for redheads, and Macy was no exception. And yet as he glanced over at her as they walked up the street, he felt more in love with her than the first time he realized she was the one for him.

It took no time at all before they were entering the building. Macy led the way to the desk where Madeline sat talking on the phone, motioning for them to take a seat and mouthed the words, "I'll be just a minute." They sat patiently while Madeline finished her call. She placed the receiver in its cradle and beckoned them into Josh Stephens' office. She closed the door behind them and motioned for them to sit at the small conference table Josh often used for loan closings.

"I was able to retrieve the phone logs and scan through them yesterday and last night. I made note of the ones who offered what seemed like any threat at all, then cross referenced the names with their current locations using the Internet to determine which ones might still be in the area, and still holding a grudge against Josh…I mean Mr. Stephens."

"So how many suspects are we looking at?" asked Macy.

"Based on what I was able to gather, there are ten people on the list who may possibly be involved."

"Is there any way to determine whether they own a blue Pontiac," asked Spence?

"Well I suppose we could, but I'm not really sure how to get that information."

"That's okay, Madeline," said Macy. "Whoever did this could simply have rented the vehicle anyway. We'll simply have to check them all out." Macy shot a disapproving glance in Spence's direction, which caused him to smile. He knew, of course, that Macy was correct. He simply wanted to see how thorough she intended to be with her investigation.

Macy scanned the list of ten names, making notes in the margin. Of the ten names, four were female and the rest were male. According to Madeline's records, the four women were married at the time of the calls, so any of these ten people had the ability to commit the murder, either on their own, or with the help of their spouse.

"Thank you for your help, Madeline." Macy turned to Spence and said, "We might as well get started on this right away if we're going to be able to get through the entire list in time to help Josh." Spence and Macy stood up, shook Madeline's hand, and excused themselves from the office. Macy waited until they were outside before she spoke.

"I didn't want to get too involved in front of Madeline, but I suggest we cross-reference this list to see if any of these people own a blue Pontiac and start there. Then if we don't find our murderer, we can begin looking at the others who may have rented one, or otherwise had access to one."

"That's my girl," said Spence with a smile, wrapping his arm around her waist while they walked back to the hotel. As soon as they were back inside their room, Macy enlisted the help of one of her contacts to check the DMV records for any on the list who owned a blue Pontiac. It was only a matter of minutes before she had the information. Apparently, three people on the list owned blue Pontiacs. Two were women and the third was a man.

"Let's start with the women first," said Macy. "Usually a woman calms down faster than a man, so hopefully we can weed these out fairly quickly."

"That's a rather sexist attitude, don't you think?" said Spence.

"Sorry, dear, but we women know what hotheads you men are," said Macy, and burst out laughing.

"You're a laugh a minute, Mace. I'll remind you the next time you show your temper."

"I was just teasing," she said, taking hold of his arm. "But seriously, I think we should start with these two women first."

"Fine, whatever you say," he said, pulling his arm away from hers in mock disgust.

"Now don't be that way," she said, grabbing his arm again. "Nobody likes a pouter."

That caused them both to break out in laughter. Spence suddenly felt warm all over as he realized just how much he enjoyed Macy's company, even when she was being mischievous.

The first person on their short list of Pontiac owners was Sandra Hill. Macy picked up the local area map she had purchased in the gift shop downstairs and scanned the street listing until she found Chestnut Street. She highlighted the location, and did the same for the other two Pontiac owners. Once she was ready, they left the room and headed to the parking garage. Macy asked Spence to drive while she navigated for him. It was a short drive from the hotel downtown over to Chestnut Street. She noticed several older duplexes that lined the street on either side as she scanned the house numbers. Just before they reached the driveway, she indicated to Spence which place it was, so he slowed down as they approached. Spence let out a huge sigh as he eased the car into the driveway. She sighed almost in unison with him when she also saw what he did. There in the back yard was a blue Pontiac resting on four jack stands with the hood up, no wheels, and no motor. The motor was hanging from a tree by a steel chain. Although the car was painted blue, there was almost as much rust as there was paint.

"Think positive, Mace," said Spence. "After all, we don't know how long this car has been out of commission."

Macy just rolled her eyes as they climbed out of the car and headed to the front door. Since there was no doorbell, Spence tapped his knuckles loudly against the glass of the storm door. They immediately heard the barking of a dog from within as if it wanted to lunge through the glass and rip their lungs out. Someone inside yelled at the dog and began opening the door. Through the glass they could see a woman in her mid-forties with short dark hair wearing a housecoat printed with pink and blue flowers. She was a little heavyset, but not obese, with a cigarette hanging from the corner of her mouth. She stood behind the glass staring at Spence and Macy, apparently waiting for them to speak before uttering a sound. Finally Macy spoke up.

"We're sorry to bother you, ma'am, but we're looking for Sandra Hill."

"Well you found her," she said, still holding the cigarette in her mouth. "That sorry excuse for an ex-husband of mine better not have sent you over here to beg for money. That no good bum left three months ago without fixin' my car, just left it there in the back yard with the engine hangin' in the tree. He ran off with some bimbo from the bar down the street without so much as a note. I had to find out about it at the laundromat when I saw the two of them together. Darn near broke his nose, and would have if he hadn't moved so quick. He came back once about a month ago tryin' to get money out of me, but I chased him off with the fryin' pan. I got me a dog since then to keep pests away," she said, nodding her head in the direction of the Rottweiler standing beside her. "I get a check each month on account of my disability, and all he ever wanted to do was mooch off me. I guess that bimbo offered to take him in, so he left. Well as far as I'm concerned he can stay gone."

Macy and Spence looked at each other as if to say, "That was a little too much information, lady."

Spence spoke up, "So your car hasn't been driven lately?"

"Are you deaf? I just told you he left it that way three months ago," she said with a snort, the cigarette still firmly in the corner of her mouth, now with almost two inches of ash clinging to the end. Obviously, they could scratch this one from their list of suspects. Spence asked for her pardon and excused himself and Macy from her front stoop. Once back inside the car, Macy broke the silence.

"If I ever let myself go like that, just shoot me please," she said, shaking her head.

"I don't think you have to worry about that, dear. Besides, you mean you didn't think she looked sexy," he said with a chuckle, which prompted a rather sharp punch in the arm from Macy. He winced and flexed his arm as if in pain, and chuckled again, pulling out of the driveway and heading back toward town.

The next name on the list was Chandra Norris. She lived on Centennial Street, so they had to cross back through town and head north. Macy continued to provide directions for Spence as he made his way through traffic. When they drove along Centennial Street, she noticed the houses seemed to be nicer than the ones on Chestnut. After a few minutes, she nudged Spence and pointed to the next house on the right. "This is it." Spence eased the car into the driveway, but there was no vehicle parked at the house. They made their way to the front door and rang the doorbell. There was no sound from within and Spence rang the bell again. After ringing it a third time and waiting for a few minutes, it was apparent no one was home.

As they stepped off the porch and walked back to their car, a man next door shouted in their direction. "They don't live there anymore."

Spence and Macy stopped and looked over at the gentleman with a questioning look, which the neighbor obviously took for "what?"

"I said they don't live there anymore?"

"Who," asked Spence?

"The Norris,' that's who you're looking for, ain't it?"

"Yes, sir. Do you know where they moved to?" asked Macy.

"Sure, they bought a house over on Skeet Club Road. They were renting here, but I think he got a new job or something so they bought a house."

"Do you know the house number?"

"Nope, I'm afraid I don't, but I saw the realtor who stopped over there for a visit while they were house hunting. The sign on her car read "HOMax.""

"Thanks for the information," said Macy.

"They're not in any kind of trouble, are they?" he asked.

"No, not at all," said Spence as they climbed back into the car. Macy waved at the gentleman as they backed out of the driveway. Spence continued north on Centennial Street while Macy used her cell phone to call information for the address of the HOMax office. Finding the real estate company was located just off Eastchester Drive in a small office complex, she instructed Spence to continue north on Centennial until they reached Eastchester Drive. Turning right, she began looking for the small side street that HOMax was on. As it turned out, the HOMax office was located just before Skeet Club Road intersected with Eastchester Drive, so it should be fairly easy to locate the Norrises once they got the street address.

"Do you have any ideas on how we're going to get that address from the real estate agent?" asked Spence.

"You just leave that to me and follow my lead," replied Macy.

They climbed out of the car and walked into the HOMax office. A lady at the front desk was busy talking on the phone, so they waited patiently for her to finish her conversation. As soon as she hung up, Macy went into action.

"My husband and I are looking for a house somewhere in this area. We're from out of state and he just got a new job at the hospital, so we need to find something quickly."

The lady instructed them to wait while she called an agent to come to the front. After a few seconds, a young lady in her early thirties dressed in a smart navy blue business suit approached from one of the back offices. She extended her hand to Macy and said, "Hello, my name is Catherine Fowler. How may I help you?"

"Hi, my name is Amy Moss, and this is my husband, Jerry. He just got a new job at the hospital, and we're looking for a house to relocate to."

"Where are you relocating from?"

"Tennessee."

"Why don't we step back to my office and see what we can come up with?" The realtor led them down the hallway to her office, stepped inside, and motioned for them to have a seat. She sat down and began punching keys on her computer.

"Now, what type of property are you looking for?"

"Well, my sister and I were looking at listings on the Internet and found some houses on Skeet Club Road that sounded nice, that is if it's a good neighborhood," said Macy. "It's just me and my husband right now, but we're thinking of having at least two children, so I guess we need to look at either a three or four bedroom house.

"Oh, that is an excellent area, and it has been growing a lot recently. Let me see what is available there," she said as she continued typing. "Well, there are a couple of houses for sale there that sound like they may be what you are looking for." Then the realtor let out a sigh. "This one would have been perfect, but it sold the other week."

"Oh really," said Macy, feigning disappointment. "Can I see it?" she asked as she stood and peered around the computer monitor. She made mental notes of the appearance of the house so she would recognize it again when she saw it. She smiled and sat back down.

"I can show you some properties if you like," said the realtor.

"Well, we just got into town and are kind of tired. Can you print off the information on those two houses so we can talk about them tonight? Then I'll call you tomorrow morning and set something up," she said, grabbing one of the realtor's business cards.

"Sure, that would be great," she replied, punching a few more keys and the printer behind her suddenly sprang to life. She handed Macy the papers, shook their hands, and escorted them back to the front lobby. Along the way, she asked Macy for a contact number where she could reach them in case something came up, to which Macy complied by giving her a bogus number.

Spence and Macy left the office and climbed into their car, heading in the direction of Skeet Club Road. As they turned left onto the street from Eastchester Drive, Macy noticed that many of the houses sat far enough back from the road it was hard to see them. Luckily, she remembered the address number from the listing at the realtor's office, and began to look for the number on the mailboxes. They rode for a little more than a half mile before she spotted the number. Spence pulled into the driveway and continued until he stopped just behind a blue Pontiac Sunbird. There was a black and white medium-sized dog lying on the front porch that stood up as he saw them approach. Before they could get out of the car, the dog walked down the steps and approached the car. Since they were unsure as to how friendly the dog was, Spence blew the horn before they got out, seeing if anyone was home. A lady opened the front door and made her way to the car. He rolled down the side window.

"We're sorry to bother you, ma'am, but I wasn't sure if your dog would bite."

"Well, it's a good thing you didn't get out," she replied. "He will bite. Can I help you with something?"

"We're investigating the death of Julie Stephens," said Spence. "Did you know her?"

"Isn't she the lady whose husband killed her?"

"Well, that's what we're trying to determine," said Macy.

"Are you cops?"

"No, ma'am. We're with the prosecutor's office," said Spence. "According to witnesses, there was a blue Pontiac at the Stephens house the morning of the murder. Also, the bank records indicate you had a disagreement with Mr. Stephens at First National Bank. We're just trying to rule out any potential suspects who own a vehicle matching the eyewitness description."

"Wait a minute! You mean you think I killed this woman?"

"No, ma'am, I'm not saying that. I'm just trying to determine if your vehicle was the one at the crime scene that morning. Has the car been stolen recently?"

"No, it's been with me. And this so called disagreement with the bank happened over a year ago regarding a car they repossessed from me. Yeah, I'll admit I was pretty pissed at the time, but they came to where I work and took it without me knowing. When I came out to go home, it was gone. I've never been so embarrassed in my life, so I might have said some things in the heat of the moment, but I would never physically harm anyone."

"Is there any way you can prove you were not at the Stephens' house on the morning of the murder?" asked Spence, giving her the date.

"Yeah, I was at work that day, and my insurance company sent somebody out to repair a broken windshield on the car where a rock had hit it a few weeks ago. I saw the guy out there working on it when I was on my morning break, so I know it was there all day."

"Is there any way he could have borrowed the car without you knowing it?" asked Macy.

"No. I left it unlocked for him, and I kept the key, so there was no way he could have moved it. I even looked under the dash when I got in that evening to make sure no one had tried to hot wire it. Wait right here," she said, and walked back into the house. After a few minutes she emerged with some papers in her hand.

"Here's the invoice where they repaired it with the time and date marked on it. Is that good enough proof?" Spence looked at the paper, handed it to Macy. She took a quick look, noted date and time, and handed it back to the woman.

"Yes, ma'am, it is. We're sorry to have bothered you, but we needed to rule out all potential suspects."

"Well, I've mellowed a lot over the past year. I tend to take things more in stride, so I guess I understand you're just doing your job. I'm just glad you can cross me off your list now," she said with a smile, passing her hand across her brow in a mock sign of relief. Macy thanked her again as Spence began backing the car out of the driveway and headed back toward town.

"What do you say we grab some dinner and head back to the hotel for the evening?" asked Spence.

"What about the third Pontiac owner on our list?"

"I doubt he's going anywhere tonight. Besides, with Josh the prime suspect, if he is the killer, he probably thinks he's in the clear. This way we can get some rest and start fresh in the morning."

"Who do you think you're kidding?" asked Macy. "You just want to get back to the hotel early so we'll have plenty of time for some intimate exercises before bedtime."

"Do I hear any objections?" he said smiling.

"Not at all," replied Macy, as she smiled back and placed her hand on his neck. "Drive like the wind. The sooner we get back, the more time we have." They burst out laughing, feeling like a couple of school kids. It was a feeling they both hoped would never go away.

CHAPTER 18

The next morning, Callie and Drake picked up where they left off the night before, sharing some intimate time before heading over to Aunt Jewel's for breakfast. Although it was still early, he didn't mind being wakened like that. In fact, he rather preferred it over an alarm clock. They showered and dressed quickly in order to get over to Aunt Jewel's on time. She did not want to offend her aunt by showing up late for breakfast. Callie was expecting some of the rest of the family to be there, but when they drove up, there were no other cars. She knocked once on the back door as she opened it and stepped inside. *So much for waiting to be welcomed in,* thought Drake, following behind her.

"Come on in, child," said Aunt Jewel, busy kneading dough. "I was just about to put the biscuits on to bake, then everything will be ready."

"What can I help you with?" asked Callie.

"You can set the table." She looked up at Drake and smiled. "Did you sleep well last night, Adam?"

"Yes, ma'am."

"Please call me Aunt Jewel," she said, interrupting him. "Everybody does."

"Yes, Aunt Jewel," he replied.

"That's better," she said with a wink, then motioned for him to have a seat while she put the biscuits in the oven. Drake watched as Callie knew exactly where the dishes and silverware were to set the table with. As soon as she finished, she asked Aunt Jewel what else she could do, to which Aunt Jewel patted the back of the chair beside Drake and told her to sit down. She was glad in a way, especially since her aunt was a much better cook than she was. As soon as the bread was done, she set the serving dishes on the table.

"I just whipped up a little breakfast since you two were the only ones coming," she said.

Drake looked at the large bowls of eggs, bacon, sausage, ham, grits, gravy, and biscuits, and wondered what a large breakfast would have looked like. As soon as she sat down, Aunt Jewel reached toward them, grabbing Drake's right hand with her left and Callie's left hand with her right.

"Would you say grace, Callie?" They all bowed their heads as Callie gave thanks for the food. Drake was no stranger to prayer, having heard his grandmother say grace at many family meals, but he could not help but marvel at how beautiful Callie's prayer was. It was a side of her he had not seen to this point, a side he found very interesting and appealing. After last night's exercise, and this morning's, he was hungry, and dug right in, eating until he thought he would burst. Aunt Jewel looked at him, then back at Callie and smiled. She loved to see a man eat hardily, and viewed it as a compliment to her cooking. When everyone had finished eating, there was still quite a bit of food left.

"What are you going to do with all of this leftover food?" asked Drake.

"Well, I usually cook breakfast for the jail one day each week, and I was hoping I could get you to take it over there while Callie and I cleaned up."

"I'd be glad to." Aunt Jewel told him how to get there, and once everything was boxed up, he left on his mission. The directions were quite easy, and he had no trouble finding it. He smiled at the reaction of the police officers, having obviously been eagerly expecting Aunt Jewel's cooking. He lingered at the station for a little while talking to the officers about the crime in Dalton. He found it interesting comparing crime rates and types between a small town and a larger city. Sometimes he thought it might be nice to live and work in a small town, but then realized that as a defense attorney, he would have trouble finding work. He decided that for his line of work he needed to stick with a more populated area.

He left the station around mid-morning and headed back to Aunt Jewel's. She and Callie were sitting in the swing on the front porch when he drove up. As he walked toward them, Aunt Jewel stood up and moved to one of the rocking chairs.

"Please, you don't have to move for me."

"Nonsense," she said. "You two should sit together. After all, you are going to marry my niece, aren't you?" He felt his face turn red.

"Yes, ma'am, I intend to," he replied, sitting down beside Callie, smiling at her.

"Good, because I think you make a great couple."

That comment made Callie turn red also. They felt like a couple of high school kids before the prom. She changed the subject by asking Aunt Jewel about the day's events. This was the day before her uncle's funeral, so the family was expected to be at the funeral home this evening for the visitation. That was where friends and family would come to pay their respects to the family. Uncle Harry had planned his funeral several years ago, requesting a military burial complete with an American flag draped over the coffin. He was a veteran of the Vietnam War, and wanted everyone to know. Uncle Harry was one of those southern conservatives who believed in supporting your President, especially in a time of war. He requested the casket not be open for viewing, but instead had selected a picture and had it framed for the occasion. The visitation was supposed to last from seven until nine, but the family had to be at the funeral home by six-thirty. Aunt Jewel told Callie to be prepared because given the number of friends Uncle Harry had, she knew people would begin arriving before seven and would not leave until well after nine.

Drake excused himself for a moment to phone Macy to see how the investigation was going. He knew Josh would probably call sometime today, and he wanted to have an update for him.

"Hello," said Macy.

"Macy, this is Adam. How is the investigation for Josh coming?"

"We've got a list of people who had a disagreement of one kind or another with Josh, but so far we haven't uncovered any viable suspects for Julie's murder. There are only three people on our list who own a blue Pontiac, but the murderer could have rented one. We are going to the last Pontiac owner on our list this morning."

"Thanks. I just wanted to check with you in case Josh calls me. Please keep me posted."

"Will do," said Macy as they ended the call. Drake returned to the porch swing beside Callie and continued with their visit. About twenty minutes had passed when his cell phone rang. He excused himself quickly and walked off the porch as he answered the call.

"Adam, this is Josh. Are they hunting for me yet?"

"Not yet. We were able to get a two week continuance, so no one knows you're on the lam."

"Well, at least I can stop looking over my shoulder for a few days. I met with your friend, but I haven't heard anything since our initial visit. Has there been any progress?"

"Not so far, but she is following up on some leads your assistant gave her. I just spoke with her this morning and she promised to keep me updated."

"Thanks, I just thought I would check in."

"Why don't you just come back in, Josh?"

"You know why, Adam. I'll be in touch." Then the line went dead as Josh ended the call.

Drake stood motionless for a moment, thinking about the situation and how he had kept silent when he knew his client had skipped town. Hopefully, this would not come back to haunt him. As he walked back to the front porch, Drake noticed Callie and Aunt Jewel were not there. He walked over to the screen door and peered inside calling, "Hello?"

"Come on in, honey," said Callie. "We're in the kitchen." He opened the door and stepped inside, making his way to the kitchen where he found Callie and Aunt Jewel busy making sandwiches.

"I didn't want to just barge in," he said rather sheepishly.

"Nonsense," said Aunt Jewel. "You're just like one of the family now, child."

"We came in to fix a little lunch," said Callie.

This time Aunt Jewel asked Drake to say grace, which he did as best he remembered from when he was a child. Although he stammered once, he felt proud to make it through with what he believed to be an adequate yet brief prayer.

After lunch, they headed down to the funeral home for one last viewing of the body before the evening visitation. The immediate family was allowed to see the body per Uncle Harry's instructions, although the casket would not be open for public viewing. As she peered into the coffin, Callie thought Uncle Harry looked rather peaceful, as if he were simply asleep. She whispered a gentle goodbye to him as a tear rolled down her cheek. Turning, she walked out of the parlor while Aunt Jewel remained behind to say her last goodbye.

Callie and Drake waited in the foyer for Aunt Jewel, who only spent a few minutes alone with Harry. When she walked out of the parlor, it was as if she read their minds by saying, "When you've been together as long as we have, it's not goodbye, but rather see you later. I know he'll be watching over me, so I can talk to him every day." And with that she walked out of the funeral home and back to the car with Callie and Drake following close behind.

They had just enough time to rest a few hours before getting ready for the visitation. Callie had brought along a stylish black dress that fit the part of a mourner, without sacrificing her physical attributes. Drake stood silent as he stared at her, taking in all of her beauty. Suddenly, he felt like the luckiest man on earth.

He donned his black suit. They left the Bed and Breakfast and stopped by Aunt Jewel's to take her to the visitation. Aunt Jewel was also wearing a black dress and although it was clearly from another era, it still looked appropriate for the occasion. They arrived at the funeral home at twenty minutes after six, and people were already arriving. The funeral director escorted them to where they should stand, then the visitation began.

The last time Drake had witnessed such a large turnout for a funeral home visitation was when Tony DeRoche, one of High Point's most prominent businessmen, died. People were lined out the door and down the side of the building for the viewing. This was no exception, as the line extended all the way out into the parking lot. At nine o'clock when visitation was supposed to be over, the line was still backed up to the inner door. It took an extra hour for the remainder of the guests to go through the line and pay their respects. Drake could tell from the look on Aunt Jewel's face that she was exhausted, but she felt it was her duty to stay through the entire event. It was just one of those things you do as a member of the family.

When the last visitor passed by and walked out, Aunt Jewel kicked her shoes off and sat down on a nearby sofa, completely drained from the exertion of standing for so long. Callie and Drake joined her on the sofa as they all took a minute to rest their legs. After a few minutes, they helped Aunt Jewel to her feet and escorted her to the car. By the time they got back to her house, she had almost fallen asleep in the back seat. Callie decided it might be best if they spent the night with her just to make sure she was okay, so Drake went to the Bed and Breakfast and retrieved the personal items they would need for the night. Even though they were young, tonight would definitely not be a night for intimate exercise, especially after four hours on their feet having to greet hundreds of people.

They slept in the guest bedroom just down the hall from Aunt Jewel. He fell asleep almost immediately and slept straight through the night. Callie, however, kept waking up every couple of hours to check on Aunt Jewel. Every time she peered into her bedroom, though, Aunt Jewel was sleeping peacefully. She was glad they had spent the night with her, and felt it was probably the reason she was able to sleep so soundly. Callie remembered her mother telling her how that was the most difficult thing after her father died—sleeping. After checking on her one last time around four o'clock, Callie finally succumbed to the exhaustion that enveloped her body and fell soundly asleep, not waking until morning.

Chapter 19

At five in the morning, Macy finally gave in to the fact she was not going to get any more sleep, climbed out of bed and headed to the bathroom for a quick shower. It was not unusual for her to become wired while working a case, even to the point of insomnia. As the water flowed over her head and shoulders and ran down the length of her body, she was thinking about the day ahead. For some unexplained reason, she felt like this last blue Pontiac owner was the murderer, and yet, she had not even met him. Maybe it was wishful thinking on her part, or the fact she had talked Spence into delaying their vacation to take on this case. Either way, she was determined to turn over as many stones as it took to prove Josh Stephens was innocent.

She dried off, got dressed, and quietly sat down in front of her laptop to do a little research, hoping her movements would not disturb Spence from his sleep. She searched for any information on Mark Jacoby, the last of the three blue Pontiac owners, hoping to find anything at all that might help them with their questioning once they located him. At first nothing came up when she did a simple name inquiry. She next checked the archives of The High Point Enterprise, the local newspaper, for articles mentioning Jacoby. She narrowed her search to around the time of the threatening phone calls made to Josh Stephens. Unfortunately, she was unable to find any articles mentioning him by name.

When Spence began stirring around seven-thirty, she woke him up so they could get started. She finished mapping out their day while he showered and dressed. They would visit the Jacoby residence first, and if nothing came from that, they would start working their way down the rest of the list of ten names Madeline Jones gave them.

Since Jacoby lived north of downtown, she stopped at Alex's House for breakfast. Alex's House was a local restaurant that was open twenty-four hours a day. It was a rather small place with a few booths and an old fashioned counter with stools. The local police could often be found there eating when they were not at the Krispy Kreme doughnut shop. Alex's was not very crowded when they stopped in, and they were able to get a booth at the far end of the diner. Because the restaurant was so small, the aroma from the kitchen permeated the dining area, increasing their hunger. They refrained from ordering a large breakfast in order to avoid feeling lethargic and overly full later in the morning. Besides, in their business you never knew when you might have to break out into a full run. She went over the day's schedule with Spence while they ate. After they finished their meal, Spence drove while Macy navigated, just like yesterday.

Their first stop was Mark Jacoby's place. He lived in an apartment on the north end of town on Northgate Court. It was a small apartment complex, so it took very little time to locate. There was no blue Pontiac parked in front of the apartment building when they arrived. She noticed how quiet the neighborhood was as they made their way to his apartment door. Once there, Spence knocked loudly, and they waited for an answer. He knocked two more times, but still heard no response from inside. As they turned to leave, the door across the hallway opened ever so slightly, and a fragile voice came from within saying, "He don't live there anymore."

Macy turned in the direction from where the voice came and asked, "Who?"

"Mr. Jacoby. I assume that's who you're looking for."

"Yes, sir. Do you know where he moved to?"

"Nope. All I know is he went to live with his daughter and her husband when they evicted him from here."

"Why was he evicted?" asked Spence.

"Because he was a drunk and a bum who wouldn't pay his rent. If you ask me, the neighborhood's better without him." And with that, he closed the door before they could ask anymore questions. They returned to their car and climbed in, waiting a few moments to collect their thoughts before either spoke.

"Well, what do we do now 'Ms. Avenger'?" asked Spence with a slight smile.

She rolled her eyes and shook her head. "What we do is find out where the daughter lives and track this guy down," she said with a sigh, as if stating the obvious. Spence just smiled as he backed away from the curb and drove out of the apartment complex, turning south onto Main Street. As they approached Eastchester Drive, he began eagerly searching the buildings until she spotted it.

"Quick, turn in here," she said, as Spence pulled the car into a Starbucks parking lot.

"You suddenly have an urge for coffee?

"No, silly. They have Wireless Internet access here, and I just happened to bring my laptop along. We can have something to drink while I search the web to find this woman."

"I understand now, master," said Spence in a poor imitation of Caine from Kung Fu. Macy just shook her head as they entered Starbucks. She took a seat at one of the tables and opened her laptop while he went to the counter and ordered a couple of coffees. By the time, he returned with the coffee, she had already uncovered the name of Jacoby's daughter, Margaret. According to the neighbor, though, she and her husband took her father in, so Jacoby would not be her last name now. Hopefully, she was married in Guilford County, thought Macy, as she hurriedly typed on the keyboard. She searched the marriage records for Guilford County for a Margaret Jacoby between the years she would legally be able to marry. She let out a sigh of relief as the information appeared on the screen. According to the county records, a Margaret Jacoby married Phil- lip Estes on June 10, 1992. She did a quick address search for Phillip Estes in Guilford County, but there was no record of a Phillip Estes living in the county. Macy searched The High Point Enterprise archives for the wedding announcement from June 1992. She found their wedding announcement and quickly scanned the article until she read that the parents of the groom were from Cherryville, North Carolina. Another quick search revealed Cherryville to be located in Gaston County.

She searched for the last name Estes in Gaston County, but was only able to locate a couple of families in Gastonia. She tried a search based on the city address of Cherryville without the county information. Three names appeared in the search results, with one being Phillip Estes. According to the records, he lived on John Cline Road. Macy pulled a quick map search and soon discovered why the Gaston County search had not shown his record. John Cline Road was actually in Cleveland County, but was close enough to Cherryville to have a Cherryville address. According to the map, the Estes lived between Kings Mountain and Shelby, just north of Moss Lake.

Scribbling down the address information, she looked over at Spence with a smile, and said, "Road trip!" She packed up her laptop and they headed out the door. Based on the information she retrieved, it would take approximately two hours to drive to Cherryville from High Point.

He eased out of the parking lot and headed south on Main Street to Interstate 85. From there, they headed south toward Charlotte until they reached the Shelby exit, which would take them around Kings Mountain to Shelby. Then they would head north toward Cherryville and wrap around the north side of Moss Lake. Hopefully, after two hours of driving it would not lead to a dead end, but Macy had certainly ran into her share of them since she began her crusade as 'The Avenger.'

Macy made notes while Spence drove as they discussed potential questions for Mr. Jacoby. Since the neighbor offered such limited information, it was imperative they determine how long it had been since he lived in High Point, especially if he was now living two hours away. It might be difficult to prove he was at the crime scene given the distance between the two locations. Besides, he may very well have a solid alibi for the time of the murder. Macy still had a strong feeling about him, but was unable to interpret it to mean she believed he was actually the murderer. Usually she was clear with her instincts, but for some reason she believed him to be linked to the crime, but lacked the overwhelming sensation of his guilt. Although her instincts had been right many times in the past, she knew she could not totally rely on them alone. Much would be determined from the information she learned once they were able to speak with Mr. Jacoby. Until then she would need to keep her feelings and emotions in check until she could weigh all the facts and make an educated analysis.

Spence took the exit onto Highway 74, heading toward Shelby. As they bypassed Kings Mountain, he wondered if perhaps there was a shorter route, but since he was unfamiliar with the area, he stuck to the directions he had. As they reached the edge of Shelby, he turned right onto Highway 150 and headed north toward Cherryville. From here, there were a couple of small twisty roads, until finally they reached their destination.

Phillip and Margaret Estes lived in a brick house on the corner of John Cline Road and Haven Way. Macy could see Moss Lake from the house as they climbed out of the car and headed to the front door. As they neared the front porch, she could hear a dog barking from within the house. She rang the doorbell, which sent the dog into a frenzy, then heard the lock click on the door as someone cracked open the front door. At first, the woman spoke through the glass of the storm door.

"Hello?"

"Hi, my name is Macy Merit. I'm looking for Margaret Estes."

"I'm Margaret Estes. What can I do for you?"

"I wanted to talk to you about your father. May we come in?"

"Yes, please," she answered, pushing open the storm door and motioning them inside. Macy spotted the source of the barking as a Bichon Frise stood guard just inside the foyer. Margaret spoke to the dog sternly as she told Macy, "Joey is really a good dog. He's just a little aggressive when it comes to strangers, especially men." She looked over at Spence when she said that. "I'll let him out the back so we can talk in peace." She ushered the dog outside while Macy and Spence sat down on the living room sofa.

As Macy looked around the beautifully decorated interior, she thought it must be the work of a professional decorator. Everything complimented each other, from the draperies, to the carpet, and even the sconces on the wall. There was also a lot of hardwood flooring, which added a nice touch. But the thing that caught Macy's eye the most was a beautiful mural painted on one wall that extended to the double doors leading to the adjoining sunroom. When the doors were closed, the scene matched up perfectly, but when the doors were open, as Margaret did when she let the dog out through the back door, the mural still looked complete.

"Did you paint this?" asked Macy, indicating the mural. "Heavens, no," replied Margaret. "There's not an artistic bone in my body I'm afraid. I had a friend in Shelby paint it for me."

"It's beautiful, and really adds to the décor."

"Thank you. Now, you said you were here about my father. Is there any news?"

"News?"

"Yes, you are with the police, aren't you?"

"No, we're independent investigators working on a case that may involve your father."

"Oh no, what has he done now?"

"Nothing that we know yet," said Macy. "Why?"

"My father has a tendency to drink sometimes, then doesn't remember things he does."

"Like what?"

"He has been known to get into fights, especially at bars."

"You asked if we were the police and if there was any news," said Macy. "What were you referring to?"

"My father got on one of his drinking binges a few weeks ago and left without saying where he was going. When he didn't come home a few days later, I called the police. They told me that since he was an adult there wasn't much they could do, and suggested he was probably sleeping it off somewhere. They did promise to keep an eye out for him and let me know if anything turned up. That's why when you said you wanted to talk to me about him I just assumed you were with the police."

"Has he ever disappeared like this before?" asked Macy. "Not for this long. The longest he was gone before was a week. Of course, that's since he started living with us. I don't know what his habits were before that."

"Why did he come to live with you?"

"Well, actually, I brought him home to live with me when he was evicted from his apartment in High Point. He really is a good man. He's just had a rough time of it over the past three years. First he lost his job when the furniture plant he worked for closed. Then the bank foreclosed on their home. That's when my mother left him for another man. She said she needed to be provided for, and if he couldn't do it, she would find someone who would. I haven't spoken with my mother for awhile, especially after the way she treated my father. Besides, my relationship with him was always closer since I was little. He began drinking shortly after he was laid off, and it steadily progressed to the point where he is today. I guess drinking helps him forget his troubles for a little while."

"Did he ever mention a man named Josh Stephens?" asked Macy

"Did he ever! It was as if he was obsessed with this man. Dad said he was the reason he lost everything because he wouldn't work with him on the mortgage. He said Stephens couldn't wait to foreclose on his home so he could sell it to one of his buddies who owned the property beside of it and build an apartment complex. Dad would get drunk and then swear to get revenge on Stephens, but I don't really think he meant it. I believe he just needed someone to blame for his troubles and a banker seemed like a likely target."

"Did your father ever say anything about Mr. Stephens' family?" asked Macy.

"The only thing I remember was one time when he was drunk he said something to the effect of how he would take away everything Stephens loved, the same way he took everything from him, and see how he liked it. But I still believe it was simply the ravings of a broken drunken man, and that he had no intention of harming anyone. If you knew my father like I do, you would know he could never hurt another human being. Besides, his health has suffered so from his drinking that I don't believe he is physically capable of doing much."

"How did your father leave? Did he take a cab or drive?"

"He still has the car he owned before he lost everything else."

"What kind of car does your father drive?" asked Macy. "A blue Pontiac Grand Prix."

"Do you have any idea where your father could have gone?"

"Like I told the police, the only place I know he frequents is Louie's Bar & Grill over on Lafayette, but my husband and I have been by there several times and haven't seen him," said Margaret. Then she changed direction, asking, "So, what is this case that you want to speak to my father about?"

"I'm afraid we're not at liberty to divulge any details at this point," said Spence, hoping that would appease her. It didn't.

"What do you mean you can't divulge any details? After all of the things I just told you, you can't at least tell me what you think my father may be involved in?"

"Someone killed Josh Stephens' wife a couple of weeks ago," said Macy.

"And you think my father had something to do with it?"

"At this point we don't know. An eyewitness saw a car matching the description of your father's at the scene earlier that same morning. We're just trying to rule him out as a suspect."

Margaret placed her head in her hands and began rocking back and forth, then looked up and said, "He did it, didn't he? I just thought he was ranting on in a drunken rage, but he really did want to make this guy suffer. I should have called someone. Oh no, it's all my fault." Macy put her arm around Margaret trying to comfort her as she began to sob.

"No, Margaret, it's not your fault. We don't even know for sure your father did anything. Let's not jump to conclusions before we get a chance to talk to him."

"But what if he did do it? What will I do then?"

"I suggest you cross that bridge when, and if, you get to it. In the meantime, if your father comes back, or you hear from him, please call me," said Macy, handing her a business card.

Margaret glanced down at the card. "The Avenger. So you help people, do you?"

"I try. And I'll try to help your father any way I can, too, if you need me." She patted her on the shoulder before she and Spence left. He could tell by the look in her eyes she felt sorry for Margaret.

"Snap out of it, Mace. You've seen enough of this by now not to get personally involved."

"Oh, I'm not. I just had this strange feeling that something's not quite right, but I can't put my finger on it."

"So you're not feeling sorry for Margaret?"

"Maybe a little, but that's not what's bugging me."

"Then what is?"

"When I find out, I'll let you know."

Chapter 20

Drake awoke the next morning before Callie. She was still sleeping soundly when he got up and headed into the kitchen. Aunt Jewel was already up and fixing breakfast when he walked in.

"Good morning, Adam. Did you sleep well?"

"Yes, Aunt Jewel. I guess I should go wake Callie up for breakfast."

"No, let her sleep. She was up all night checking on me. Besides, this will give me a chance to get to know you a little better."

Aunt Jewel had prepared a smaller breakfast this morning since she would not be taking any food to the jail. After they sat down at the table, she grabbed his hands and said grace, then she began passing dishes of food to Drake while he filled his plate. An attorney during cross examination could not have done a better job of questioning someone than Aunt Jewel did with him. By the time they were halfway through breakfast, she knew more about him than Callie. He did not mind, though, because she was a very interesting woman to talk to, and he was also learning a lot about Callie in the process. They were almost finished eating when she came walking in rubbing her head and yawning at the same time.

"Did you sleep well, child?" asked Aunt Jewel. "Not really."

"Probably cause you were checking on me all night."

"Wait, how did you know...never mind," said Callie, waving her hands as she sat down beside Drake and gave him a quick peck on the lips.

Aunt Jewel poured her some coffee and sat the food dishes where she could easily reach them. Aunt Jewel stood up and motioned for Drake to follow her saying, "Let's go finish our little chat while Callie eats."

She gave a questioning look as they headed for the front porch. Once they were outside, Callie could only hear mumbling followed by several outbursts of laughter. She just shook her head and continued eating until she was full, then topped off her coffee and carried it with her to join them on the front porch.

The funeral was not until two o'clock, allowing plenty of time to visit before getting ready to go to the church. Uncle Harry had requested his funeral be held at First Baptist Church, where he was a member and a deacon. He had also requested specific songs and readings, and had scheduled the length of the service, long enough for people to remember, but not too long to cause people to forget. He told Aunt Jewel about many funerals he had seen that lasted so long that by the time they were over, people almost forgot who had died. He did not want any special notoriety, but he did want people to remember him.

"So what were you two talking about?" asked Callie.

Aunt Jewel looked at Drake and winked saying, "What did I tell you?" And at that, they both burst out laughing while Callie looked back and forth at them with a puzzled look on her face. Then Drake answered, "I see now. I hadn't noticed that before."

"Noticed what?" asked Callie, causing another eruption of laughter between Drake and Aunt Jewel. She snorted and stood up in a huff, but Aunt Jewel grabbed her by the arm before she could stomp off, still shaking with laughter.

"Listen, child, I was just telling Adam some things about you from when you were young, like the fact that you always were a nosy little thing," said Aunt Jewel.

"I am not nosy. I'm just very interested in people and what they are saying."

"That sure sounds like nosy to me," he said, as he glanced at Aunt Jewel and winked. They both chuckled again causing Callie to turn a little red from embarrassment.

"Okay, maybe I am a little nosy," she conceded. "But is that so bad?"

"Not at all, honey," replied Drake, leaning over for a kiss. "I like you just the way you are."

"So what else did you talk about?"

"I just wanted to get to know Adam a little better," said Aunt Jewel.

"And now that you do, what do you think?" asked Callie. "I think you made a very wise choice."

"Why thank you, Aunt Jewel," said Drake.

"You're welcome, child," she replied with a nod and a smile.

They sat and visited for another hour until Aunt Jewel stood up and announced she was going to get ready. That was Drake and Callie's cue to head back to the Bed and Breakfast to shower and get dressed, too. On the short drive over, Callie tried to get Drake to tell her more of the conversation between him and Aunt Jewel, but he just smiled and shook his head.

Once inside, Callie whispered in Drake's ear, "We've got time," then locked her lips on his, pulling him down on top of her. They made love, making up for last night, and headed into the shower together for round two. They dressed and made it back to Aunt Jewel's with ten minutes to spare. They all climbed into the car and headed to the church.

Uncle Harry had planned such a beautiful service that Aunt Jewel admitted she could not have made it any better. One of the ladies in the church choir sang two hymns. One was Uncle Harry's favorite *How Great Thou Art*, and the other was *In The Garden*. Each song brought a tear to Aunt Jewel's eyes as she remembered Uncle Harry singing beside her in church.

The pastor did an exceptional job of memorializing Uncle Harry, which demonstrated how well he knew him personally. Callie remembered the many funerals she had been to where the preacher did not really know the deceased, so the service felt canned and impersonal. This was a proper send off, she thought.

After the service, they walked the short distance to the cemetery outside. It was unusual to find many churches with their own cemetery today, but First Baptist was established at the turn of the century when it was more common to have your own cemetery on church property. Uncle Harry made sure he got two plots before they were all gone, since the church had no other land on which to expand. The pastor offered the typical graveside eulogy, then passed by the family to express his sorrow for their loss.

After the pallbearers placed their lapel flowers on the casket, the family stood and visited with the people who stopped by to offer their condolences. They left the cemetery before the body was lowered into the ground. Everyone was invited to come by Aunt Jewel's where people had dropped off a lot of food. Many people came by to visit with Aunt Jewel for a short while and grab a bite. She was glad to see so many friends, and hoped there were no leftovers by the time everyone had eaten.

Later that evening, it was only Aunt Jewel, Callie, and Drake who remained. Aunt Jewel asked them to take her back to the cemetery for one last time today since the body would now be interred. They walked up to the gravesite where some of the flowers had been laid upon the fresh dirt now covering the grave. Aunt Jewel got down on her knees and patted the top of the grave, telling Uncle Harry she would see him later. She stood up and silently walked back to the car. Even though she had held up extremely well over the past few days, Callie could tell she was grieving inside. She gently reached over and took Aunt Jewel by the arm, causing her to place her hand over the top of Callie's. They remained silent all the way back to the house. Once there, Aunt Jewel told Callie she would like to be alone tonight, and for her and Drake to have an evening alone together. Callie knitted her brow in concern, but Aunt Jewel reassured her that she would be all right. Callie gave her a hug and a gentle kiss on the cheek, and climbed back into the car with Drake. She waved to Aunt Jewel as they drove off toward the Bed and Breakfast. Callie was in no mood for sex tonight, so they simply cuddled until they drifted off to sleep.

The next morning they arrived bright and early at Aunt Jewel's for breakfast. Aunt Jewel seemed like her old self again, and even insisted that Callie and Drake not spend all their time at the house looking after her. She wanted to get back to her normal routine as much as possible, and felt they should enjoy themselves some while they were here.

Callie left Aunt Jewel's briefly and swung by the library to use their internet access. Then she returned and insisted Drake come with her. She blew a kiss and waved goodbye to Aunt Jewel, and headed out of town. It would take about an hour and a half to get to Atlanta from Dalton, which gave Callie plenty of time.

He asked where they were going, but she insisted it was a surprise. When they pulled into the parking area outside Turner Field, Drake began to get excited.

"Are we going to a Braves game?"

"We sure are," Callie responded with a wry smile across her lips. Drake leaned over and planted a big wet kiss on her. She knew the Atlanta Braves was his favorite baseball team, and went online and found out they were playing an afternoon game against the Dodgers. She purchased the tickets online using her credit card so she could surprise Drake.

He was like a kid in a candy store, twisting his neck all around to take in as much as he could see. He had always wanted to go to a live game, but had never made the trip. The seats were behind home plate, with an excellent view. Callie smiled as he called out different players' names to her. She had never seen him so happy, which made her feel warm inside. He even had a hotdog and a pretzel to complete the stadium experience. And to cap off the evening, the Braves won the game.

He talked almost nonstop about the game on the ride back to Dalton When they got back to the Bed and Breakfast, Callie topped off the night with an unforgettable lovemaking session. Afterward Drake had trouble falling asleep, his mind racing as he tried to think of some way to pay her back for such a wonderful day. As if she read his mind, she reached over, touched his face, and said, "One more time is all the thanks I need," as she pulled him over onto her, locking her soft wet lips onto his. The next morning they had breakfast at one of the local restaurants since Aunt Jewel would be making her usual morning rounds at the hospital as a volunteer. Afterward, Callie asked Drake what he wanted to do next. They had another week of the continuance left, and he left it up to Callie. She wanted to go to the beach. They packed up, checked out of the Bed and Breakfast, and headed to Jekyll Island. Since it would take approximately six hours to get there, they took their time to enjoy the scenery as they rode through Georgia.

Callie called Aunt Jewel and told her where they were heading. She sounded glad they were able to take a little minivacation. She told Callie there was no need for them to drive all the way back to Dalton. They could simply return to North Carolina when they needed to, provided she promised to come for more visits later. Callie told her they would definitely visit her more often, especially since Drake loved the small town charm and Aunt Jewel's cooking. Callie could see Aunt Jewel smiling in her mind's eye as she said goodbye. Now it was just her and Drake on their own little adventure.

When they arrived at Jekyll Island, they were able to find a rental cottage at one of the rental agencies. It was a small two bedroom older house, but perfect for the two of them. There was a screened porch that faced the ocean, providing a beautiful panoramic view. Before they unpacked, Callie insisted they try out the bed. After their love making session, she wanted to walk on the beach. Suddenly, they realized they had not packed swimsuits since they did not know they would be going to the beach. Luckily, there was a beachwear shop just down the road, and they drove there, trying on suits until they found what they wanted, then headed back to the cottage where they changed and went out onto the beach. They walked along the edge of the water, which was still rather warm from the after- noon sun. After walking a couple of miles, they realized it had been a long time since they ate. Fortunately for them, there was a small burger shack just ahead, and immediately walked over and ordered a burger apiece and a soda. Luckily, Drake had tucked some money away in the Velcro enclosed pocket on the back of his swim trunks, giving them enough money for their meal plus an ice cream cone afterward.

Drake alternated looks between the rolling waves of the ocean, and the beautiful face of Callie as the ocean breeze wafted through her hair. It was as if time stood still whenever he looked at her, and suddenly he was becoming aroused. He tried to take his mind off sex, but when his eyes surveyed the way her body filled every curve of her bikini perfectly, he lost the battle.

Feeling he needed a swim to cool him off, he grabbed Callie by the hand and led her to the water where they both dove in. It didn't take long for the feelings to overcome him there also, as he scooped her into his arms and began kissing her until a large wave crashed over them. She started laughing and ran out of the water back toward the cottage. Drake was much faster, though, and soon caught up with her. They walked hand in hand quickly back to the cottage, easily removing their swimsuits once they were inside. Between the food and the sex, they both were exhausted afterward, and fell asleep in each other's arms.

They were awakened to the sound of Drake's cell phone around nine o'clock that evening. "Hello," said Drake sleepily.

"Adam, this is Macy. I didn't wake you, did I?"

"No, what's up?" he lied.

"We've got a potential lead on the mysterious blue Pontiac that was seen at Josh's house the morning his wife was murdered. I was hoping you could have Betty check and see if there is any record of this guy having checked into a hospital or been arrested lately."

"Sure, hang on and let me grab something to write with," he told her. He grabbed a pen from the dresser and a magazine to write on. "Go ahead."

"His name is Mark Jacoby. He used to live on Northgate Court in High Point, but recently moved to Cherryville to live with his daughter. According to his daughter, he had an issue with Josh over his house being foreclosed by the bank."

"I'll call Betty first thing in the morning and get her working on it."

"Thanks. In the meantime, Spence and I are going to hang out around Shelby to see if we can spot him at some of the local bars."

"Okay, I'll let you know what Betty finds out," said Drake, and hung up.

"Who was that?" asked Callie.

"Just someone helping me with a case," he replied. "Now go back to sleep."

"But I'm awake now," she said with that sparkle in her eye.

"A night swim would be nice."

"That's exactly what I was thinking," she said, climbing out of bed totally naked and heading for the door.

"Whoa, aren't you forgetting something?" asked Drake, holding up her bikini.

"It's nighttime, remember?" she replied with a coy giggle, and out the door she ran. He followed closely behind her, naked as well. They both jumped into the ocean which had cooled down considerably since the sun went down. They embraced and kissed as the cool water swirled around their naked bodies, invigorating them. There were a few people walking along the beach, which only added to their excitement. Finally, they ran back to the cottage where they made love once more, tasting the salt water on each other's skin as their bodies writhed rhythmically together. After expending a lot of energy once again, they fell asleep tangled together and didn't wake up until morning, when the sun illuminated the room.

Chapter 21

The next morning both Drake and Callie were famished, and headed out early for breakfast. There was a small local restaurant a couple of blocks from where they were staying and they ate there. Drake waited until he knew Betty would be in the office before calling her.

"Drake Law Offices," said Betty when she answered. "Betty, this is Adam. I need a favor."

"Anything for you, boss."

"I need you to see if you can track somebody down for me. His name is Mark Jacoby. According to Macy, he used to live on Northgate Court in High Point, then moved in with his daughter in Cherryville. It seems this guy may have had an axe to grind with Josh."

"Hmm…that name sounds somewhat familiar, but I can't quite put my finger on it. But I'll get right on that."

"Thanks. Just call me on my cell when you find out anything."

"Will do," said Betty as she hung up. She sat there for a moment repeating the name under her breath, but finally shrugged her shoulders when she could not think of where she knew the name from, and began typing on her keyboard. She checked the DMV records for the last known address, and also got the name of his insurance company, just in case they had a new address for him. According to the latest records, his address was listed as the Cherryville house where his daughter lived, and his insurance was with Independent Auto Insurers. Betty called them to see if they had a different address for him. As she dialed the number, it seemed vaguely familiar, but when the receptionist answered, Betty knew she had spoken with these people before. She asked to speak with the agent who handled Mr. Jacoby's insurance, and after being placed on hold for a few seconds, a man came on the line and asked who she was. When Betty gave him her name, he said, "Ma'am, I've already spoken with your insurance company about the accident and I assured them we will process the claim as soon as we can."

Betty hesitated before she said, "I'm not sure I understand."

"You were calling about the accident where Mr. Jacoby ran into you?" Betty immediately began shuffling through some papers on her desk, finally pulling one out of the stack.

"Yes, sir. I'm sorry to bother you, but I need to replace my car as soon as I can."

"I understand, ma'am. You should have your check within the next three business days."

"Thank you," said Betty, and hung up. She stared for a moment at the paper in her hand, realizing midway through her phone call where she knew the name Mark Jacoby from. He was the man who ran through the intersection and hit her car. Now that she knew who he was, it would be easy for her to tell Drake where to find him. He had been unable to post bail, and was therefore being held at the county jail pending a hearing. Betty dialed Drake's cell phone.

"Hello?"

"Adam, this is Betty. You're not going to believe who Mark Jacoby is."

"What do you mean?"

"I mean, he's the guy who ran through the intersection and hit my car."

"You're kidding!"

"No, I'm serious. So as far as where to locate him, that's easy. He's in the county jail awaiting his hearing."

"Thanks, Betty. I owe you one." And with that he ended the call and immediately dialed Macy's number.

"Hello?"

"Macy, this is Adam. I found Mark Jacoby."

"Great! Where is he?"

"It just so happens he is the guy who ran into Betty that morning when she had her accident. He's in the county jail as we speak."

"I appreciate the info. Spence and I will head back to High Point right away."

Drake had no sooner ended the call when his cell phone rang again.

"Adam, this is Josh. Do you have any leads from the list Madeline gave Ms. Merit?"

"Actually we do, Josh. It seems one of the people on your phone log is responsible for running a red light while intoxicated and hitting my assistant. According to his daughter, you foreclosed on his home after he lost his job, then his wife left him, and now he blames you for his troubles."

"Mark Jacoby," said Josh.

"Right. Boy, you sure have a good memory."

"We're a community bank, Adam. We don't foreclose many homes."

"I never thought about it like that," said Drake. "So where is Mr. Jacoby?"

"He's in the county jail awaiting his hearing."

"Do you think he may be the one who killed Julie?"

"I don't know at this point. I guess we need to have the police search his car, since it's probably still in the impound lot."

"Why don't you get Ms. Merit to do it?" asked Josh. "At this point I don't trust the police very much."

"I see your point. I'll call her right now." Drake ended the call and quickly dialed Macy's number.

"Macy, this is Adam. Listen, I was wondering if you think you should search Jacoby's car to see if there is any evidence linking him to Julie Stephens' murder?"

"Why don't we just have the police or the DA's office do it?"

"Josh seems to have a trust issue with the local police right now."

"Oh, I see. Well, it will be difficult to gain access to the impound lot."

"Let me check on something and I'll call you back," said Drake. Then he turned to Callie and filled her in on what was going on. He asked if there was any way she could have someone from her office assist them with the search. Callie made a couple of quick phone calls, then told Drake she would have someone from the office search the vehicle in the presence of Macy. That way she could verify what they found to Josh. Drake called Macy back.

"Macy, the Assistant DA has agreed to have someone from their office meet you to search the vehicle. He'll perform the actual search, but you can verify the contents for our case."

"Sounds great," said Macy. "Who do I ask for at the impound lot?"

"Just give them your name. They will be expecting you.

Oh and Macy, thanks for your help."

"All in a day's work," replied Macy as she ended the call. As they were getting ready to leave, Macy called Margaret Estes to let her know they had located her father. As soon as she filled her in, she and Spence packed the car and checked out of the hotel. They were supposed to meet with the representative from the DA's office at three o'clock that afternoon, so they had a couple of hours to kill. When they reached Salisbury, they stopped for a bite to eat, then continued on their way. Macy pulled driving directions from the Internet before they left, and drove straight to the impound lot. They arrived shortly before three o'clock and checked in with the guard. After a couple of minutes, the man from the DA's office arrived and escorted them inside the gate. The attendant directed them to Jacoby's car, which had not been touched since it was brought in. The DA's assistant unlocked the vehicle and began taking an inventory of items found inside the car. As he made his way around the inside of the vehicle, he found very few things, mainly old fast food wrappers, a couple of paperbacks, and some empty cigarette packages, but nothing of real importance. Macy requested they look inside the door panels, so he had one of the uniformed officers dismantle the doors. Unfortunately, there was nothing inside them either. The last place they searched was the trunk. As soon as he opened the lid, they could see what appeared to be a pile of clothes. Upon closer examination, they appeared to be a pair of coveralls. The assistant removed them, holding them up in front of him. There was an embroidered logo on the left front pocket which read 'TruAir.' As the coveralls unfolded, a pair of latex gloves fell onto the ground. They were covered in what appeared to be blood, and the assistant carefully placed them inside an evidence bag. He also sealed the coveralls inside a separate evidence bag. There was a ball cap the same color as the coveralls that also had the

'TruAir' logo, and a pair of sunglasses. A couple of empty cigarette packs, just like the ones found inside the car, were lying on top of the coveralls before he removed them. The assistant to the DA made notes concerning all he found, handed Macy a copy, then took the evidence he had collected with him to the police lab for analysis. Macy and Spence briefly scanned the inventory list, but having seen the items first hand, they were well aware of the contents of Jacoby's car. With the evidence now beginning to point in another direction, Macy decided it was time to meet Mark Jacoby.

She and Spence made their way over to the county jail where they requested to meet with Mr. Jacoby. The guard punched some keys on the computer then looked up at Macy. "I'm sorry, ma'am, but he was just released on bail thirty minutes ago."

"Who posted his bail?" she asked.

"According to the records a Margaret Estes made his bail." Macy rolled her eyes as she exhaled upward causing her red bangs to lift and fall. Apparently Margaret left as soon as Macy called her, drove directly to the jail, and bailed out her father. She thanked the officer and hurried out of the jail with Spence following close behind her.

"I guess we're on our way back to Cherryville," said Spence.

"You guessed right. We'd better hurry. She already has a head start on us."

They climbed into the car and sped off toward the Interstate. Spence drove as fast as he dared and not risk drawing attention from area law enforcement. They drove straight to the Estes house without stopping, but as they pulled into the drive, there was no sign of Margaret's car. Macy told Spence to pull around the corner and park where they could see the house without being seen. They waited for a couple of hours before Margaret pulled into the driveway. As she exited her vehicle and went inside, Spence pulled the car up behind hers, blocking any potential exit. Then he and Macy climbed out of the car and headed for the front door. Macy rang the doorbell twice rather impatiently. It took Margaret no time at all to open the door. She looked at them and offered a coy smile.

"Where is he?" asked Macy.

"Who?"

"You know who, your father."

"You told me he was in jail in High Point."

"Look, Margaret, we know you bailed him out this afternoon," said Macy.

"Well, he's not here, so I don't know what to tell you."

"You can start by telling me where you drove him to."

"Look, I bailed him out and offered to bring him home, but he insisted he had some other place to go, so we parted company in High Point," said Margaret.

"I don't believe you. Now where is he?"

"I've been as nice as I can about this, but now I'm going to have to insist you leave or I'll call the police," said Margaret, closing the door in their faces.

Macy rang the bell a few more times, causing Margaret to shout at them to go away. It was obvious they were not getting any further cooperation from Margaret Estes. As they walked back to the car Macy said, "I know she's lying."

"Most children will cover up for a parent in trouble," said Spence.

"I know. I guess I was hoping that Margaret might be different from most people."

"Wishful thinking," he replied. "So what now?"

"Well, since he's not driving, there's no use driving through the area hotel parking lots looking for his car. I think we should get a room for the night and come back here early tomorrow morning. If we're lucky, Margaret may lead us to him."

"Oh boy, a stakeout," cried Spence excitedly. Macy simply rolled her eyes.

"We probably should make a run through the local bars tonight just in case he decides to have a nightcap," he continued.

"Hey, that's not a bad idea. After a few days in the pokey, he may be in dire need of a drink, that is if Margaret didn't stop by the ABC liquor store while they were out."

"Well, we've got nothing else to do, so we might as well at least take a look."

They left the Estes house and drove to one of the local hotels where they booked a room for the night. They waited until later in the evening before heading downtown to check out the local bars. Macy had made a list from the phone book inside the hotel room before they left, and placed a checkmark beside each one as they made the rounds. They stopped first at Louie's since Margaret told them that was her father's favorite watering hole. Unfortunately, there was no sign of him. The bartender told Spence he had not seen him in over a week.

They continued their quest until they had made it to all of the bars on their list. They went back to Louie's for another look, just in case Jacoby went out late. By the time they got there it was fairly empty with no sign of Mark Jacoby. Spence nodded at the bartender who simply shrugged his shoulders and shook his head. Obviously Jacoby had not been by since they came in earlier. It was one-thirty in the morning when they walked out of Louie's and headed back to the hotel. They were both exhausted when they went to bed, but that didn't prevent Macy from rolling over onto Spence for a little intimate exercise. When they finished, both drifted off to sleep soundly. Macy had asked the front desk for a wake up call at five o'clock so they would have plenty of time to get to Margaret's house early.

Suddenly, they were awakened by the sound of a car alarm. Spence recognized it as their car, and sprang from the bed. He ran over to the window just in time to see someone running away from the car across the parking lot. It was too far away for him to see the person clearly. He tossed on a pair of jeans and ran outside. Someone had slashed their tires and left a note under the windshield wiper. Spence removed the paper and read, "Leave town tomorrow before someone gets hurt." There was no signature and no names listed on the paper. By the time he turned around to go back inside, Macy was standing behind him.

"What is it?" she asked.

"Apparently someone doesn't want us snooping around here for Jacoby," he replied as he handed her the note. She read it quickly, shaking her head.

"You know, something like this makes me want to work harder on the case."

"I know what you mean. Let's go get some sleep and we can deal with this tomorrow. Looks like we won't be watching the Estes house early this morning."

"That's okay. I doubt they're going anywhere." Macy walked by the front desk on their way back in and canceled the wake up call. She decided they may want to sleep in.

Chapter 22

M acy awoke the following morning to the smell of coffee. Spence had been kind enough to brew a small pot in the room with one of those hotel coffee makers and complimentary coffee packs. She leaned on one elbow, smiling up at him as he handed her a cup. He placed a call to his auto club for a tow to the nearest tire store.

He and Macy began formulating a plan while they waited for their car to be picked up. After about an hour there was a knock on their door. Spence opened it to reveal a man in greasy blue coveralls with an equally dirty cap on his head. He smiled at Spence, revealing three missing teeth with the remaining ones in need of major dental hygiene. He introduced himself as Carl, and told Spence he was there to haul his car to the tire store, asking if Spence wanted to ride with him. Spence shrugged his shoulders and kissed Macy goodbye before leaving the room behind the man. Macy was not sure how long Spence would be gone. She quickly showered and dressed to be ready to leave when he got back.

Carl hauled the car onto the flatbed truck and they headed to the tire store. It was a short drive into town, arriving at the store just after it opened. Spence was fortunate to be first in line, so once he told them the tires he wanted, they began working on the car immediately. He signed the necessary paperwork for the auto club and thanked him for his service.

He flashed another toothless smile at Spence. "Probably be best if you head on back home when they get them new tires on your car, lest whoever slashed them tires decides to come back. It seems you're not welcome in these parts." Then he winked and patted the pouch hanging from his belt, which held a folding lock-blade knife, turned and walked out of the store.

Spence stood silent for a moment, realizing he had not told Carl about the note. For all he knew it could have been a random act of vandalism. Yet it was clear Carl knew it was more than that. Spence hurried to the door and read the name and number from Carl's truck. Racing to the counter, he grabbed a pen and paper from in front of the cashier, and scribbled the information quickly before it left his memory. He looked at the counter attendant and asked, "Do you know that man?" pointing in the direction where Carl had just walked out. One of the mechanics who was standing near the side door of the garage spoke up.

"Everybody around here knows Carl." He turned and walked back into the garage.

The lady behind the counter glanced in the direction of the mechanic. "He's right. Everybody from these parts knows Carl Estes."

"I've heard that name before," said Spence.

"You might have heard someone mention his brother, Phil. Phil is the good one."

"And let me guess," interrupted Spence. "Carl is the black sheep."

"You could say that. He's been in trouble with the law off and on ever since high school. Mostly petty theft and vandalism, small stuff in most people's eyes. He spent some time in juvey when he was thirteen. After he dropped out of school, he ended up serving some hard time for assault. Seems he beat up some old man for one of the local loan sharks. Anyway, I wouldn't get on his bad side, if you know what I mean."

"I understand," Spence replied with a nod of his head. "Does he and his brother get along? I mean do they pal around together?"

"I wouldn't put it like that exactly, but they are close. You see, Phil is a year older than Carl. When Phil was six years old, their daddy left town and never came back. Their mom became an alcoholic and began abusing Carl. Phil tried to protect him as much as he could, and I guess under the circumstances they became closer. Phil put himself through college and now works for an insurance company. I guess it was too much for Carl, so he dropped out of school and left home. After his run-in with the law, Phil was able to get Carl a job at the garage as a tow truck driver. Carl seems to be walking the straight and narrow these days, but he still gives me the creeps," she said, shuddering as she finished the last statement.

After about forty minutes passed, the clerk informed Spence his car was ready. He paid the bill and thanked her for the information about Carl. He left the store and headed back to the hotel. When he walked into the hotel lobby, he spied Macy sitting on one of the sofas with their bags in front of her. As he walked toward her, she immediately stood up and began to speak.

"You're not going to believe what happened!"

"Let me guess. The hotel no longer wants to extend us their hospitality," said Spence.

"They knocked on the door fifteen minutes after you left and informed me they had made a serious booking error and would need the room immediately. I asked if there were any other rooms available, but they said no."

"Sounds like we're not welcome here," he said with a wry smile.

"Well I'm glad to see somebody finds all of this amusing," said Macy, almost snorting the words as she placed her clenched fists firmly on her hips.

"Relax, honey. I got a similar reaction from the tow truck guy. In fact, I believe he's the one who slashed our tires. It turns out he is Phil Estes' brother."

Macy suddenly got that 'I see' look in her eyes as she and Spence gathered their luggage. Neither spoke another word until they were in the car.

"Okay, what do we do now?" asked Macy.

"Don't look at me," replied Spence. "You're 'The Avenger.' I'm just your trusty sidekick, remember?"

Macy shot a quick 'drop dead' glance at Spence. "Let's head back toward Kings Mountain. I'm sure the Estes don't have enough pull there to get us thrown out. In the meantime, I'll call Adam and see if the D.A. is considering Jacoby as a possible suspect. Maybe they'll decide to put out an APB so the local police can pick him up. It would sure make our job a little easier."

"Now that's 'The Avenger' I've come to know and love," said Spence, as he smiled and winked at Macy. He winced in mock pain as she reached across the front seat and punched him in the shoulder. As Spence drove, Macy called Adam.

"Drake," said Adam as he answered the call.

"Adam, this is Macy. Have you heard anything from the D.A. about the stuff they found in Jacoby's car?"

"Not yet. I'm waiting on the results from the lab."

"Well hurry them if you can. We seem to have run into a roadblock here and I don't want Jacoby to disappear before the D.A. considers him a suspect."

"I'll keep you posted," said Adam as he ended the call.

Macy closed her cell phone and exhaled a frustrated breath upward, causing her red bangs to lift and fall slightly. She told Spence what Adam said, then they drove the rest of the way to Kings Mountain in silence. There was a hotel just off of I-85, so they booked a room and waited patiently for Adam to call.

* * *

Drake and Callie cut their little vacation short, especially with the recent turn of events in the Stephens' case. They left before sunrise, and pulled into High Point around eleven o'clock. She dropped Drake off at his house before heading home for a shower. He took a quick shower as well, and headed to the office to touch base with Betty. When he walked through the door, he could see the look of surprise on her face.

"Relax, Betty. Everything's okay between me and Callie. We just decided to cut our trip short. Some new evidence has come to light in the Stephens' case, and we both wanted to get back so we can fully review everything before the trial resumes."

Betty exhaled a long sigh of relief. "Good. I'm glad nothing happened between you two."

"Well, I wouldn't say nothing happened," said Drake with a slight chuckle.

"I don't need to hear about all that, just as long as you two are happy."

"Ecstatic," replied Drake. He told Betty about Mark Jacoby, the vehicle search, and the contents recovered from the trunk.

"Surely they'll investigate this Jacoby and drop the case against Mr. Stephens?" she said.

"Well, that's what I'm hoping for. But let's not count our chickens before they hatch. I've seen stranger things happen, especially in a murder case."

Drake went to his office and picked up the phone. He thought Callie would have had enough time by now to discuss the new evidence with her boss, and hopefully be ready to drop the charges against Stephens. Of course it all depended on what the lab tests revealed. He confidently punched the numbers on the phone. After a couple of rings, he smiled when he heard her voice on the other end.

"Callie Devane."

"Hey, it's me. Have you found out anything yet on the stuff they pulled out of Jacoby's trunk?"

"I have the report right here. It seems the blood on the gloves and coveralls is a match for Julie Stephens."

"I knew it," said Drake. "So when will you cut Josh loose?"

"Whoa, not so fast, Adam. I've got to meet with my boss this afternoon to discuss this new evidence, but there is no guarantee he'll drop the case against Josh."

"You can't be serious. That evidence is all I need to create enough reasonable doubt in the minds of the jurors to get Josh acquitted and you know it."

"Maybe. But there are still a lot of gaps and inconsistencies in your client's case that raise a lot of questions about his innocence. Personally, I believe he may be innocent, but ultimately it's not my call."

"I understand. Will you let me know as soon as your boss makes a decision?"

"You'll be the first to know," she said, ending the call. Drake leaned back in his chair and let out a big sigh, running his hands through his hair. All he could do now was to wait. He grabbed some lunch at the café. He took his time eating, knowing it would be awhile before he heard back from Callie. When he returned to the office, he dove into some of the contract work Betty had prepared that needed his signature, trying to get his mind off of the Stephens' case.

He soon was caught up again, however, and without any more work to do, he began pacing inside his office. He was never one for patience, and waiting on Callie's call seemed almost unbearable. Then the phone rang.

Drake almost jumped on top of the phone, grabbing the receiver before Betty could answer. It was one of Betty's friends, so he placed the call on hold and buzzed her. She immediately picked up.

He started to pace again, breaking out in a sweat from a combination of nerves and steady movement. The phone rang again. This time he allowed Betty to answer, just in case it was not for him. As soon as she buzzed his office, he grabbed the receiver and punched the button that was blinking on the phone.

"Adam, I'm afraid I have some bad news," said Callie.

"You're kidding?"

"I wish I were," she continued, "but my boss insists he believes your client is somehow involved, even if Jacoby was the one who committed the murder."

"So he wants to continue with the trial."

"Actually, he said he would consider a plea deal for Mr. Stephens if he gives up Jacoby and makes a full statement as to his involvement in the crime."

"And just what does your boss propose?"

"He's willing to reduce the charge to conspiracy to commit murder, and recommend a sentence of twenty years."

"That's ridiculous," said Drake, his voice rising. "Why should he admit to something he did not do in order to serve twenty years?"

"Adam, I understand your disappointment, but he would be eligible for parole in about seven years. That would be better than life in prison, or worse yet, the death penalty."

"Well, we're not taking any deal," Drake insisted. "Shouldn't you discuss this with your client first?"

"Of course, I'll discuss it with him, but I know he will say no."

"I'm sorry."

"It's okay, honey. I know it's business and not personal, and it's not your call. I'll see you later, right?"

"You betcha," she said, and hung up.

Drake sat back and sighed again as he digested what Callie had just told him. Picking up the receiver, he punched at the buttons. After a couple of rings, Josh answered.

"We need to meet," Drake told him.

"When and where?"

"Can you get to the office?"

"Sure. Give me twenty minutes."

It took Josh only fifteen to get to Drake's office. Drake ushered him into his office and closed the door.

"I hope you have some good news regarding the other suspect you told me about," said Josh.

"Actually, the D.A. has offered a deal."

"What do you mean a deal? I'm innocent!"

"I know, but they believe you are at least an accomplice with this other guy. By law, I have to make you aware of their offer."

"I don't care what it is. I'm not taking it."

"Let me just go over the details with you," said Drake. "If you testify against Jacoby, and admit the details of your plan, they will reduce the charge to conspiracy to commit murder and recommend a sentence of twenty years. You would be eligible for parole in about seven years, maybe less on good behavior."

"Okay, you've presented the offer and I still say no."

"Are you sure?"

"What do you think, Adam? Can't we raise enough reasonable doubt for an acquittal?"

"Well, it certainly would appear that way, but I have to warn you. There is no way to accurately predict what a jury will decide. It's quite possible that even with this new evidence the jury may still convict you, which could mean life in prison or the death penalty."

"What would you do?" asked Josh.

"I can't tell you what to do, Josh. This is a decision you must make on your own."

"Well, I say we proceed with the trial."

"Would you like to think about it? The trial doesn't resume until Monday."

"No, I don't need any more time. I'm innocent and I'm not going to admit to something I didn't do."

"Fine. I'll let the D.A. know of your decision," said Drake. He stood and shook Josh's hand and asked if he needed anything, but Josh told him Macy was taking good care of him. After he left the office, Drake grabbed the receiver and punched in Callie's number. He sat back in his chair and waited for her to answer.

"Callie Devane."

"Hey, Callie, it's me. Josh said no to the deal, so I guess we'll see you in court."

"I understand."

"Oh, Callie, I'll need everything you have on the contents taken from Jacoby's car."

"Certainly. After all, we don't want to violate discovery.

I'll bring it with me tonight."

"See you then," said Drake as he hung up. Feeling there was nothing more he could accomplish today, he told Betty he was leaving, and headed home to rest and meditate before Callie got there.

CHAPTER 23

Macy and Spence were playing a game of contract rummy when her cell phone rang.

"Macy, this is Adam. Just thought I would let you know that the D.A. plans to pursue the case against Josh. He thinks Josh at least had something to do with his wife's murder, and was possibly working with Jacoby. Trial resumes Monday."

"Have you told Josh?"

"Yes. The D.A. actually proposed a deal, which Josh rejected, so I am supposed to receive the information on the evidence found in Jacoby's car tonight."

"Great. That should go a long way in helping you establish reasonable doubt. In the meantime, Spence and I will continue to look for Jacoby."

"Thanks, Macy. I would really like to find him and get him on the stand."

"We're on it," she said, and hung up. Spence looked at her. "What's up?"

"They're going ahead with the trial. Adam said the blood on the gloves and coveralls found in Jacoby's trunk match Julie's, but the D.A. is convinced Josh is still involved somehow."

"Well, if Adam is as good as I think he is, he should have no problem establishing enough reasonable doubt with this new evidence to win his case."

"I hope you're right," said Macy. "So what do we do now?"

"We find Jacoby," she replied, tossing the car keys to Spence.

They left the hotel and headed back toward Shelby. Since it was only four-thirty, she knew there was no need to check the bars yet. They did a little snooping around town instead. They stopped at the insurance company where Phil Estes worked, hoping to meet with him and maybe rattle him enough to get some information. As they pulled into the parking lot, they noticed several vehicles parked over to the far left side, probably employees. There were no other cars there. Spence and Macy walked into the building and made their way to the receptionist, where they asked to see Mr. Estes. They were asked to have a seat in the waiting area while she informed Mr. Estes they were there. It took less than a minute before Macy saw a man approaching. He was dressed in navy blue slacks and a herringbone patterned sport coat. Spence noticed he was roughly the same height as his brother Carl, which was about five feet nine inches. As he drew closer to them, he extended his hand, smiled, and introduced himself. Spence was glad to see Phil used better dental hygiene than Carl.

"I'm Phil Estes," he began. "How can I help you?"

"Can we speak somewhere more private?" asked Macy.

"Certainly. Right this way." And with that, Phil ushered them to one of the offices in the back, closing the door behind them. He gestured toward the two seats in front of the desk, walked around and sat down behind it.

"Now, how may I help you?"

"Well, Mr. Estes, we're working with an attorney on a case in High Point and we have reason to believe your father-in-law may be a witness to the crime."

"Really? What crime is that?"

"A woman was murdered," said Spence, watching closely to observe his reaction. Estes never flinched.

"And just how do you believe my father-in-law would have any knowledge of this crime?"

"We're not at liberty to divulge the details of the case since it is still ongoing," said Macy.

"In that case, how can I help you?"

"It would be very helpful if we could speak with Mr. Jacoby. Do you know where he is?" asked Spence.

"I'm afraid I don't," he answered. "He stayed with us for a little while, but I haven't seen him since last week."

"We could have you subpoenaed," said Macy.

"And I will tell them the same thing I told you. Look, I don't know where he is. And even if I did, I wouldn't tell you. My wife told me somebody was snooping around trying to railroad Mark into something. Let me give you a little advice. You're barking up the wrong tree. Mark didn't have anything to do with this woman's murder, so back off!"

"Or what, Mr. Estes?" asked Spence.

"Just don't say I didn't warn you," he replied, and repeated. "Back off." He stood and motioned toward the door, indicating the interview was over. Macy and Spence did not offer to shake his hand, but simply turned and walked out. They did not speak until they were in the car.

"He's lying," said Spence.

"Really? What was your first clue?" replied Macy rather sarcastically.

"Since you're the pro at this, what's our next move?"

"Oh we're just getting started," answered Macy. "We've awakened the monster. Now let's poke it with a stick."

Macy grabbed the car keys from Spence and climbed in behind the wheel.

"Let me drive for a while," she said as she started the car. She asked Spence to navigate as she drove, requesting directions to the garage where Carl Estes works. It was just before quitting time when they pulled up a few yards away. Macy parked at the curb and turned the ignition off while they waited for Carl to leave. After ten minutes Spence spotted Carl walking out of the garage and heading toward an old Chevrolet panel van. It was a faded white color with rust spots all over it. As he drove out of the parking lot, Macy pulled in behind him, careful not to follow too closely for fear of being spotted. He drove out of town heading west toward Asheville. He turned onto a dirt road and continued for another three miles, stopping at a secluded old shack in the middle of nowhere. Macy stopped just inside a bend in the road where the car could not be seen from the shack. She and Spence walked through the trees on the right side of the road until they could get a good glimpse of the shack. They assumed this was where Carl lived, but you know what they say about assuming.

Peering through a pair of binoculars, she saw a man exit the shack and meet Carl halfway from the van. The man was smartly dressed in a dark silk suit. He and Carl shook hands and exchanged pleasantries. The man gave a motion with his right hand and two other men appeared from within the shack, each dressed almost as nice as the first man.

She could see them talking, but could not make out what they were saying. They nodded, shook hands again, and Carl walked back to the van while the other men returned inside the shack. Macy and Spence quickly scrambled to their car and headed back out the road, hoping they were far enough ahead of Carl not to be noticed.

"I want to get a closer look at that shack," said Macy.

"I don't know. They didn't exactly look like the friendly neighbor type," said Spence.

"That's why I'm planning on waiting until tonight."

"What?"

"Relax, darling. It'll be just like old times in special ops."

"That's what I was afraid you would say," said Spence, letting out a big sigh.

"Trust me, Spence. I know what I'm doing."

"I know. I just feel so helpless when you do these things. Besides, isn't the man supposed to protect his woman?"

"Did I hear a hint of male chauvinism?" asked Macy with a laugh. "Don't worry. You're going with me."

Spence was speechless for a moment. "Are you sure?"

"Of course I'm sure. We're in this together. Just remember our little training sessions and you'll be fine," said Macy, alluding to the hours she spent teaching Spence certain combat techniques and martial arts maneuvers, just in case he found himself in a sticky situation. Of course, he did not have a fraction of the skills Macy possessed, having been trained by the best the military had to offer. But she felt confident it was enough for him to be able to take care of himself. Besides, she intended to be right there with him should he need her.

They headed back to Kings Mountain for dinner, then returned to the hotel room where they donned black outfits for their covert operation. Macy placed several items she thought they may need into a duffle bag, and once it was dark, they left the hotel and drove back to that dirt road. She felt it best to park the car in a nearby parking lot and walk through the woods to the shack to avoid their car being seen sitting on the side of the road. She climbed out of the car, grabbed the bag, and walked over to Spence, smearing grease under his eyes.

"There, that should conceal you better."

He grunted his disapproval, but made no attempt to remove it. They made their way carefully through the woods, moving slowly to avoid creating too much noise. Soon they were at the edge of the woods overlooking the shack.

"Stay right behind me," she whispered, as she moved slowly toward the building in a half crouch position. Spence followed just behind her, bending low as he tried to mimic her stealth approach.

Macy made her way around the back of the building, where there was a small window about ten feet above ground level. She surveyed the surroundings hoping to find something she could move under the window and climb onto in order to see inside. There were several metal barrels bunched together in some overgrown brush about ten yards behind the building. She looked at Spence and motioned in the direction of the barrels. Making her way to where they sat, she began moving them to see if they were empty. Luckily the first three she examined appeared to be empty, or at least light enough they could move.

She motioned for Spence to grab one while she took another, tilting them on edge and working them back and forth until they were directly under the window. Macy moved back for a third barrel, and after returning with it, motioned for Spence to help her lift one of them on top of the other two. He pushed the barrels against the wall, using his weight to steady them, while she climbed first onto one of the lower barrels, then onto the top one. Spence kept one hand on the top barrel to help steady it for Macy while she peeked inside.

There were two men in dress shirts and slacks playing cards at a small table. Each one had what appeared to be .45 caliber pistols secured inside shoulder holsters. Another man was located near the door holding an automatic rifle. He kept peering through the door window, and occasionally stepped outside for a few minutes. Macy figured they must each take turns standing guard, since he also had a pistol strapped inside a shoulder holster. She quickly scanned the room and spotted another man lying on a cot. She could tell from the picture she had seen before that this was Mark Jacoby. She also noticed several fast food bags strewn about.

The building was a simple one-room structure with no running water, and they had to eat takeout and have any other essentials brought to them. Since there was no bathroom inside, Macy quickly realized the source of the strong odor she smelled near the barrels. Obviously, they had been using them as an outdoor privy. She reached into her vest pocket and retrieved a small digital camera. She took some close up photos of the other men inside, hoping to identify them later.

The best way to get down from the top barrel she was standing on was to jump to the ground since it was not too high off the ground. As she started to jump, her shoe heel caught the rim of the top barrel causing it to twist in a clockwise position. Unfortunately, Spence was unable to correct the position of his hand in time as the top barrel spun wide and crashed to the ground. His immediate reaction was to reach for the falling barrel, which left the other two free to tumble themselves as they all crashed together in a heap. Macy heard voices from within the shack as the men scrambled outside to investigate the noise. She grabbed Spence by the arm and led him quickly back into the woods before they were spotted. They waited and watched as the men found the barrels and realized someone had been there. The men looked around trying to see any signs of movement, but Macy and Spence remained perfectly still. After a few minutes, one of the men took out a cell phone and placed a call while the others returned inside the building. She nudged Spence and motioned for him to follow her. After they were halfway back to the road, she quickened her pace, not concerned about noise.

When they reached the car Spence asked, "Why are we rushing?"

"Unless my instincts are wrong, the one on the cell phone was calling someone to tell them their location had been compromised."

"So?"

"So, they'll move Jacoby to another location as quickly as possible. If we don't make our move now, we may never get another chance."

"What move?" asked Spence.

"We need to grab Jacoby now before he gets away."

"And just how do you suggest we do that?"

"With these," said Macy as she pulled a couple of automatic rifles from the car. She also had some flash grenades and smoke canisters in her duffle bag. She handed a rifle and a back up pistol to Spence. She grabbed the bag and another rifle, and closed the trunk. She motioned for Spence to follow as she made her way quickly back to the woods. This time when they reached the edge of the trees, two men were standing watch outside. The third man was still standing at the back of the building.

"So much for sneaking up on them," thought Spence.

Macy reached into her bag and retrieved a pistol, taking aim at the man behind the building and firing, but there was no sound. He could make out what appeared to be feathers from a dart as the man reached for his neck then fell silently to the ground. She motioned at Spence to follow and they worked their way along the tree line until they could safely approach the rear of the building without being seen by the other two.

Macy made her way around the opposite side of the building with Spence directly behind her. When she reached the front corner, she motioned for him to stay where he was, then spun around the corner with her dart gun and squeezed off two quick shots. He heard a short blast of automatic weapon fire, and peered around the corner in time to see the second man fall to the ground in a heap. Motioning for Spence to fall in behind her, she made her way to the door. She eased the door open gently, just in case she had missed someone in her count. Swinging the door wide, she stepped inside. Jacoby was sitting on the edge of the cot, but he was unarmed. Macy walked over to him, pulled him to his feet, and handcuffed his wrists behind his back. She grabbed him by the shoulder and pushed him toward the door. "Let's go!"

The three of them made their way through the woods back to the car and climbed inside. Macy pulled the car out of the parking lot and headed back toward Kings Mountain. Just after turning onto the main road, she glanced into the rearview mirror in time to see a dark sedan turn onto the dirt road.

She looked over at Spence, and nodded toward the back of the car. "Looks like we got out just in time."

He turned around in time to see the car speeding down the dirt road. Macy sped up, just in case. Jacoby looked up at Macy and Spence with a slight grin. "You don't know who you're dealing with."

"Oh, yeah?" asked Spence. "Why don't you enlighten us?"

"Oh, you'll see," he replied, and repeated, "you'll see." Macy pulled into one of the parking spaces at the rear of the hotel and left the car running. Spence jumped out and used his door key to enter the rear of the building. After a few minutes, he came walking out carrying their luggage. She opened the trunk from inside the car and he tossed the bags inside, slamming the trunk lid shut. He climbed inside and they headed for the interstate.

Chapter 24

Drake almost jumped out of bed as the phone rang incessantly on the nightstand. He reached over and grabbed it, hoping not to disturb Callie. The clock glowed twelve a.m. "Hello."

"Adam, this is Macy. We've got Jacoby and are only a few miles outside of High Point."

Callie rolled over beside Drake, having obviously been awakened by the call.

"Great! Take him directly to the police station."

"Are you sure? What if he gets out again?"

"That's not very likely this time," said Drake. "After Josh turned down the D.A.'s proposal, they issued an APB for Jacoby. They plan to charge him along with Josh, depending on how Josh's trial ends."

"I see," said Macy. "If they can't convict Josh, they'll probably throw the book at Jacoby."

"You got it," replied Drake. "I'll meet you guys there." As he hung up the phone, Callie asked, "Who was that?"

"Macy. She has Jacoby and they're on their way to the police station as we speak."

"I should be there, too."

"I agree, but let's drive separately so as not to raise suspicion." Callie waited a couple of minutes after Drake left before leaving so they would not arrive at the same time. Macy arrived just after Callie, and escorted Jacoby inside the police station. Callie took over from there and requested Turner and

Brogden question Jacoby about the death of Julie Stephens. At this point they wanted to see what information, if any, Jacoby would give them before arresting him. As they led him into one of the interrogation rooms, Callie took her place in the adjoining room behind the two-way mirror.

"Mr. Jacoby, can you tell us where you were on Wednesday, May fifth?" asked Turner.

"What time?"

"Just run down the day for us as best you can."

"I was at my daughter's house most of the day," said Jacoby. "Do I need a lawyer?"

"That's up to you, Mr. Jacoby," said Brogden. "But we really just want to talk to you."

"You said most of the day you were at your daughter's?" said Turner. "When were you not there?"

"About seven o'clock I headed up to Louie's," answered Jacoby. "The last time I looked over at the clock it was eleven-thirty. Then I passed out. I woke up at Maggie's place the next morning."

"Can anyone verify you were at your daughter's house during the day?" asked Brogden.

"No. I was alone and I didn't talk to anyone I remember that day."

"Do you know Josh Stephens?"

"The name sounds familiar, but I can't place him."

"He works for First National Bank," said Brogden. "Remember him now?"

"Oh, yeah. He's the creep who foreclosed on me. Why, is he dead? Not that I would shed a tear or anything."

"No, but his wife is. In fact, she was murdered in her home on May fifth. The same day you say no one can verify you were at your daughter's house."

"This interview is over, gentlemen. I'd like to call my attorney now," said Jacoby, folding his arms across his chest.

Callie rapped on the window so the detectives would cease their line of questioning and leave the room. Afterward, Jacoby was placed in a holding cell until his attorney could be contacted. The current charge against him was conspiracy to commit murder. Since they were pursuing first degree murder charges against Josh Stephens, they had not yet charge Jacoby with the same crime. Of course, Callie would make it clear to Jacoby's attorney that depending upon the outcome of the Stephens trial, the charges could be amended to include first degree murder.

Drake headed home to try and catch a few winks before time to go to work, however, Callie stayed behind at the station, eager to see who showed up to defend Jacoby. As she waited, in walked Brandan Price, whom she knew to be a field agent supervisor for the Organized Crime Bureau. He spied her almost immediately and headed straight toward her. As he drew near, he flashed a bright smile and extended his hand.

"Callie, it's certainly a pleasure to see you again."

"What brings you down here so early?"

"Actually, I came to get Mark Jacoby."

"What do you mean you came to get him? He's been charged with conspiracy to commit murder. I'm afraid he's not going anywhere."

"Well, I see you still have that fiery spirit, Callie. However, Mr. Jacoby is a key part of an ongoing investigation by the Bureau. I'm sure you will agree it's in the best interest to release him into my custody. After all, you know a federal case trumps yours," he said, all smiles. She restrained herself from punching him right there in front of everyone.

"We'll just see what Judge Abernathy has to say about that," she replied.

"I'm way ahead of you, Callie. In fact, the Judge should be arriving anytime."

Callie stepped away for a brief moment while she tried to contact Drake. After a couple of rings, he answered his cell phone. He was still in his car, but had just turned into his driveway.

"Hello?"

"Adam, it's Callie. Listen. You need to get back here right away."

"Why?"

"There's no time to explain. We can fill you in when you get here. Just hurry!"

Adam flipped the phone shut and backed out of the drive, spinning his tires as he sped off toward the city. He parked as close to the door as possible, and practically ran inside. He immediately asked the desk sergeant where

Callie was, and was directed to one of the conference rooms. He opened the door to find her and some gentleman seated at a table next to Judge Abernathy. He closed the door behind him.

"Mr. Drake, it is very good of you to join us at such an early hour," said Judge Abernathy. "Of course, you know Ms. Devane from the District Attorney's office." He gestured toward Brandan. "This is Agent Brandan Price from OCB. He has just informed me that Mark Jacoby is a key component in one of their major cases and he was about to explain to me why we should release Mr. Jacoby into his custody. Of course, this means you can't use him as a witness in the Stephens' trial."

Drake stood there for a moment, staring in disbelief as the words from the judge resonated in his head. "Your Honor, I'm not sure I will need to call Mr. Jacoby as a witness, but we definitely need to be able to present the evidence that was obtained from the search of his car."

"I understand your predicament, Mr. Drake," said Judge Abernathy. "First, though, let me hear what Mr. Price has to say." He waved his right hand in the direction of Agent Price indicating he should present his argument.

"Your Honor," he began. "Mark Jacoby has been working as an informant for the Bureau on a major case. He is very deep within our suspect's organization, and at this point, is in a position to provide the crucial information we need to bring this man and his associates to justice."

"Mr. Price, you know I'm going to need more than that," said the judge.

"Your Honor, I'm afraid it will jeopardize my client to give out more information regarding our suspect."

Judge Abernathy smiled at Agent Price, his expression changing to a grimace. "Don't hand me that nonsense, Price. We are all officers of the court, so spill it."

Agent Price was taken aback by the judge's candor, but quickly regrouped before continuing. "Very well, Your Honor. Mark Jacoby has been able to infiltrate the organized crime operation of Harry "Two Hats" Marconi. Marconi moved to Cleveland County from Chicago ten years ago, and has been operating every illegal business he can get his hands on, from gambling to prostitution to drugs, and even murder. Two kids can't match quarters in the school playground without Harry getting a piece of the action. And Harry is involved in many more deaths than one single person. Jacoby has been working as one of Harry's bookies. That's why he hangs out at Louie's bar. Harry's got a betting parlor in the back. We're just trying to get enough dirt on Harry to bring him down for a capital offense and send him away for good."

"Why would a Chicago mobster relocate to rural North Carolina?" asked the judge.

"Too much heat," replied Price. "We were putting a lot of pressure on him, until he found out about one of our undercover agents working within his family. The next thing you know, our agent floated to the top of Lake Michigan and Harry took off for North Carolina. I guess he figured Southern money spends the same anywhere."

Drake snickered under his breath before asking, "Why do all these guys have such odd nicknames like 'Two Hats' or 'Bugsy'?"

"Actually," said Price, "it's almost a right of passage among these guys to have a reputation that earns you a nickname. Harry "Two Hats" got his from the distinctive fedoras he wears. Most days he wears a gray one. Some days he wears black, but only those two colors. People say Harry wears black when someone is about to die."

"All right, enough of the cloak and dagger stuff," interrupted the judge.

"Surely you can understand our position, Your Honor," said Price.

"Ms. Devane, I'm afraid I must agree with Agent Price on this one," said Abernathy. "This Marconi character is much too evil to risk jeopardizing the Fed's case against him for one man. Of course, Mr. Price, I do hope you are able to see justice eventually served to Mr. Jacoby. That being said, I am ordering the release of Mr. Jacoby to Agent Price. There will be no paper trail, nor will any of what has been said here today be repeated. Do I make myself clear?"

"Yes, Your Honor," said all three.

Drake spoke up. "Your Honor, will the evidence found in Mark Jacoby's trunk be admissible in the Stephens' trial? After all, it definitely goes a long way in establishing reasonable doubt."

"You've got a point, Mr. Drake. You can introduce the evidence, provided that whomever you question is only allowed to verify these items were recovered from an abandoned automobile with no ties to your client. You cannot ask them who the owner of the abandoned vehicle is. In fact, I would stress the fact that the vehicle was not your client's, and move on. The identity of Mr. Jacoby must remain a secret, but the fact that these items cannot be directly linked to your client should provide the same benefit."

"Thank you, Your Honor," said Drake.

The judge looked at Callie. "I'm sorry, Ms. Devane, but it appears you lost all the way around this morning. Now, if we're through, I'm going back to bed." And with that, Judge Abernathy said his goodbyes and left the building.

Callie instructed Turner to hand Jacoby over to Price, and watched as he was led from the station. Jacoby offered a smug sneer and a wink saying, "I told you so" when he walked past Callie.

Since it was now four o'clock, Drake abandoned the idea of more sleep, and instead went to the office, where he began writing instructions for Betty. The trial would resume Monday morning and he wanted to be ready.

When Betty walked into the office, she did a double take, obviously surprised to see Drake this early. She gave him a rather questioning look as she eased over to her desk. He walked toward her with a fresh cup of coffee.

"Good morning, Betty."

"Is everything okay?"

"Everything's fine. I just happened to be up early and decided to get a head start on the day. By the way, here's a list of things I need for you to do before we go back to trial on Monday," he said, handing her a sheet of paper.

She took the paper slowly, still looking at him as if he were an alien. He smiled at her before heading back into his office. He worked on more notes for Monday, and around eleven-thirty he telephoned Macy.

"Hello?"

"Macy, this is Adam. Are you and Spence free for lunch?"

"Sure. What's up?"

"I'll fill you in when you get here."

"Okay. We'll be there in about twenty minutes."

Drake hung up and leaned back in his chair, covering his face with his hands. The adrenaline rush he was working on earlier had left him, and now he realized why he normally did not come to the office at four o'clock in the morning. He walked to the restroom and splashed cold water on his face, before returning to his office to wait on Macy and Spence. While waiting, he wrote out a few preliminary questions for them, just in case he needed to call them as witnesses. Macy told him when she took the case that she and Spence preferred to be left out of trial testimonies, especially since they liked to keep their profession a secret from public scrutiny. Drake was hoping the assistant from the D.A.'s office would provide all the testimony he needed regarding the new evidence to establish reasonable doubt in the minds of the jurors. But he wanted to make sure he could count on Macy in case that was not enough.

As Macy and Spence walked through the door, Drake left his desk and walked out of his office to meet them. He escorted them back outside to his car, where they all climbed in and headed across town.

"I'm glad you could make it," he said, then made small talk until they arrived at Nolan's, an upscale restaurant located in the heart of downtown. Nolan's was a favorite among the salesmen when they visited High Point during the two yearly furniture markets. It was also a favorite of many of the local attorneys and bankers as a place to conduct business over a nice meal. Once they were seated, and the waiter left to retrieve their drink order, Drake began the conversation.

"Thank you for finding Jacoby so fast and bringing him in," he said.

"Hey, it's what we do," said Macy.

"So how's the case looking? Did he tell the police anything?" asked Spence.

"Well, actually, the D.A. cut him loose."

"What?" asked Macy, obviously surprised. "Why?"

"It appears there were some complications with the search. Anyway, we can still use the evidence. We just can't say whose car we found it in."

Spence shot a questioning look at Macy. "By complications with the search, I assume there is more that you're not telling us." Drake just nodded as he took a sip of water. Spence leaned back in his chair, nodded back at Drake acknowledging he understood, then leaned over and touched Macy on the arm as if to say, "I'll tell you later."

"So, where are we now?" she asked.

"I plan to call the assistant from the D.A.'s office to testify to the contents of Jacoby's car. That should cast enough reasonable doubt for an acquittal."

"And if it doesn't?" asked Spence.

"Well, that's where I was hoping you two could help. I may need to call you as witnesses."

"Whoa, Adam. I told you we prefer to avoid that sort of thing unless it is absolutely necessary," said Macy.

"And believe me, I promise only to call you to the stand as a last resort."

"That's okay, Adam," said Spence, reaching over and placing his hand over Macy's. "We know you'll do your best. In the meantime, is there anything else we can do to help?"

"Yes," replied Drake. "Will you please make sure Josh is in the courtroom on Monday? I don't want to have to explain to Judge Abernathy that my client has jumped bail. It definitely will not look good to the jury."

"Don't worry, Adam," replied Macy. "Now that the evidence is strongly in his favor, I'm sure we can convince him to show up."

They finished their meal and Drake drove them back to the office where they shook hands and parted company. Macy and Spence left for the hotel to speak with Josh while Drake went back inside the office to finish preparing for Monday.

CHAPTER 25

Drake saw very little of Callie over the weekend. She needed time to prepare for the testimony about the new evidence and he needed time to plan his strategy. Knowing it would be too much of a distraction to spend the entire weekend together, they ate dinner Saturday at Drake's and lunch Sunday at Callie's. Other than that, they worked alone preparing for Monday. When he arrived at the courthouse early Monday morning, he noticed Josh's car in the back of the parking lot. He pulled in the space alongside his, motioning for Josh to join him. Josh stepped out of his car and climbed into Drake's. As he closed the passenger door, Drake extended his hand. "Glad you could make it."

"Macy convinced me I had nothing to worry about. I hope she's right."

"Well, we've got a strong chance, especially with this new evidence."

"What about Jacoby?" Josh asked.

"That's a story for another day," replied Drake. "All I can tell you is we can use the evidence, but no one can know where it came from."

"Is he going to get away with killing Julie?"

"No. He'll face justice one day. It just may not be as soon as we would like."

Josh looked down, somewhat perplexed at what Drake said, but then quickly regrouped, raised his head, and exhaled a deep breath. "I think I'm ready."

"Good. Let's go."

They exited the car and made their way to the front door.

There were no reporters outside as the story was now old and no longer front page news. There would be some reporters in the courtroom following the case, but their stories would be buried behind more current headlines. Drake and Josh took their place behind the defense table and waited for the court to convene. He noticed Macy and Spence seated in the gallery. Drake leaned over and said to Josh in a hushed tone, "I'm going to call their assistant to testify as to the evidence found in Jacoby's car. That should raise enough reasonable doubt for an acquittal."

"What about my testimony?" Josh asked.

"With this new evidence, I don't believe you should testify."

"Are you sure?"

"Trust me."

"Okay. I believe in you, Adam, and this case. We will win. We have to."

Callie walked in about fifteen minutes after Drake. She looked over in his direction, but did not make eye contact. She offered Drake a nod, indicating her relief to see Josh in the courtroom. No sooner had Callie sat down than the court was called to order. Judge Abernathy made his way to the bench and took his place, instructing Drake to proceed with the defense. Drake called Jim Scott, an assistant in the District Attorney's office, to the stand.

"Please state your full name for the record."

"James Henry Scott."

"Mr. Scott, you work for the District Attorney's office, is that correct?"

"Yes, sir."

"I'd like for you to look at defense exhibits F and G. Do you recognize these items?" asked Drake, handing the bagged coveralls and gloves to the witness.

"Yes. These items were recovered from an abandoned vehicle."

Drake held the items up where the jury could see them. "I ask the jury to note this bag contains a pair of coveralls and the other bag contains a pair of latex gloves, both are covered in blood." He turned back to the witness. "And where was this vehicle abandoned?"

"I'm not certain."

"Then how do you know these items came from that vehicle?"

"Because the vehicle is currently in the county's impound lot. I was present at the time the search of the vehicle was made."

"Mr. Scott, were there any forensic tests performed on these items?"

"Yes, sir."

"And would you please tell the court the results of these tests?"

"Yes. The blood on the coveralls and the latex gloves were a match for Julie Stephens."

"The deceased wife of the defendant, Josh Stephens?"

"Yes, sir."

"Was there any other forensic evidence found on these items?"

"Well, there appeared to be older blood stains with a similar DNA pattern, but there was not enough for a positive match."

"Was this evidence recovered from Mr. Stephens' car?"

"No, sir."

"Then whose car was it recovered from?"

"Objection!" shouted Callie.

"Sustained," said Judge Abernathy, then he looked at Drake. "Careful, Mr. Drake."

"I apologize, Your Honor," said Drake. "Mr. Scott, can you at least verify for the court that the vehicle these items were recovered from have no connection to the defendant, Josh Stephens?"

"Yes. There appears to be no connection between the vehicle and Mr. Stephens."

"One more question, Mr. Scott. Is it your understanding that the identity of the owner of this abandoned vehicle cannot be disclosed at this time because it is part of an ongoing police investigation?"

"Yes, sir. That much I can say."

"I have no further questions for this witness."

"Ms. Devane, does the state have any questions for the witness?" asked the judge.

"No, Your Honor."

"Very well. Mr. Scott, you are excused," said Judge Abernathy, then glanced at Drake. "Mr. Drake, call your next witness."

Drake called the pathologist who performed the tests on the coveralls and gloves in order to substantiate the prior testimony. Again Callie did not cross-examine this witness.

Once he finished with the witness, Drake said, "Your Honor, the defense rests."

Court was adjourned for the day to allow both the prosecution and defense to prepare their closing arguments. The next morning, Callie went first, outlining the state's case against Josh, retracing the evidence of the drill and fingerprints. She concluded that, although the coveralls and gloves were not found in the possession of Josh Stephens, that alone did not mean he was innocent. Now it was Drake's turn, as he pointed out where the fingerprints were on the drill. He restated the lack of additional evidence at the crime scene. He covered Mr. Stephens' background, strong community presence, and his devotion to family. Finally, he concluded that the discovery of the coveralls and gloves, which corroborated witness testimony regarding the person seen at the Stephens' home that morning, proved that Josh Stephens did not kill his wife. He went on to explain reasonable doubt, and how it was the jury's duty to convict his client only in the absence of reasonable doubt. Then he paused and looked at each juror, before turning and heading back to the defense table.

Judge Abernathy then turned his attention to the jury and instructed them regarding the possible verdicts, deliberations, and other technical matters facing them in their duty to dispense justice. After he finished, the jury was led away to the jury room to begin deliberating on Josh Stephens' fate. The judge recessed court until the jury came back with a verdict. Drake knew from experience that it could be a matter of minutes, or could last several days before a verdict was reached, if a unanimous decision was made at all.

He grabbed Josh and headed over to where Macy and Spence were seated, asking them if they would like to have lunch with he and Josh. Spence seemed eager to talk, so he accepted before Macy could respond. Drake knew the bailiff would call Betty, and she in turn would call him on his cell, once the verdict was in. Drake recommended they eat at The Opening Act, a nice restaurant that offered a more private setting where they could freely talk as they lingered over a nice steak.

On the way to the restaurant, Drake noticed a dark sedan following close behind. He made a few unnecessary turns onto different streets just to confirm he was being followed. The sedan stayed with him, so he continued on to the restaurant without telling the others. As they climbed out of the car, he looked over at the sedan as it parked in a space a couple of rows behind them. The windows were tinted enough to prohibit him from seeing inside. No one exited the vehicle, and he could not be certain how many people were inside.

Macy noticed Drake staring at the sedan and asked, "What's wrong Adam?" as she turned her gaze toward the car he was watching.

"Nothing," he answered, failing at being a convincing liar.

Macy let it go, but was now on full alert for anything out of the ordinary. She squeezed Spence's hand and motioned with her head toward the sedan. Spence merely nodded his understanding, took her by the arm and escorted her to the front door. They entered the building and walked directly to the hostess stand, where Drake requested a quiet table in the back.

After the waiter left to get their drink order, Drake spoke up. "Well, what do you guys think?"

"I believe you've got a strong case," replied Spence. "I'm curious, though, Adam. Why didn't you ask the judge for a dismissal after your last witness? I mean, it seems after what he testified, the judge could have very well determined the state did not have sufficient evidence to satisfy the burden of proof."

"Well actually, Spence, I was going to, but Josh insisted I proceed with the trial."

"Why?" asked Macy.

"Double jeopardy," said Josh, speaking up. "If the jury acquits me, I can't be tried again for Julie's murder." Macy shot an inquisitive look in Spence's direction.

"And if they don't acquit you?" asked Spence.

"I'm confident they will," replied Josh.

"And if they don't, we can always appeal. Right, Adam?"

"Of course," said Drake. "But we're not going to need an appeal, are we?"

"I don't think so," said Macy, raising her water glass in a mock toast.

They finished their meal and left the restaurant. Drake casually looked in the direction of where the sedan had parked, but it was not there. He eased out into traffic and headed back to the courthouse so the others could retrieve their cars. Josh planned to come back to the office to wait with Drake for the rest of the afternoon in case a verdict came in quickly. Macy and Spence drove back to the hotel to wait for news from Drake.

As he headed up Main Street, Drake checked his rearview mirror just in time to see the black sedan pull out from a side street and fall in behind him. He didn't say anything to the others until they reached the courthouse. Once there, Josh climbed in his vehicle and headed off for the office while Macy and Spence headed toward the hotel. Drake remained behind for a minute to see who the sedan would follow.

As Spence drove out of the parking lot, Drake saw the black sedan fall in behind him. Drake followed them to see if they were really following Spence, or just hanging back behind Josh. As soon as Josh turned into the parking lot at Drake's office, Drake had his answer. The black sedan continued behind Spence. Drake pulled into the office parking lot and reached for his cell phone.

"Macy, you guys have a tail."

"I know. I spotted them after we left the courthouse."

"Any idea who it is?"

"Not yet, but I think we'll soon find out. They just followed us into the parking deck."

"Be careful," said Drake as he hung up, then went inside to wait with Josh.

Spence pulled slowly into the parking space as Macy considered their options. Her bag was in the trunk, which unfortunately did her no good at this point. The black sedan stopped directly behind them, blocking any chance of exit. Before Spence could open the door, two men jumped out of the sedan and approached both sides of the car. Macy watched the one on her side through the side view mirror, noticing his bulging muscles underneath his silk suit. The men immediately pulled open the doors and shoved a pistol in their face, motioning for them to get out. Spence and Macy exited the vehicle, slowly looking for an opportunity to break free and run, but there was another man standing behind the car with a shotgun. At this point escape was futile.

Spence and Macy were escorted to the black sedan where one of the men climbed in the back seat with them and placed a blindfold on each, while the other one joined the man with the shotgun in the front. They sped off, exiting from the parking garage and heading south out of town. As they rode in silence, Macy used her special ops training to estimate the number of miles they had driven based upon assumed speed and time, allowing as best she could for stoplights. She could tell as soon as they were out of town because the car did not stop again until it reached its destination. Her best estimate was approximately thirty to forty miles when the car finally stopped. They were led to a building with the blindfolds still intact, until the door closed behind them. One of the men removed their blindfolds and instructed them to sit down, gesturing toward two empty seats in the middle of the room.

It took a few seconds for her eyes to adjust, but soon Macy was able to make out a figure standing in front of her. He was an older gentleman, probably in his mid-to-late fifties, wearing a navy blue suit and a matching fedora. Harry "Two Hats" Marconi, she thought. At least he was not wearing black today, but then again, the hat color code could just be a myth.

"Good afternoon, Ms. Merit," he said, smiling at Macy.

"Do I know you?" she asked.

Harry let out a huge laugh as he looked at his cronies. "Does she know me?" he asked rhetorically. "I'm sure you've heard of me. Harry "Two Hats" Marconi is my name. I am quite well known," he said, obviously trying to stoke his ego.

Macy seized the opportunity. "I'm afraid I've never heard of you."

The smile quickly faded from his face, replaced by red from the sudden rush of blood to his brain. "I assure you, Ms. Merit, that before we are through, you will come to know me very well." Some of the red drained from his face and the smile reappeared.

"What are we doing here?" asked Spence.

"Ah, Spencer Rawlings," said Marconi. "Tell me, Mr. Rawlings, how does one retire from a law practice at such a young age? Did you get lucky at the track?"

"You could say that," said Spence, offering a half smile.

Harry swung his right arm swiftly, striking Spence on the side of his face with the back of his hand. A slight trickle of blood ran from the right corner of Spence's mouth as his head bobbed first to the left and back in place.

"I'm a very busy man," said Marconi. "I don't have time for games. Now, tell me why you are so interested in Mark Jacoby?"

"Who?" asked Spence, obviously trying to take most of the punishment in order to spare Macy.

Harry's arm swung again, this time with greater force as he almost knocked Spence out of the chair. His lip was bleeding much heavier now, but he showed no signs of pain. Macy wanted to jump up and take this guy out with her bare hands, but knew his cronies stood ready to cut her in two with automatic weapons if she so much as looked the wrong way. All she could do was bite her lip and hope Spence did not push Marconi too far.

"Perhaps I'll have better luck with you, Ms. Merit. Why did you attack three of my men and steal Jacoby away in the middle of the night? Did you not realize the danger in such action?"

"We were trying to help out a friend," said Macy. "We believe Jacoby killed a woman whose husband is on trial for her murder."

"Ah, the Josh Stephens' case," said Marconi with a sigh. "And how is the case going?"

"The jury just got it today. Of course, I'm sure you already knew that."

"You're very perceptive, Ms. Merit, and smart, too. Unlike your husband, who seems to enjoy bringing out my fiery temper."

"I assure you he meant no disrespect," said Macy. "He was just being a little cautious in giving out information."

"Is that true, Mr. Rawlings?" asked Marconi. "Do you really respect me?"

"Go to hell!" said Spence, spitting blood with the words.

This time Marconi punched Spence in the stomach, then punched him across the face, causing his nose to bleed.

"Please, Mr. Marconi," said Macy. "I'll tell you anything you want to know. Just talk to me and leave Spence out of this."

"Okay, Ms. Merit. Tell me more about Jacoby and how he might be involved in this murder case."

Macy told Marconi about the evidence they found and why they took him from the shed that night. She also explained he had been released, which she believed Marconi already knew. As she spoke, Marconi gently rubbed his chin as if trying to digest everything she was telling him. He waited for a few seconds after she finished before he spoke.

"Why was Jacoby allowed to leave the police station without being arrested?"

"Well, actually, he was arrested at first, but his attorney pointed out an irregularity in how the evidence was obtained and was able to convince a judge to disallow the search. The evidence could be used to assist Mr. Stephens' defense, but was inadmissible against Jacoby," answered Macy.

"Doesn't that strike you as odd?" asked Marconi.

"It happens," said Spence, raising his head from his chest. One of his goons moved over to strike, but Marconi raised his finger, stopping the man in his tracks.

"Thank you for your honesty, Ms. Merit. I'm afraid now we must leave you for a little while until I can decide what to do with you."

He instructed the men to tie Macy and Spence to the chairs and place duct tape on their mouths, then he and his men left the building. Macy looked at Spence's bloody face as she heard two cars speed away.

Chapter 26

Macy could see the concern on Spence's face, not for himself, but for her. She wanted so desperately to hold him and tell him it would be okay, but even if she was not bound and gagged, she still could not offer that assertion. And yet he yearned for the same thing—a chance to hold Macy and assure her that everything would be all right.

They could tell it was nearing dark as the shadows in the room became longer and the brightness from the one small window high upon the rear wall gave way to a pale gray. Macy struggled against the bonds that held her tightly against the chair, but it was of no use. These guys definitely knew how to restrain someone, obviously from years of experience, thought Macy. How she wished she had some of her gadgets from her bag. She swore to herself that if she ever got out of this alive, she would definitely find a way to conceal at least some important items that would come in handy in a predicament such as this.

Spence also struggled for a moment, then realized he was getting nowhere. He looked over at Macy and winked, but his eyes betrayed the feeling of despair in his soul. They both knew that since Marconi had gone to the trouble of kidnapping them, and allowing them to see his face, he would surely have them killed.

She recalled her military training as she prepared her mind to be ever vigilant for the slightest opportunity which might arise. All she needed was one mistake and she would make them pay. As the gray hue of twilight was enveloped by black, they heard a noise outside. From the sound, Macy could tell there were two automobiles. She listened as the doors opened and shut, revealing more than one person had exited the vehicles. Then the lock on the building door turned and someone stepped inside. As the bright beam from a flashlight blinded her vision, she heard Marconi speak. When he stepped in front of the light, her eyes locked on Marconi. This time he was wearing a black fedora.

"You brought these people upon us, Mark. They wouldn't give you up, but I'm not convinced you're not working with them. We never had any trouble from Feds or private investigators until you showed up. Now I'm wondering whether you should join them."

"If you believe that, Harry, then take your gun out and shoot me in the head now," replied Jacoby. "And if you don't believe it, then shame on you for saying it."

"Sorry, Mark. I had to test you. I'll tell you what, you get rid of these two for me, and I'll never doubt you again."

"It would be my pleasure, Harry. You just go on back home, relax, and leave everything to me. By tomorrow morning, they'll be history."

"I knew I could count on you, Mark," said Marconi, then walked out of the room. Macy heard the car door open and shut, and then it sped away.

Jacoby walked closer, and bent down in front of her face. "You two have made a real mess for me. It's time I took care of you for good." He motioned for the two thugs to loosen the bonds on Macy and Spence and pushed them toward the door. They were escorted to the other car, where Jacoby climbed in the back seat with them, while the other two sat in the front.

"Let's go," Jacoby ordered, and the car took off.

They drove out in the country for about fifteen minutes before coming to an abrupt stop. The two goons jerked Macy and Spence from the rear seat and pushed them ahead in front of them with Jacoby following closely behind.

"You know, when I worked in furniture I never got to see much of the state I live in," he said. "But since I started working for Harry, I've seen a lot of North Carolina. And you know what I learned? There are a lot of abandoned gold mines in Randolph County. A person could get lost out here, fall down one of those old mines, and never be heard from again." He looked at the two henchmen. "I'll take it from here, boys. The boss wants me to take care of this personally."

He shoved a pistol into Macy's back and urged her and Spence forward. From the flashlight beam she could make out the entrance to what appeared to be some kind of tunnel. They walked through the entrance and continued for another twenty feet.

Jacoby grabbed Macy by the shoulder hard, causing her to stop in her tracks. He leaned closer and said in a hushed voice, "Okay, you two. We should be far enough inside so Tweedle Dee and Tweedle Dum out there can't hear. You guys have really complicated things for me. I had to do some fast talking to get Harry to believe me. Now the only way for me to keep my cover is for you two to disappear. Since I'm no killer, though, I'm gonna need your help."

"You're the one holding the gun," said Spence. "Do you expect us to just jump down the mine shaft willingly?"

"Oh, sorry about that," said Jacoby as he put the pistol in his pocket. "No one is going down a mine shaft. I told you, I'm not a killer. I just have to make it look good for Harry and his goons, so here's what I want you to do." He leaned over and instructed them in a low voice. After about twenty minutes, he turned to leave. Macy and Spence let out a scream, allowing the sound to trail off as if they were falling then Jacoby appeared outside of the mine.

"Well, that's that," he said as he looked at the two men. "Let's go guys."

He and the two men climbed into the car and sped away, the tires spitting up dust and gravel as they went. As soon as they were certain the car was out of sight and gone for good, Macy and Spence stepped through the mine entrance and into the still night air. She paused for a moment while she perused the night sky. Once she had her bearings, she took Spence by the hand and began leading him away from the mine. Jacoby told Macy to head northeast until they got to Asheboro. There they should be able to hole up until someone could get their things to them from the hotel in High Point, then they could head back to Kentucky. He was kind enough to have given her a flashlight, but without knowing much about the terrain, it was taking a long time to reach their destination.

After walking for about an hour, they appeared to be nearing a paved road. Macy carefully walked up to the road sign and shined the light on it, revealing the letters HWY and the numbers 64. They continued walking alongside the highway until they saw a sign indicating Asheboro twelve miles straight ahead. Several cars passed but no one stopped. After another mile of walking, Macy heard a vehicle approaching from behind them. Since she and Spence were becoming tired, and the night was passing, she stuck out her thumb as she spun around and faced the vehicle. The vehicle passed by, then the brake lights flashed as the driver brought the car to a stop, and backed up until it was beside Macy. The passenger window opened and the driver shouted to Macy, "Where to?"

"Asheboro," replied Macy.

"Get in. I'm headed there myself."

Macy and Spence climbed in the back seat among the empty fast food wrappers and various other trash.

"Don't mind the mess," he said, wiping a few crumbs off the seat. "The kids like to eat in the car when we go on trips." Smiling at Macy, he told her about his wife and three kids in Charlotte, and how he was traveling on business.

She smiled back as he went on about his family. He was a pleasant gentleman, in his early forties, mostly bald on top with just a little hair around the sides, which he kept trimmed very short. She could tell he was well suited for sales, since he seemed to have no problem with shyness or the ability to converse with people.

"What brings you this far out walking at night?"

"Our car broke down several miles back," said Macy. "We were lost on some dirt road, and it died on us so we started walking until we got to the highway."

"You guys weren't out trying to find one of those gold mines, were you?"

"Well, actually we were," said Spence. "I'm sort of a history buff, and well, a friend of mine told me about them. I had no idea how easy it would be to get lost."

"At least you got lost out here and not in one of those mines. You could wander around in there for days and no one would ever find you." He paused a moment before asking, "So where in Asheboro can I take you?"

"Well, actually we need a place to stay for the night until we can get our car repaired tomorrow," said Spence. "Do you know where any hotels are?"

"I'll do you better than that. I'm on my way to the Holiday Inn Express. It's a nice enough place, and one of the newer hotels in town. You can get a room there for the night."

"Thanks," said Macy as she looked over at Spence and winked. He smiled back at her and took her hand, squeezing it gently.

After about twenty-five minutes, the man pulled into the hotel parking lot, stopping in front of the entrance. Macy and Spence climbed out of the back seat and thanked the man for his help. Spence offered to pay him, but he refused saying he was headed this way anyway and it was no extra trouble or expense for him. In fact, he liked the company, especially after several hours on the road. He drove the car back out to the parking lot and looked for an open space while Macy and Spence went inside.

As they approached the front desk, a young man in his early twenties looked up and motioned he would be with them soon, as he cradled the telephone receiver on his shoulder. He was obviously assisting someone with a reservation, and appeared to be the only one working the desk. Macy seemed to barely look at the man, but Spence was somewhat taken aback by the man's appearance. His head was clean-shaven and he had a mustache and goatee. Spence could see tattoos emerging from the top of his shirt and onto his neck. He also had multiple piercings in his lip, ears, and eyebrows.

Spence gave Macy a sideways look, gesturing toward the guy, but she just smiled and shook her head. He obviously could not believe a business establishment would hire someone who looked like that, but just as he was about to speak, she leaned over and said, "Relax, honey. This is the twenty-first century. People are more accepting of individual tastes and fashions, even in the workplace." She smiled and gently squeezed his hand.

After a few seconds, the man finished his telephone conversation and turned to them. "Can I help you?"

"We would like a room for the night," said Spence.

"Certainly. Would you prefer a queen or two doubles?"

"Queen, non-smoking," replied Spence.

The man began typing on the keyboard in front of him, looked up at Spence and asked, "How will you be paying for this?"

Macy gave Spence a nervous look as she realized she had left her purse in the car at the hotel in High Point. He smiled at her and nodded as he removed his wallet from his back pocket. Luckily, the men who took them earlier had not bothered to remove it. He retrieved a credit card and handed it to the man. The hotel clerk continued typing, swiped Spence's credit card through the machine, and then handed it back. He asked Spence to sign the slip, and handed him two keys. He grabbed a hotel diagram from the counter and instructed them on the best way to get to the room, thanking them as they turned and headed toward the elevator.

As the doors were closing, Macy saw the gentleman, who gave them a ride to Asheboro, enter the lobby. She quickly tossed a wave in his direction, but he did not see her. They rode the elevator to the third floor where they stepped off and made their way down the hall to room 323. Once they were inside, Macy began stripping off her clothes. "What are you doing?" asked Spence.

"If we're going to have to wear these clothes for an extra day or two, I would prefer to air them out a little," answered Macy, pulling down her panties. Spence grabbed her wrist and pulled her to him.

"But I like it when you're a little dirty. It's sexy."

He placed his lips on top of hers, firmly interlocking them into a long intimate kiss. Macy ran her fingers through his hair as she returned the favor, kissing him deeply as she began unbuttoning his shirt. In no time they were lying on the bed, their bodies intertwined as one as they moved rhythmically to their own animal instincts. It seemed that coming so close to death kindled the passion Spence had for Macy, as he realized how fleeting life was. He held on to her as if he never wanted to let go. She, too, held on tightly, sensing his deep love and desire for her.

After several minutes of unbridled passion, their bodies separated as they lie on their backs panting for air. Macy laid her head against Spence's chest as he stroked her hair. Neither said a word while they basked in the afterglow of true love. For a few minutes they were able to suspend time with no thoughts or cares for Mark Jacoby, Josh Stephens, or Harry "Two Hats." For this moment in time, all that mattered was each other.

Spence soon fell asleep. Macy, on the other hand, was still wired, and called Drake to let him know where they were. Since Spence paid for the room with a credit card, she could make a long distance call and have it charged to the room.

"Hello?"

"Adam, this is Macy."

"Are you guys okay? The last I saw you those goons were trailing you."

"We're fine for now," said Macy, telling Drake about their adventure and how Jacoby had actually saved them.

"We need a favor, Adam."

"Name it."

"Can you find a way to get our things and car from the hotel in High Point and send them down here to us? It would be nice to have a change of clothes."

"Sure. I'll get Betty to take care of it. No one would probably pay her much attention, so she shouldn't be followed. And don't worry, I'll keep your whereabouts secret. As far as I'm concerned, I haven't heard a word from you guys since court, just in case anyone should ask."

"Thank you, Adam," said Macy. She hung up and walked to the bathroom. When she returned to the bed, Spence was awake.

"Who was that on the phone?"

"I called Adam to let him know we were okay and see if he could get our things to us."

"You did tell him we're supposed to be dead?"

"Yes. He said as far as he was concerned, he has not heard from us since court."

"So when will we get our stuff?"

"What's your hurry?" asked Macy. "I thought you liked me when I'm dirty?"

"I do. I just don't like myself that way."

"Well I do," said Macy with a sly giggle as she quickly jerked the covers off his naked body, exposing him in the faint light that shone through the bathroom door.

"Looks to me like you're ready for some more action," she said, eying Spence's body, then climbed in beside him, locking her lips on top of his. Spence brushed her red hair with his fingers as they kissed relentlessly. Soon they were in the middle of round two.

CHAPTER 27

That afternoon after the jury had been given the case to deliberate, it was apparent they would not reach a verdict any time that evening. The judge ordered they be sequestered to a nearby hotel for the night, and be brought back to the jury room the next morning to continue their discussion of the case. Josh left Drake's office and went home, while Drake remained behind his desk for a little while. It was his experience that in most trials the longer the jury took, the greater likelihood the verdict would go in his favor. Jurors who took very little time deliberating tended to side with the prosecution, believing there was little need to examine the evidence in detail, and often might have missed some minute detail which could exonerate a defendant.

Drake placed his hands over his face and moved them backward, rubbing his fingers through his hair. It had been a tedious trial, but waiting for the jury to reach a decision was almost torture. He finally packed it up and headed home. As he drove, he thought about Callie. They would not see each other until after the trial was over now that it was in the jury's hands. He was looking forward to the end of this trial and the opportunity for him and Callie to be able to openly pursue their relationship. She would still be able to work for the District Attorney, provided she and Drake were never working the same trial. Of course, there was no guarantee the District Attorney would continue her employment once the news of their marriage became public, but being a strong attorney she would have no trouble securing a position elsewhere.

His mind wandered back to their visit to Dalton and how peaceful it was. He had never felt so relaxed in his life, and wondered what life would be like to live and work in a small town. Of course, with the crime rate almost nonexistent there, he would have to vary his practice to include contract and corporate work in order to make a living. Oh well, he was just thinking anyway. He had no plans to move and leave his established practice in High Point.

Drake arrived at home alone and in the dark. Sam was there as usual to greet him. He spent a little quality time playing with the dog before eating a frozen dinner for supper. Afterward, he watched a little television before calling it a night. He had just drifted off to sleep when Macy called. Now that he was fully awake, he tried to process what she had just told him about their encounter with Harry "Two Hats" Marconi and Mark Jacoby. After mulling it over in his mind for another hour as he tossed and turned, Drake finally succumbed to the lack of sleep and drifted off. He was jolted awake by his alarm clock blaring an old 80's tune as he desperately reached for the off button. Slowly climbing out of bed and heading for the shower, he hoped it would wake him up. After all, he wanted to be sharp in case the jury came back with a verdict today. After breakfast and a brief romp with Sam, Drake headed to the office.

Betty was already busy at her desk when he walked in.

"I need a favor, Betty," he said as he stopped in front of her desk.

"Okay. What is it?"

He explained the situation with Macy and Spence, then, after swearing her to secrecy, drove them over to the hotel. He remained in the car while Betty went inside. She walked over to the front desk and pretended to be Macy, stating she had lost her key but accurately told them the room number. She must have appeared to be genuine because after a few swipes of a new key card and the punch of some buttons, the clerk handed Betty a key. She punched Drake's number on her cell phone as she headed for the elevator.

"Okay, I'm in. Take the car around to the parking area, find Spence's car, and let me know where to meet you at."

She made her way to the hotel room where she packed up all of their belongings and waited for Drake to call. Soon her cell phone rang and he told her where in the parking garage to meet him. She took the elevator to the parking level and exited through the back to avoid being seen by the front desk. As she emerged into the parking area, he sounded his horn once and flashed his headlights so Betty would see him. She hobbled toward Spence's car, holding the extra set of keys she found in the night stand, exactly where Macy told Drake it would be. She climbed in and stuck the key into the ignition with a turn, causing the engine to spring to life. Pulling out of the garage, she headed south toward Asheboro. He called Betty on his cell phone and maintained contact with her until she reached the hotel where Macy and Spence were staying. Once he was certain she was safe, Drake hung up and headed back to the office. Betty carried the luggage into the hotel and made her way directly to their room. She knocked on the door and waited for a couple of seconds before Spence appeared.

"Betty, thank you so much for this."

"I was glad to do it," replied Betty as Spence ushered her into the room. Macy jumped up from the chair and threw her arms around her.

"Finally some clean clothes!"

After exchanging a little small talk, Betty told them she needed to get back to the office.

"How will you get back?" Spence asked.

"Oh, don't worry. I'll take a cab. Adam can pick up the tab." As soon as she left, Macy headed for the shower, eager to change into something fresher. Spence waited patiently for her to finish before cleaning up himself. Once they were clean and refreshed, they headed out for some breakfast. Macy felt confident that as long as they stayed away from High Point, Harry "Two Hats" would believe they were dead.

When Betty returned to the office, Josh was there with Drake.

"Any word from the jury?" she asked.

"Not yet," replied Drake.

Betty quickly became immersed in her work again as Drake and Josh continued their discussion of small talk. Drake asked her to order in pizza for their lunch in order to keep Josh away from public scrutiny. As soon as they finished their meal, though, Josh told Drake he needed to get some air, especially if the verdict did not go their way and he ended up cooped up for life. Drake assured him that would not be the case, as Josh headed to his car. As he pulled out of the parking lot, Josh rolled the window down and breathed in a deep breath of fresh air, then headed to the cemetery to visit his family. Ever since he was arrested and on the run, he had not had the opportunity to spend time with his loved ones.

Julie was buried beside Rachel, just as they had planned. There was an empty lot beside Julie reserved for Josh. He spoke first to Julie, then to Rachel, unable to control the tears that traced down his cheeks. Soon he was sobbing almost uncontrollably as the emotions of losing them, coupled with the ordeal of the trial, had finally taken their toll. He spent the next two hours crying until he was able to regain control of his emotions. He spent another hour of quiet time reflecting upon their lives in silence. He kissed the fingers of his right hand and gently touched them to Julie's headstone, did the same to Rachel's before turning and walking back to the car. He was now ready to accept his fate, whatever it may be.

Instead of driving back to Drake's office, Josh headed back to his house. He no longer needed the hotel room Macy had provided. He sat in his favorite chair and turned on the television, hoping to find something to take his mind off the trial. After flipping through several channels, he chose an old John Wayne western and settled in for the afternoon. It wasn't long before he drifted off to sleep, his body spent from the overflow of emotional depletion he suffered at the cemetery. He did not wake up until after dark.

He made his way in the dark to the kitchen where the illuminated panel on the microwave displayed the time as eight-thirty. Josh made a quick sandwich, took a sleeping pill, and retired to the bedroom. He curled up in a fetal position and the pill soon took effect, pulling him back down into the realm of unconscious dreams.

Meanwhile, Drake was spending another night alone. He played with Sam for awhile, and then ate dinner, which consisted of a delivered pepperoni pizza and cold soda. After dinner he took a nice hot bath, hoping to relax his tired and tense muscles. Since the trial ended and the jury took the case, Drake had been knotted up inside as he pondered the fate of his client. When he finished his bath, he rifled through his CD collection, retrieving the soundtrack to *Philadelphia*. Although he normally used this to fuel his creative and emotional spirit before and during a trial, sometimes he found that listening to it helped to ease his troubled soul while awaiting the outcome of jury deliberations. He closed his eyes as the music filled his head, picturing Tom Hanks in his pivotal role. Drake felt a tear roll down his cheek during the opera aria as he remembered Hanks' character crying at that same point in the movie. He suddenly realized how empty he was without Callie, but the thought of the rest of his life with her ceased the flow of tears and brought a smile to his face. Yes, she was good for him and he knew it. Just then the phone rang.

"Hey, babe. Whatcha doin'?" asked Callie.

"Believe it or not, I was thinking of you," he said. He could hear the smile in her voice as she said, "That's so sweet. I just wanted to tell you how much I love you."

"I love you more," he replied.

"I love you most," she said with a slight chuckle. It was a little game they played. After one would tell the other they loved them, the other would say they loved them more, only to be trumped by the first one saying they loved the other most. Occasionally, one would break protocol and completely skip the 'more' stage, instead opting to go straight to the 'most' stage. Either way, they always got a good laugh about it and it was one of the things they shared together that helped forge a stronger bond between them. They exchanged a few more sweet nothings then ended the call. Drake certainly felt better after their conversation, as he grabbed the remote and turned on the television. He wanted to catch the late news before going to bed.

Callie had curled up with a book, and having just read a romantic part, called Drake again for some intimate phone time. After they ended the call, she returned to her book. Many nights she preferred to avoid the television and shield herself from the outside world, if only for a few hours. Working in the D.A.'s office provided enough reality during working hours to last her through the remainder of the day.

Placing the book down, she walked to the kitchen to fix a cup of hot tea. Green tea was her favorite. She filled the kettle with enough water for a couple of cups, and placed it on the stove. As she reached in the cabinet for the green tea, she spied the box of orange spice tea she bought for Drake. He liked to drink tea with her, but found the green tea not to his liking, so she bought orange spice, which he decided was actually quite good. It was one more thing they could share together—a relaxing hot cup of tea to go with their conversation. Callie took her tea to the living room and returned to her book.

Meanwhile, Macy and Spence decided to take in a movie. After it was over, they returned to the hotel. She called Drake to see if he had heard anything from the jury.

"Adam, this is Macy. I hope I didn't disturb you."

"No, I was just watching the news. What's up?"

"Have you heard anything from the jury?"

"Not yet, but one of my sources told me the judge spoke with them this afternoon and asked how the deliberations were going. Apparently, he wanted to make sure they had not reached an impasse without notifying him. They informed the judge they were fairly close to reaching a unanimous decision, so they wanted at least one more day to deliberate. My source feels confident we will see a verdict sometime tomorrow."

"I guess we need to just sit tight then?"

"Well, considering dead people aren't supposed to be up walking around, I guess you'd better," he said with a laugh.

"Thanks for sending Betty with our things. Now that I have my cell phone back, you can call me whenever the jury comes back with a verdict."

"Will do," said Drake, ending the call.

Drake began channel surfing again once the news was over. Since he was awake now, he watched an old comedy. During the first commercial, he grabbed a soda from the fridge and a bag of chips. It was going to be one of those nights, or so he thought. Shortly after he finished the soda, the combination of released adrenaline, and the fact that it was very late, soon overtook his body and he fell asleep in the recliner. He did not even move when Sam jumped up to join him.

As Callie sipped her tea, she suddenly realized she might very well lose this case. And since they could not go after Jacoby, Julie's murder would probably be unsolved. Then she thought about her impending marriage to Drake and how her boss would take the news. With the recent loss of a high profile case, coupled with the romance between her and the attorney she lost to, Callie began to think her job might be in jeopardy. Now she was more awake than ever. She put her book down and walked over to her computer.

Realizing this was all very premature, she updated her resume. She enjoyed her job very much, but she loved Drake more. And if it meant giving up her current position to be with him, then it was worth it.

Once she finished updating her resume, she began surfing the Internet just to see what was out there. She did not know why, but for some reason she found herself thinking about Dalton. She made a quick inquiry as to the employment possibilities in Dalton, but as she read through the few postings, she realized attorney positions would not be posted like other jobs. Usually, these were obtained by networking with influential connections, then being called for interviews. Knowing this, Callie began working on a list of contacts, both in North Carolina and Georgia. Who knows, maybe she could talk Drake into moving there. Then she remembered him telling her about his conversation with the police department and the fact there was very little crime there. He told her a criminal defense attorney such as he would probably starve to death trying to drum up enough business. Oh well, it was nice to dream about a more simple life, even if it was not in the cards.

Callie looked at the clock, and seeing it was three o'clock in the morning, knew she had better try to get some sleep. After all, Drake told her earlier that day what his contact said about the jury, so they would probably reach a verdict before the close of business tomorrow. Although her boss did not plan to appeal should the verdict go against them, she wanted to be alert during the proceedings. She lay down and curled up as she thought about Drake. As she drifted off to sleep, she was dreaming about the two of them on Aunt Jewel's front porch, their two children playing in the yard. She dreamed about them the rest of the night until the alarm clock rang and wiped away the images from her mind. Until then, she was at peace.

CHAPTER 28

Drake awoke the next morning and jumped out of bed. His stomach churned with nervous apprehension as he realized today would probably be the day the jury came back with a verdict. He felt confident when the new evidence was discovered, but now that the verdict was imminent, he began to have doubts. He started second guessing his moves in the last days of the trial, and even replayed his closing argument in his mind, trying to alleviate the almost overwhelming premonition that he missed something. As he splashed cold water on his face, he tried to tell himself this was how he always felt right before a verdict, which usually came back in his favor in spite of the self-inflicted doubt and lack of confidence. Today was no different as he struggled to control his nerves. After years of doing this, he thought it would become easier, but when someone's life hung in the balance, he could not shake the feeling that somehow he was responsible should one of his clients be sent to prison, or worse yet, be put to death.

Drake showered and dressed, and let Sam out for his morning routine as he wolfed down some dry toast. Heading to the office to await word from the courthouse, he was on his second Camel of the day by the time he pulled into the parking lot. He tossed the butt to the side as he stepped inside the building. Betty greeted him when he walked through the door, and handed him a cup of coffee. She knew how he was just before a big verdict, and tried to make things as easy as she could for him.

"How's Josh holding up?" she asked.

"Actually quite well considering what he is facing."

"You know you did the best you could, no matter what the outcome."

"Did I really, Betty? If we lose I can't help but think it was somehow my fault."

"And yet you know that's not true," she said, touching his shoulder.

"Why do I torture myself like this, Betty?"

"Because you're human," she replied. "And because you care about your clients."

She offered a reassuring smile as he turned and walked into his office. He knew he would not hear from Callie until after the trial was over. He so desperately wanted to talk to her, to hear her sweet voice telling him that everything would be okay. He longed to hold her in his arms and smell the sweet fragrance of her perfume mixed with the scent of her body as he buried his face in her long dark hair. He closed his eyes, picturing her standing in front of him looking as beautiful as ever. Warmth suddenly flooded over his body like an ocean wave as he contemplated their future together. He had never felt this way about anyone before, but instead of feeling scared or apprehensive, he was fully at peace, almost as if this relationship with Callie had always been. This must be true love, he thought, leaning back in his chair.

Suddenly, he was startled from his daydream when the telephone rang. He glanced at his watch and realized he had actually been lost in thought for over an hour. The time read ten o'clock. Betty answered the phone and spoke briefly before hanging up. The look she gave Drake told him everything he needed to know. The jury was back.

As he gathered his papers, Betty called Josh and instructed him to come to the office. Josh arrived a few minutes later and they headed for the courthouse. As they drove, Drake quickly phoned Macy.

"Macy, this is Adam. The jury is back and we're on our way to the courthouse. I'll call you as soon as I can."

"Thanks, Adam," replied Macy when he ended the call. She informed Spence the jury was back and they began packing their bags. Once the trial was over, and if Josh was acquitted, they could continue on to the beach and their vacation. If he was convicted, Macy knew Drake might need their help in preparing an appeal.

When they arrived at the courthouse, Drake saw the line of reporters waiting by the front entrance. Obviously, someone had tipped them off and Josh was once again front page news. Drake offered no comment while Josh remained mute as they made their way past the throng of reporters shouting questions as they passed by. Once inside, they were able to escape the line of news vultures and turn their attention to the matter at hand. As they walked inside the courtroom and took their place behind the defense table, Drake stole a quick glance in the direction of the prosecutor's table. Callie was already seated, her dark hair falling down in front of her shoulders as she was busily scribbling notes. She looked up quickly at Drake, obviously feeling his eyes burning a hole through her. She offered a slight smile, and returned to her work.

Drake turned and faced Josh, trying to provide some comforting last minute phrase to ease his client's anxiety. Josh looked steady as a rock, however, seemingly unfazed by what was going on around him. What Drake lacked in confidence regarding his defense of Josh, Josh made up for with his confidence in Drake.

"Madame Foreperson has the jury reached a verdict?" barked Judge Abernathy.

A lady in a blue dress, appearing to be in her early forties, stood from the front row of the jury box. "Yes we have, Your Honor."

The bailiff stepped toward the lady, retrieved a sheet of paper from her, and took it over to Judge Abernathy. The judge opened the paper and read over the contents, then handed it back to the bailiff to deliver it back to the lady. Once it was back in her hand, Judge Abernathy asked, "In the case of the State of North Carolina versus Joshua Dale Stephens, on the sole count of murder in the first degree, what is the verdict of the jury?"

"We, the jury, find the defendant not guilty," she answered. Immediately, there was a wave of noise that spread throughout the courtroom as people began mumbling to their neighbors. The judge rapped the gavel to restore order. "Based upon the findings of this court and the ruling of the jury, Mr. Stephens, you are hereby released. You are free to go." He pounded the gavel again and announced this session of court was concluded.

Josh grabbed Drake in a bear hug. Drake turned toward Callie, who crossed the aisle, extended her hand, and said, "Congratulations."

He led Josh from the courtroom and into the throng of reporters. Once outside, he paused to speak to the crowd. "We are pleased with today's verdict," said Drake. "An innocent man was finally exonerated. Now maybe the police can start searching for the person who took this man's wife away."

One of the reporters asked Josh how he felt, to which he replied, "I just want my wife's killer caught and brought to justice." Then he looked directly into the camera and said, "If there is anyone out there with any information as to who killed Julie, please call the local police."

He and Josh continued to the car without further comment. They drove back to Drake's office where Betty had ordered in lunch as a celebration. As soon as they walked into the office, Drake reached for his cell phone, dialed Macy's number and waited for her to answer.

"Macy, this is Adam. We won!"

"That's great," said Macy. "Do you need anything else from us before we head to the beach for vacation?"

"Well, actually, I was hoping you guys would come help us celebrate at dinner tonight. Besides, Josh still has the cell phone you gave him and he wanted to return it to you."

"What about the ongoing investigation into Marconi? We are supposed to be dead, you know?"

"Let me check on that for you. Just hang tight and I'll call you right back."

Drake ended the call, and immediately dialed another number.

"Agent Price, this is Adam Drake. Can you give me any kind of update on the Marconi case?"

"What concern is it of yours?" snapped Price.

"Well, I'm calling for my friends, Macy Merit and Spencer Rawlings. I suppose Mark Jacoby told you about his meeting with them the other night."

"He didn't tell me anything," said Price. "A couple of joggers found his body in a park in Shelby this morning. Apparently, Harry "Two Hats" decided to put a bullet in his skull. Why? What do your friends have to do with my case?"

Drake explained how Harry had abducted them, and ordered Jacoby to kill them. He told him about the meeting at the mine and how Jacoby had allowed them to leave as long as they stayed out of town. He also told Price what Macy said about the conversation between Jacoby and Marconi and how it appeared Jacoby had belayed any suspicions Marconi had.

"Well, obviously something else stirred his lack of trust in Mark," said Price.

"Sorry about your case," said Drake.

"Me, too, but we've just about got enough to bring Marconi down. If we can just tie Jacoby's murder to him, then at least Mark will get some justice."

"Maybe its fate's way of dealing with him for Julie Stephens' murder," said Drake.

"Look, I know Mark Jacoby wasn't the model citizen," said Price. "But I can now tell you without a doubt, he did not kill that lady. The reason he had no alibi for the time of the murder was because he was in a meeting briefing me on the Marconi case. He couldn't tell you that at the time for fear of blowing his cover. But now that he's dead there's no reason you shouldn't know."

"If that's true, how do you explain the evidence we found in his car?"

"I don't know. Maybe Marconi had one of his goons put it there as a test. Or, maybe whoever killed this lady knew about the situation between Stephens and Jacoby, and framed him. Either way, unless they find the real killer we will never know."

"I guess you're right," said Drake.

"Look, tell your friends that as long as they keep a low profile, they should be okay. But since they saw Harry "Two Hats," if he sees them again he will finish the job."

"Okay. Thanks, Agent Price."

He hung up and punched Macy's number on the keypad. "Macy, its Adam. I just spoke with Agent Price and he said as long as you guys keep a low profile, you should be okay."

"Thanks, Adam," said Macy. "When and where do you want us to meet?"

"Just come to the office when you get ready and we can go from there. Since Marconi operates mostly in Cleveland County, you should be safe here. Oh, by the way, they found Mark Jacoby's dead body in a park in Shelby this morning."

"I guess he didn't have Marconi as convinced as I thought," said Macy.

When she ended the call, she looked over at Spence. "Jacoby's dead."

"I guess justice was served after all."

"But I thought you believed he was innocent."

"That's what my gut told me when I first saw him. But who knows, I guess my gut was wrong."

"We're all entitled to a mistake now and then, dear," said Macy with a giggle.

They began getting ready for the evening before driving back to High Point, leaving their luggage in the hotel to return for it later before heading to the coast tomorrow. After a quick shower and a change of clothes, they were on their way to High Point.

Meanwhile, Drake, Josh, Betty, and a few of Josh's coworkers had just finished their luncheon celebration. Josh's boss walked over to him, shook his hand, and said, "Josh, I was sure you were innocent. I know how difficult this ordeal has been for you, so please take a couple of weeks off. You haven't had time to grieve for Julie, what with the trial and all."

"Thanks. I'll do just that."

"Well, I have to get back for a meeting. I'll see you in two weeks," he said to Josh, then left the office.

The other employees began leaving as well, until there was only Josh, Drake, Betty, and Madeline, Josh's assistant. Josh bent down and whispered into Madeline's ear, and she also left to go back to the bank. Drake told Josh that Macy and Spence were on their way to the office to join them for dinner later that evening. He seemed pleased, telling Drake again about needing to return the cell phone Macy gave him. Josh went home for a little while to unwind and refresh before dinner. Betty returned to work while Drake sat in his office staring at the ceiling. Then the phone rang. Betty transferred the call to Drake.

"Hello?"

"Hey, sweetie," said Callie.

He felt his legs go limp at the sound of her voice. It was a good thing he was sitting down. "Well hello there."

"Congratulations again," she said softly. "I was wondering if you had plans for the evening."

"Believe me, I would rather do nothing else than be with you, but I promised Josh I would take him out to dinner to celebrate his acquittal. Macy and Spence are driving up from Asheboro to join us."

"Asheboro? What are they doing in Asheboro?"

"It's a long story. I'll fill you in later."

"Speaking of later, I don't suppose this dinner will last the entire evening?"

"Not when there's the prospect of seeing you. I assume that prospect will be open for later tonight?"

"You assume correctly," she said with a laugh.

"I'll call you as soon as I am on my way home," he said.

"I'll be waiting."

Drake hung up and stood up from his desk. He walked into the reception area and stopped at Betty's desk. "I believe we've done a good day's work today, Betty. What do you say we pack it in and start again in the morning?"

"I say that sounds like a wonderful idea to me. By the way, I made your dinner reservations for seven o'clock at Alejandro's."

"Are you sure you won't join us?"

"Positive. I need a quiet night all by myself."

"Okay, then. Have a good evening," said Drake as he walked through the door. As soon as he stepped outside, he lit a Camel and walked slowly to the car. As he drove toward home, Drake pulled the half-smoked cigarette from his lips, looked at it, and said, "I really need to quit these." He tossed the unfinished cigarette out the window and turned the radio up. He pulled in the drive and almost ran into the house. Since he had a few hours before dinner, he spent some time playing with Sam, then he headed for the shower to get cleaned up for dinner.

CHAPTER 29

Macy and Spence arrived at Drake's office around six-thirty. He was already there waiting on them. "I'm glad you two could make it."

"We're glad we could help," said Macy.

They walked into Drake's office and took a seat as they waited for Josh to arrive.

"I'm glad this one's over," said Drake, picking up the file laying on his desk and tossing it back down hard, causing some of the papers to shift out of the edges. A small clear pouch fell out of the file and onto the floor in front of Macy.

"What's this?" she asked, picking up the packet.

"Oh, that's one of Julie's earrings," answered Drake. "I found it inside one of her purses when I searched the crime scene. Josh said she lost the matching one and was going to take it to the jewelers the day she died to have another one made."

Macy held up the ruby and diamond earring, staring for a few moments as it glistened in the light. "It's beautiful," she said softly, handing it back to Drake.

"I forgot it was in there. I'll give it back to him tonight."

"So, Mark Jacoby's dead," said Spence.

"It appears so. According to Agent Price, he was shot in the head."

"Well that will close the case on Julie's murder," said Macy.

"I'm not so sure of that."

"What do you mean?"

"According to Agent Price, Jacoby was with him during the time of the murder. He insists there was no way Jacoby could have killed Julie."

"But what about the coveralls and gloves we found in the trunk of his car?" Spence asked.

"I don't know. Price thinks that maybe whoever killed Julie knew about the bad blood between Jacoby and Stephens and framed him for the murder."

"If that's true then what was the motive?" asked Macy.

"That I cannot say with certainty," said Drake. "All I know is my client is innocent and Jacoby's dead. If Price is correct about Jacoby, we may never know who killed Julie."

"That's got to be eating at Josh," said Macy.

"I don't think it's really had enough time to sink in for him yet. Hopefully, he'll be able to move on. So where are you two headed now?"

"Well, we're going to spend the night in Asheboro and drive to Myrtle Beach tomorrow," said Spence.

"That sounds nice. Callie and I just got back from the coast in Georgia."

"Callie? Is that Callie Devane with the District Attorney's office?" asked Macy.

"Oops, I guess I just let the cat out of the bag," said Drake, covering his mouth in mock surprise.

"How long have you been seeing each other?" Spence asked.

"A few weeks, and I know what you're going to say, but we kept it strictly on the Q.T. and remained objective in our professional lives. Neither of us compromised the case in any way. Now that it's over, we can be more open about our relationship. Of course, we can no longer be on opposing sides in the courtroom."

"You sound as if you're planning on getting married."

Drake smiled a mischievous grin. "Well, as a matter of fact, we are."

"Congratulations," said Spence, jumping up to shake Drake's hand.

"Congratulations for what?" asked Josh, having just entered the office.

"Uh...for your win of course," said Macy.

"I found this in your file, Josh," said Drake, handing the earring to Josh.

"Thanks. I've been looking all over for this. This was a special pair of hers and I wanted it as a keepsake," said Josh, clutching the packet to his chest before carefully placing it in his suit jacket pocket.

They left the office and drove together to Alejandro's. It was an upscale restaurant famous for their Italian and Mexican cuisine, but they also had a fine assortment of seafood and steaks. Josh had already paid Drake for his services, so he was buying. As they dined, they continued their conversation.

"Adam tells me you're planning on taking some time off, Josh," said Macy.

"Yes, my boss wants me to take a couple of weeks, what with the loss of Julie and the trial. The problem is I have been so engrossed with the trial that I won't know what to do with myself now that it's over."

"Were you thinking of going away somewhere?" asked Spence.

"I don't know where I would go at this point. Besides, I haven't been on a vacation without Julie in years," he replied, frowning as he glanced down at the floor.

"I've got an idea," said Macy. "Why don't you come to the beach with us? We stay in a condo our friend owns and there are two bedrooms with plenty of room. That way you won't have to be alone all of the time, but there's room enough for privacy when you want it."

"I wouldn't want to intrude on you two. I'm sure Spence would rather be alone with you."

"Nonsense. Uh...not that I don't want to be alone with you, dear," Spence said rather sheepishly, trying to recover from his recent faux pas. "What I mean is, there is plenty of room at this place where Macy and I can still be alone, but we can also socialize when we want. We really would like for you to join us."

"I appreciate your kind offer, but I insist you two enjoy your vacation together, alone. I'll be okay."

After they finished eating, they rode back to Drake's office where they said their goodbyes and parted company. Macy and Spence headed back to Asheboro while Drake and Josh went home.

Josh began packing immediately for his trip. A few days away from home might do him good, he thought. He would have plenty of time to deal with sorting through Julie's things when he got back. Besides, he would probably donate her things to a local shelter to help those less fortunate. She would have liked that.

Drake phoned Callie from the car on his way home. By the time he pulled into the drive, she was already there. Since she had a key, she was waiting inside when he walked through the door. She immediately pounced on him in the dark before he could flip the switch. They began kissing and groping each other, coiling and recoiling in a heated frenzy as they removed each other's clothes. There was so much pent-up passion between them, they could not wait to make it to the bedroom, but rather collapsed in a heap on the kitchen floor.

When they finished making love, Drake scooped Callie into his arms and carried her to the bedroom. After a few moments, they were ready for an encore. Drake felt complete when he was with Callie and never wanted her to leave again. He felt as if the world had been lifted off his shoulders as now they would be able to continue their relationship out in the open rather than hiding under the cover of darkness. Drake drifted off to sleep with his arms around Callie and a smile on his face.

The next morning, Macy and Spence checked out of the hotel in Asheboro and continued on to Myrtle Beach, stopping once for lunch. When they arrived at the condo, Macy unlocked the front door while Spence unloaded the luggage from the trunk. The place was huge with a large great room and dining area, plus an extra sitting area where one could curl up with a book instead of watching television. There was one bedroom downstairs and a second one upstairs, each with its own private bath.

Once everything was in place, Macy turned to Spence and flashed a wry smile. Spence reached out, took her by the arm, and pulled her soft body to him, pressing hard against her. Something about the salt air seemed to invigorate them, so they took full advantage of their alone time. They spent the afternoon making love.

Later that evening, Macy and Spence left the condo to grab some dinner. As they were eating, Spence looked up at Macy, only to see a blank look on her face as she stared off into the distance.

"What's wrong?" he asked.

"Nothing," she replied, blinking her eyes.

"Don't hand me that. I know that look. You're not satisfied with the outcome of this case."

"I am, but I just wish we could have found Julie's killer. I feel like we didn't finish the job. Like we forgot something, or missed something."

"You did everything you could. We did our job. Josh was found innocent. What more do you want?"

"I want justice for Julie Stephens. You know me, Spence. You know that I became The Avenger, not only to help people in need, but also to make sure justice is served. I may operate outside of the law when necessary, but it is always in the interest of true justice. I feel like I let Josh and Julie down."

"So what do you want to do? The police have all but closed the case. Even with what Agent Price told them, they still consider Jacoby their prime suspect now and with him dead, they'll do very little looking at anyone else. They have too many other hot cases to work on and they're certainly not going to ask you to investigate it any further."

"You're right. I'll get over it eventually. Just give me a little time."

"No problem, but please try to relax and enjoy our vacation," he said. "You've earned it."

Macy smiled at Spence and resumed her gaze into the distance. Spence had seen it before, but not often. Most cases she solved completely, but there had been a couple she believed she missed something on. This was one of those cases, so he knew he would have to let her work through it the same way she did on the others. He wanted to take her into his arms and make everything all right, but whenever she was in one of these states, it was best if he gave her some space.

They finished their meal in silence and headed back to the condo. They watched television for a little while, then Spence suggested they take a walk on the beach. The full moon reflected off the water, giving the beach a twilight effect. They walked down toward the pier since it was well lit and easy to navigate toward. Once they reached the pier, they turned around and walked back to where they started from. When they reached the walkway in front of the condo, Spence took Macy by the hand and led her to the water's edge. There they waded into the shallows, allowing the small waves to roll over their ankles. Darkness had cooled the sand and water, making it quite refreshing.

"Care to take a late dip?" asked Spence.

"Not tonight," she replied. "Maybe tomorrow night. Besides, we have all week."

They remained standing in the moonlight for a few more minutes before walking back to the condo.

"I hope Josh is okay," said Macy.

"Don't worry. He's a big boy."

"Yes I know, but with everything he's been through lately, I hope he doesn't do something stupid."

"You don't believe he would commit suicide?"

"No, nothing like that. But he might drink too much in order to drown his sorrows. I've seen it happen too many times"

"Well, let's hope he's stronger than that," said Spence. "He'll have to deal with everything on his terms."

After watching the evening news, they went to bed. Spence was fast asleep in no time, another benefit of the salt air. Macy, on the other hand, tossed and turned most of the night. She could not get the images of Julie Stephens out of her mind, and yet, she knew that regardless of what Agent Price said, Mark Jacoby was the likely killer. After a few hours of wearing out the bed, Macy got up to drink some warm milk, hoping it would help her sleep.

She walked into the main room and sat down on the sofa, turning on the television to see what was on. Since she was wide awake, watching a movie might help her become drowsy enough to eventually slip back into sleep. After settling on an old mystery movie, she drained the last of her milk, placed the cup on the coffee table, and leaned against the arm of the sofa, stretching her legs out. Before the identity of the killer in the movie was revealed, she was sound asleep.

CHAPTER 30

It was barely dawn when Josh headed toward the airport. He booked his flight and hotel for Miami the night before, and hoped he would somehow be able to enjoy the trip. Once the plane touched down, he rented a car and headed to the hotel. He carried his bag inside, surveying the room. It was a typical hotel room, complete with a small fridge, where anything he consumed would be added to his bill. He grabbed one of the small liquor bottles and a soda, mixed the two in a glass, and made his way to the balcony overlooking the Atlantic before collapsing in a resin chair. He scanned the beach through his Oakley's as he sipped his drink. It was like a huge weight had suddenly lifted off him, as he exhaled a long sigh.

It took a few seconds for Josh to realize the noise that stirred his sleep was his cell phone. He had fallen asleep on the balcony, succumbing to the combination of relieved stress and alcohol. He recognized the number on the display, when he opened the phone.

"Yeah," he said in an irritated tone.

"Hi, honey. How are you?"

"I'm fine," he replied, keeping his end of the conversation short. After a short pause, the caller continued.

"I miss you. Where are you?"

"Look, I told you, it's over," he said, closing the phone.

Josh drained the rest of his drink, which was already warm from sitting on the small table beside his chair. Standing up, he walked back inside to mix another. Suddenly, his cell phone rang again. It was the same number, so

Josh ignored it. After a few seconds, he heard the familiar tone announcing he had a voice mail message. He stuffed the phone back into his pocket and walked to the balcony, sipping his drink as he leaned over the rail. After a few minutes, he walked back inside, took off his pants, and put on his swimsuit. He left his cell phone in the front pocket of his pants, headed out of the room and down to the pool area.

Josh took a seat at the poolside bar and ordered a scotch. He slowly surveyed the area as he waited on his drink. It was fairly crowded for this time of day, but eventually his eyes settled on a young blonde lying on a pool chair. She was oblivious to the noise around her, appearing to be asleep, but there was no way he could tell since her sunglasses shielded her eyes, not only from the sun, but from his view as well. She appeared to be alone, but he remained at the bar to observe. She looked a few years younger than he was, but was definitely in great shape, filling out her two-piece bikini in all the right areas, with no extra bulges seeping out. He surmised she either never had children, or worked extremely hard to hide it. Her skin was golden brown, obviously the result of much time spent as she was now.

Josh turned back toward the bar, drained the last of his second drink, and placed the empty glass in front of him. When he turned around to resume his girl watching, she was gone. *How did she disappear so quickly?* He frantically searched the crowd for any sign of this mystery girl. He was about to turn back to the bar and order another drink in defeat, when he saw her walking away from the pool toward the ocean. He slid from the barstool and made his way through the gate onto the walkway leading to the beach. He stood at the top of the steps exiting down to the sand, watching the backs of her legs as she made her way slowly down. By the time he casually descended the steps to the sandy beach below, she was at the water's edge. He sat down on the sand, watching as she swam for a couple of minutes before walking back toward the shore. He assumed she just wanted to cool off before resuming her sunbathing.

With his sunglasses on, Josh believed she could not tell he was watching only her, so he remained seated as she approached. She walked past him, slowly turned and lowered her thick pink lips toward his ear.

"Are you going to speak to me, or just look at me all day?" she whispered. "Room 405, if you're interested."

Turning, she walked back toward the pool. Josh stood, following, as she passed the pool area and disappeared inside the hotel. He waited for five minutes before stepping inside, making his way to the elevator. It stopped on every floor on the way up for what seemed to Josh an eternity before finally reaching the fourth floor. He cautiously stepped from the elevator, looking for the directional signs that would tell him which corridor to take. Moving to the right, he made his way to room 405. As he raised his fist to knock, the door flew open and a hand grabbed him by the front of his shirt, pulling him inside. She was already kissing him as she shoved the door closed behind them, pulling him down on top of her. Somewhat disoriented at first, Josh soon found his bearings, noticing she was totally naked. Together they worked at his clothes until they were both writhing in rhythm on the carpet.

When they finished, she stood up abruptly and announced, "I'm going to take a shower. You can let yourself out."

She headed toward the bathroom while Josh sat mystified by the entire ordeal. He did have his marching orders, though, dressing quickly and leaving the room, walking toward the elevators. His room was on the sixth floor, so he made the short elevator ride up to his room. Once inside, he collapsed on the bed, still trying to sort out what just happened. After a few minutes racking his brain, he headed to the shower to clean up.

When he stepped out of the shower, he looked at the clock and noticed it was three in the afternoon. No wonder he was so hungry. It had been several hours since he'd eaten a couple of biscuits on the way to the airport that morning. Maybe he'd grab an early dinner, then check out one of the area clubs later that evening.

For the rest of the afternoon, Josh could not get his mind off this mystery woman. He dropped in one of the local clubs and made his way through the throng of dancing people to the bar, amazed at how quickly one of the bartenders delivered his scotch, given the large crowd. This was definitely one of the hot spots in town. As he nursed his drink, he turned on his barstool to watch the crowd. Several couples were dancing, some men and women, others simply women, but it wasn't a gay club. A small group of men huddled at one end of the bar watching a small group of women at the other end. It was like watching the National Geographic channel where a pride of lions were deciding how to divide up a pack of wildebeests. Typically, during the hunt, they would ferret out the weakling of the herd and move in for the kill, but since these were men, they were assigning each one a woman before they made their move.

As Josh settled in to watch the show, his view of the male pack was suddenly obscured by a woman who sat right beside him. It was *her*. The mysterious blonde had returned, but had she followed him?

"Fancy meeting you here," she said with a wry smile.

"Isn't that supposed to be my line?"

"Sorry if I seemed a bit cold earlier," she continued. "By the way, my name is Janet."

"Josh."

"So tell me, Josh, what's your story?"

"What do you mean?"

"I mean, where's your wife?" she asked, pointing to his hand.

For the first time since the funeral, Josh was suddenly aware he was still wearing his wedding ring. "Dead," he replied.

"Did you kill her?"

"What...?" Josh began, startled by how perverse and abrupt this woman was.

Before he could get the words out, she continued, "Look, I don't mean to be crude, but I run into creeps all the time who lie about their marriage, or beat women, or worse. I happen to have the misfortune of being a beautiful blonde woman with no attachments, so believe me, I attract all kinds of weirdos. All of them are looking for the same thing, so I guess today I just beat you to the punch."

Josh sat silently, unable to speak, simply staring into her beautiful blue eyes.

"C'mon, let's get outta here," she said, tossing some cash on the bar and grabbing Josh by the arm.

He was still in shock as she led him outside and around the corner to a red Mustang parked at the curb. They climbed in and drove off, Josh continuing to stare at Janet, his mouth open. She leaned over and gave him a soft kiss, moving his mouth closed with her finger.

"Careful, you don't want to catch any flies," she said, smiling softly.

They made their way to a restaurant where Janet requested a private booth. There, they shared an appetizer platter while both drank scotch. He told her the story of his daughter and wife as Janet listened intently. When he finished, she told him of her three broken marriages, all with abusive husbands, the last one almost killing her.

"For the last three years, I've lived like these whoring men. Taking advantage of guys like you simply for sex, and moving on to the next," she confessed.

"So why are you still here?"

"I dunno. I'm still trying to figure that out myself."

"Well, nothing says we can't enjoy the moment, however long it lasts."

They finished their drinks and headed back to the hotel. This time they took the elevator to the sixth floor, making their way to Josh's room. Once inside, they took their time kissing and caressing as they slowly undressed. This would not be the animalistic sex they had earlier, but instead more intimate and deliberate. Julie crossed his mind for a fleeting moment, but then this felt so right. The sun was just beginning to streak the morning sky when they fell asleep.

He awoke to the sound of his cell phone, telling him he had a voice mail message. He turned the ringer off after the tenth call, but had not listened to any of the messages. He slid out of bed, trying not to disturb Janet, grabbed his cell phone, and crept into the other room. There he listened to the same messages, over and over, until he came to the last one.

"I'm not calling you again. If you don't come back now, I'm going to the police!"

Josh scribbled a quick note for Janet, dressed, and raced out of the hotel toward the airport. As he drove, he punched the numbers on his cell phone and made a quick call. He returned the rental and walked into the main terminal. Once inside the airport, he hurried to the ticket counter.

* * *

Spence shook Macy gently to wake her. It was ten o'clock and she was still on the sofa. He had already prepared breakfast. Slowly, she sat up, shuffling her feet as she walked into the kitchen. He grabbed a piece of toast and a cup of coffee, sitting down across from Macy, offering a smile as he took a bite. Leaving the table, he walked outside toward the beach.

Macy turned on the television, squinting hard as if trying to make sure of what she saw.

"Spence, come here quick!"

"What is it?" he asked, walking back into the room. "Isn't that Josh?" she asked, pointing to the television.

As the reporter continued her discourse about Miami Beach and the throngs of tourists there this week, the camera panned the crowd, capturing Josh and Janet in an intimate embrace.

"I know it's none of my business," said Macy. "But I thought he would have at least grieved a little more for Julie before moving on to dating again."

"Maybe, but we don't really know what their relationship was like," said Spence. "They may not have been very close.

For all we know they could have had one of those 'open marriages' where each one sees other people."

"Ugh…" said Macy. "The thought of something like that gives me the creeps."

"Try not to let it get to you," he said, placing his arms around her and giving her a big squeeze.

After breakfast, Macy and Spence donned their swimsuits and headed out to the beach. They spent most of the day outside, returning to the condo later that afternoon to shower and dress for dinner. They ate at one of the many seafood restaurants on Kings Highway, then came straight back to the condo for an evening walk on the beach.

"Isn't this great?" said Spence.

"Yeah, but you know what? I'm not really in a vacation mood myself."

"You're still stewing over Josh, aren't you?"

"I'm sorry, but something just doesn't feel right."

"You've got to let it go. He has his own life to live, no matter how wrong you think he may be."

"You're right. Let's try to forget about Josh and enjoy the rest of our vacation."

"Well, to tell you the truth, I kinda miss home myself."

"Well, we were planning on staying until next week, but why don't we go ahead and leave?" suggested Macy.

"We'll leave tomorrow," said Spence.

They enjoyed one more walk on the beach that evening, returning to the condo to pack before going to bed early.

CHAPTER 31

The next day, Spence loaded the car and they began their journey home. They stopped a couple of times along the way and once to eat lunch. Then when they were about an hour from High Point, Spence ran over something in the road cutting down a tire. Unable to get the jack to work, he called the auto club. They waited for almost two hours before someone showed up. By the time they were back on the road and nearing High Point, the sun was setting.

"I guess we're staying here for the night," said Spence.

"It could be worse," replied Macy. "We could be at the bottom of a mine shaft."

They shared a nervous laugh, realizing that was probably nothing to kid about. As they approached the city limits of High Point, Macy's cell phone rang.

"Ms. Merit, this is Madeline Jones. You've got to help me!" she said in a desperate half-whisper.

"Madeline? What's wrong?"

"He's breaking in now!"

Macy heard a crash in the background followed by Madeline screaming, then the phone went dead. Macy tried frantically to redial the number, but all she got was a busy tone.

"What's going on?" asked Spence.

She looked up at Spence with widened eyes. "That was Madeline Jones, Josh's assistant. She's in trouble. We need to go help her."

She called information for Madeline's address while Spence turned on the emergency flashers and sped through town. After a few minutes, they arrived at Madeline's house, but no one was home. The front door had been kicked in but there was no sign of Madeline anywhere.

Macy grabbed her cell phone and began dialing. After a couple of efforts and some mixed curse words, she called George.

"Hello?"

"Hey George, it's Macy."

"Hey sis, what's up?"

"I need your help. I've been trying to reach someone on his cell phone, but I keep getting his voice mail. I'm afraid he might be in trouble."

"Give me the number and I'll have a GPS trace run on it. If it's on, we should be able to locate it."

Macy's brother, George was a field supervisor with the FBI in Kentucky. Once she gave him the number, he relayed it to the field office for a trace. She began to pace while she waited. It took a few minutes before he came back on the line.

"I've got a location for the phone, Macy. I'm emailing it to your phone now. You should have it soon."

"Thanks, George. I owe you."

"Take care, sis, and be careful."

Macy ended the call and pulled up the email with the coordinates where Josh's cell was traced to. They climbed into the car and she punched the coordinates into the navigation system on the console. Shortly, a small map appeared giving her directions from her current location.

They sped away from the house heading north out of town. The directions led them to a small narrow winding road up a hill. They continued up the incline, monitoring the navigation screen as they drew nearer to the blinking object. Just then she spotted a car on the side of the road in front of them. Spence slowed down and eased in behind it, while Macy grabbed something from her duffle bag behind her seat and placed it in her pocket. She immediately recognized the vehicle as Josh's.

Climbing out of her car, she slowly walked up the road, telling Spence to wait in the car and keep the motor running in case they needed to make a quick getaway. As she made her way alongside Josh's car, she could see ahead the shadow of a figure bending down over the front seat of another car. Suddenly, the figure stood and turned to face her.

"That's close enough," said Josh, pointing a pistol at Macy.

"Josh, what are you doing?"

"How did you find me?"

"GPS from your cell phone," replied Macy.

"No, I mean how did you suspect me?"

"I didn't for a long time. But when Agent Price was so adamant about Mark Jacoby not being Julie's killer, I started thinking. The coveralls they removed from Jacoby's trunk were too long for him. He was only a little over five feet while you, on the other hand, are over six feet."

"I see your reasoning," Josh said. "But he could have simply rolled the legs up at the bottom."

"There were no crease marks, though. Also, I did a little digging and found out that one of the men who works at the impound lot is Madeline's brother. You obviously had her talk him into letting her place those items in Mark Jacoby's trunk."

"Great work, Macy, but all of that is just circumstantial evidence. You can't prove any of it."

"What about the earring?" Macy asked.

"You mean my wife's earring? What does that have to do with this?"

"No, I mean your daughter's earring. It didn't hit me until after we left Adam's office the other night, but I remembered the picture of your daughter in your office. She was wearing that same pair of earrings. The earring wasn't Julie's. It was Rachel's. What happened? Did Julie find the earring and realize you were the one who killed her daughter? Is that why you had to kill her, too?"

"She didn't understand," replied Josh. "Rachel and I had a special relationship. Even in her youth she was much more of a woman than Julie ever would be, so mature for her age."

"What happened, Josh?"

"Everything was going great until Rachel turned six. Suddenly, she no longer wanted to play along with our little game. She was going to tell Julie.

I couldn't let her ruin everything. Why did she make me do it? I loved her so much," Josh said, starting to cry.

"So you killed her to keep her quiet?"

"Yes. I parked a couple of blocks away from the school that evening and hid behind some bushes. When she came out, I called for her and she followed me down the street. Madeline was my alibi. She backed up my story of being in a meeting. I drove Rachel to our usual place in the woods. I made her dress up like the picture. She started crying and hitting me. In the struggle, her earring came off. I killed her and placed her body in the trunk of the car. I returned to the bank for my meeting, firmly establishing my alibi. Afterward at home, the earring fell out of the cuff of my pants when I took them off. I hid it among my personal items in my dresser drawer. Later that night after Julie was knocked out from the sedative I gave her, I took Rachel's body to the park where she was found."

"How did Julie find out?"

"She was going through my things the day before she died and came upon the earring. She remembered the picture, the same as you did, and confronted me about it. She was going to go to the police the next day, so that morning I spiked her orange juice, tied her up, and went to work as usual. I returned around ten o'clock. She was awake, which is what I wanted. I looked in her eyes as the drill sank deep into her chest. She never understood me. She was going to ruin me, so I pressed harder as the drill gnawed at her organs. She took one last gasp and she was gone. I cleaned the room thoroughly, taking the coveralls and gloves over to Madeline's house where I hid them. I went back to work, and the rest you know."

"Why did Madeline agree to help you?" asked Macy. "Because she's in love with me," answered Josh. "We had been having a secret affair for the last five years. I kept telling her I would leave Julie when the time was right, knowing full well I never intended to marry Madeline. She continued to believe me and was willing to do anything I asked. I told her about Julie and she agreed to help me. When you guys stumbled upon Jacoby, I was able to get her to plant the coveralls and gloves in his trunk. She conveniently steered you in his direction."

"So why are we here tonight, Josh? What are you doing with Madeline?"

"Madeline kept calling me, leaving messages on my cell. I told her it was over, but she wouldn't leave me alone. In her last message, she was very upset and threatened to go to the cops and tell them everything. I called her back and was finally able to calm her down enough to convince her if she did she would go to prison with me. I told her I would come home to her. I was afraid she was going to rat me out for sure this time, so that's why I left early from vacation. I waited for her to come home, took the extra set of keys and drove her car here. I called the auto club pretending to be broken down and hitched a ride back to her house. I broke in and subdued her, and now we're here. No one will suspect a single woman losing control of her car and running off the road. And once she's dead, there's no way to tie me to Rachel's murder. And of course, Double Jeopardy prevents me from being tried again in Julie's death. So you see, Macy, I've got it all figured out."

"What about me?" Macy asked. "I'm sure you didn't count on me being in the picture."

"True, but I'll decide what to do with you after I finish with Madeline."

Josh reached into the car, pulled the gear shift into drive while continuing to point his gun at Macy. The car lunged forward causing the driver's door to slam shut. Suddenly, Josh's eyes grew wide with fear as he realized the cuff of his pants was caught in the car door. He frantically pulled at his leg, dropping the gun onto the ground, but the car continued on its path careening over the edge of the embankment taking Josh with it.

Macy heard a scream of terror as he was pulled over the edge. Before she could reach them, the car tumbled over and over before coming to rest at the bottom of the ravine and bursting into flames. Macy walked over to where the gun lay and reached for her cell phone.

"Adam, this is Macy. I need for you and Callie to meet me immediately."

She gave him directions and walked back to the car to fill Spence in while they waited for them. After a few minutes, Spence saw a beam of light from the headlights of an approaching car. He waited until he was certain it was Drake and Callie before stepping out into the light, motioning for them to pull over to the side behind their car.

"Are you okay?" Callie asked.

"I'm fine," said Macy. "But I can't say the same for Josh Stephens and Madeline Jones."

"What do you mean?" Drake asked.

Macy tossed her head in the direction where Madeline's car went over the bank, then led them over to the edge of the ravine. As they looked down, they could see the car still burning.

"Oh, no! What happened?" Callie asked.

"Well, let's just say that justice was finally served," replied Macy, removing a small tape recorder from her pocket. She removed the tape and tossed it to Drake.

"Everything you need is on there," she said, pointing to the tape.

She gave a brief summary of her conversation with Josh, his involvement in both Rachel's and Julie's murders, and finally his demise. Callie and Drake stood silent for a moment as they absorbed what they had just learned.

"So, he was guilty after all," said Drake.

"Apparently so," said Callie.

"Spence was right," said Macy. "I should have trusted his first instincts."

Spence reached over and gave Macy a comforting squeeze.

"But how did you figure it out?" Drake asked.

"Well, I must admit that even though I was a strong supporter of Josh, I had my doubts, especially when Spence was so adamant about his guilt. What really made me leery was seeing him in Miami Beach on the news. It was as if he wasn't even mourning Julie's death. I started going over all of the evidence in my mind and realized the coveralls we found in Mark Jacoby's trunk were too tall to fit him, but was a much better fit for Josh. I thought about the earring you gave him that night and remembered I had seen his daughter, Rachel, wearing that same pair in a photograph in his office. By the time I connected all of the dots, Madeline called in a panic about someone breaking into her house, only she said, "He's breaking in," as if she knew who it was. I immediately suspected Josh, but when we got to her house, no one was there. That's when I began searching for him."

"And you just miraculously knew where to look?" Callie asked.

"Let's just say I have resources," replied Macy with a smile, not wanting to reveal the fact that her brother, the FBI field supervisor, traced Josh's mobile GPS location.

"So what do we do now?" Drake asked.

"Take this," Macy said, carefully handing him the gun, using a tissue so as not to disturb any fingerprint evidence. "I'm not sure if it is connected with anything, but the police should at least compare it with any unsolved cases. His confession on that tape should be enough for the police to completely close both cases. Of course, they will want to question Madeline's brother who helped her plant the evidence in Jacoby's car. But all in all I would say case closed."

"Thanks for everything, Macy," said Callie. "Without you, a murderer would still be walking the streets."

"Hey, it's what I do," replied Macy with a smile and a feigned tip of a hat. She and Spence walked back to their car and drove away.

Callie called the police, and waited with Drake for them to arrive. Once the detectives arrived, she handed them the tape, briefing them on the events of the evening, substituting herself in place of Macy as the one Madeline called to meet. She was able to recount Macy's story well enough to make it her own, so there was no need to tell the police anyone else was there tonight. They waited until the police were through questioning them, then drove back to Drake's house still somewhat in shock from the recent events. They spent the rest of the night talking about Josh, Julie and Rachel Stephens, hoping to make some sense of it all.

CHAPTER 32

Macy and Spence drove through the night in order to make it back to Kentucky. As they rode in the darkness, Macy finally broke the silence. "Okay, you can say it now."

"Say what?" Spence asked.

"I told you so," she said, looking over at Spence. "You were right about Josh all along."

"I could have just as easily been wrong."

"But you weren't."

"That's just further proof that we make a great team. Sometimes you'll be right and I'll be wrong. Other times, the reverse will be true. Either way, we always get our man," said Spence, looking over and winking at Macy.

She napped while Spence drove the rest of the way. They made it home around four o'clock in the morning and went straight to bed. Since they were completely exhausted, they slept late.

* * *

A few weeks later, Macy's cell phone rang, disturbing her late morning sleep in.

"Macy, it's Callie. I hope I didn't catch you at a bad time."

"No, what's up?" Macy yawned.

"We did it!"

"Did what?"

"Adam and I got married!"

"When? I thought you were going to send us an invitation."

"Well, we were, but then last week we decided to elope. Adam had one of his friends, who is a magistrate, do the honors."

"Congratulations," said Macy.

"Thanks. I wanted you guys to know as soon as we got back from our honeymoon."

"I hate we missed it, but I'm happy for you."

"We have some more news," said Callie.

"You're not pregnant?" asked Macy.

"No, no nothing like that. We came to Georgia for our honeymoon and stopped by to see Aunt Jewel. You remember me telling you about our trip there earlier last month?"

"Yes, I believe it was the most relaxed I had seen Adam since we met him."

"It turns out that the District Attorney in Whitfield County, Jim Jacobs, was an old friend of Uncle Harry. When he found out I was in town, he called and offered me a job."

"What about your job in High Point?"

"After my boss found out about Adam and me, he fired me. So naturally, when this opportunity came up, I jumped at it."

"How does Adam feel about all of this? I mean, he does have a thriving practice in High Point."

"Actually, it was his idea that I take it. He had been thinking about Dalton ever since our first trip, so he sold his practice there and moved here with me."

"So what's he going to do there?" asked Macy.

"I tell you, Macy, it was almost like fate. When I was discussing my job offer with Mr. Jacobs, I mentioned Adam and his practice in High Point. He told me one of his friends who had been practicing for thirty years was looking to retire, but had not been able to find someone to take over his practice. Mr. Jacobs arranged a meeting between his friend and Adam and they worked out a deal. Now Adam will still be able to try some criminal defense cases, but also has a solid practice in contract law."

"Sounds to me like everything fell perfectly into place."

"You're right. And if it had not been for the Stephens' case and meeting you and Spence, we may never have taken that trip to Dalton."

"Wait a minute. How do we get credit for all of that?"

"Simple," replied Callie. "After we saw the amount of love and happiness you two have, it made us both long for the same thing. Seeing how intimate and connected you guys are was a perfect demonstration of how a marriage should work. We both became more open minded with regard to our personal and professional options, and as a result, we are moving to Dalton. So thank you for the wonderful influence you had on us. Oh, and thank Spence, too."

"I will Callie. And Callie…"

"Yes?"

"Please keep in touch."

"You can count on it, Macy."

And with that, Callie ended the call. Macy could not help but smile as she closed her cell phone.

"What was that all about?" asked Spence. "You'll never guess."

Macy went on to tell Spence what Callie had just told her. They shared a few chuckles as she relayed the details. When Macy finished, they both lay back with satisfied expressions, not just because they were a positive influence on this young couple, but because they knew what Callie said was true. Their relationship was as good as it could get. Each had the other's best interest at heart, even if it meant sacrificing his or her own desires. They snuggled up together, basking in the moment. Then Macy's cell phone rang again.

"Macy, its George. I've got another case for you if you're up to it."

"No rest for the weary," said Macy with a huge sigh.

Spence reached over and took the phone from Macy. "Can it wait until tomorrow, George?"

"Sure, I suppose."

"In that case, we'll call you tomorrow," said Spence, flipping the cell phone closed. He placed his arms around Macy and held her tight, sealing his lips firmly on top of hers. After a long deep sensual kiss, he looked deep into her eyes. "Work can wait until tomorrow. Today is ours."

He held her body tightly against his as they began a long afternoon of intimate exploration.

About the Author

Dale Crotts is the author of *The Reckoning* and *Death Watch*, two other books in the Macy Merit/Spencer Rawlings series. Dale grew up in a small community known as Glenola, located in Randolph County, North Carolina. He attended Randleman High School, and later graduated from High Point College with a Bachelors Degree in Business Administration. After working several years in banking, Dale earned his MBA from the University of North Carolina at Greensboro. His passion for writing began early, as he wrote plays for his drama class in middle school. A professional opportunity took Dale to Kentucky, where he lived for four years, and then moved to Michigan for one year, before returning to North Carolina. Many of the locations and characters in his writing come from his travels throughout the Midwest. When not working or writing, Dale enjoys traveling, reading, and golf. He is a huge fan of the television series *House*, and also enjoys watching college basketball, especially the High Point University Panthers, his alma mater. Dale currently resides in North Carolina.